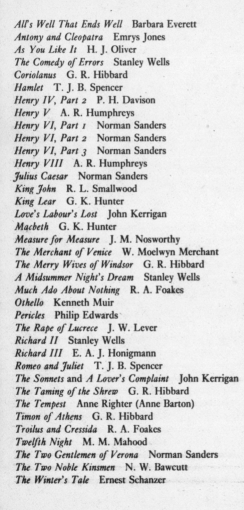

NEW PENGUIN SHAKESPEARE

GENERAL EDITOR: T. J. B. SPENCER

ASSOCIATE EDITOR: STANLEY WELLS

WILLIAM SHAKESPEARE

*

THE FIRST PART OF KING HENRY THE SIXTH

EDITED BY
NORMAN SANDERS

PENGUIN BOOKS

Penguin Books Ltd, Harmondsworth, Middlesex, England
Viking Penguin Inc., 40 West 23rd Street, New York, New York 10010, U.S.A.
Penguin Books Australia Ltd, Ringwood, Victoria, Australia
Penguin Books Canada Limited, 2801 John Street, Markham, Ontario, Canada L3R 1B4
Penguin Books (N.Z.) Ltd, 182 190 Wairau Road, Auckland 10, New Zealand

This edition first published in Penguin Books 1981
Reprinted 1987

Made and printed in Great Britain
by Richard Clay (The Chaucer Press) Ltd,
Bungay, Suffolk
Set in Monotype Ehrhardt

CONTENTS

INTRODUCTION

WHEN Queen Elizabeth I, threatened with the Earl of Essex's rebellion in 1601, said to her Keeper of the Records 'I am Richard II, know ye not that?' (thus comparing herself to an earlier monarch who had suffered at the hands of a rebellious subject), it was something more than a typical gesture of self-dramatization. For the Queen, as for her subjects, similar events in the past and the present were quite naturally brought together in the mind, because in sixteenth-century England history was neither an academic exercise nor an indulgence of antiquarian tastes: it had an awesome relevance to the lives of ruler and governed alike.

The historians of the age, such as Edward Hall and Raphael Holinshed, were governed by the providential version of history, a Christian-based view of the past, derived ultimately from the works of Orosius and Augustine, in which events manifested the unfolding of God's plan, as the fates of men and nations illustrated the workings of divine justice. Encouraged by their royal patrons, these chroniclers further connected this providential theory with what is now called the 'Tudor Myth', a blanket term that stands for the mixture of philosophy, political theory, religious justification, and official propaganda which promoted obedience to the crown as an Englishman's prime duty and defined rebellion as the worst of all crimes. It was an interpretation of fifteenth-century events that showed how the wars, dissensions, and political disasters had been brought to an end in England through the God-directed assumption of the throne by the wise-ruling dynasty of the Tudors.

When, in the late 1580s, playwrights came to produce history plays, it was to be expected that they would take over from the chronicles they ransacked for their plots many of the attitudes and assumptions they found there. But the history play, as opposed to historical fact, is by its very nature more humanly immediate; it has a much broader base of appeal; it is more emotionally vivid; and it is subconsciously more easily linked by a patriotic audience to contemporary happenings. It is surely no accident that the genre itself should have emerged and reached its popular and artistic peak in the fifteen years or so that followed the defeat of the Spanish Armada in 1588. And this initial connexion between the type of play and a great national event can often be found reflected in the relationship between individual history plays and specific contemporary happenings or political climates.

Given Shakespeare's intellectual make-up as well as his unerring sense of what would please his public, it is easy to understand that he began very early in his career to write historical dramas. Nor is it surprising that his plays are informed by the didactic purposes of history proper, and that in general they tend to underwrite Elizabethan beliefs about order, rebellion, and right rule. Yet he must also have known that for the bulk of his audience his plays offered more strongly that special excitement that comes from a vivid re-creation of the past, some patriotic stimulation, and some clear object lessons for the present. It is an appeal that the popular writer Thomas Nashe isolates in 'The Defence of Plays' in his *Piers Penniless*:

> what if I prove plays to be no extreme, but a rare exercise of virtue? ... the subject of them for the most part ... is borrowed out of our English chronicles, wherein our fore-

fathers' valiant acts, that have lain long buried in rusty brass and worm-eaten books, are revived, and they themselves raised from the grave of oblivion, and brought to plead their aged honours in open presence: than which what can be a sharper reproof to these degenerate effeminate days of ours?

*

In writing *1 Henry VI* Shakespeare seems to have had at least half an eye to events in the public mind. Towards the end of 1591 and early in 1592, England had troops in both France and the Netherlands in support of the Huguenot Henry of Navarre, who was attempting to secure the French throne following the assassination of Henry III in August 1589. Lord Willoughby led the first force to Dieppe in 1589 and took part in the capture of Vendôme, Mons, Alençon, and Falaise. Troops commanded by Sir John Norris served in Brittany in 1591; and the Earl of Essex leading a third army landed in August of the same year, took Gournay, and laid siege to Rouen in October, until he was recalled by the Queen in January of the next year.

With contemporary events such as these as a backcloth, a play recalling the triumphs in France of legendary soldiers like Salisbury, Bedford, and Talbot as they prevailed against the treachery and witchcraft of Joan of Arc, the Dauphin, and Burgundy would be likely to provide popular, topical theatrical fare. This is particularly true of the period between August 1591 and January 1592, before the Queen's disillusionment with the campaign and her recall of Essex, and before Rouen was relieved by the Duke of Parma in April 1592.

There is evidence that the play was indeed well received by numerous spectators early in 1592; for Thomas Nashe seems to be alluding to Act IV, scene 7, when, just after the passage quoted earlier from *Piers Penniless*, he writes:

> How would it have joyed brave Talbot, the terror of the French, to think that after he had lain two hundred years in his tomb he should triumph again on the stage, and have his bones new embalmed with the tears of ten thousand spectators at least (*at several times*), who, in the tragedian that represents his person, imagine they behold him fresh bleeding.

Another reference to a Henry VI play occurs in the account book of Philip Henslowe, the theatrical financier. He records that there were a large number of well-attended performances by the Lord Strange's Men at the Rose Theatre of 'harey the vi', which he designates as being a new play on 3 March 1592.

Whether these allusions are in fact specifically to the play as we now know it is still a matter for scholarly debate; for there is no general agreement on such topics as the play's relationship with *Parts Two* and *Three*, its exact date of composition, the way the three pieces were planned and written, and even the extent to which Shakespeare was responsible for their authorship. The apparently haphazard and occasionally incoherent use of the source materials, the variations in style, and the textual inconsistencies have encouraged scholars to evolve various theories of multiple authorship; Robert Greene, Thomas Nashe, and George Peele are the better-known names cited as co-authors. The argument for the presence of these writers is supported by some factual details, but mainly by parallel passages quoted from their known works, and by stylistic and technical devices commonly employed by them detected in various scenes of the play. However, the stylistic evidence is by its nature subjective and impressionistic, and the factual evidence is susceptible to different interpretations because of its paucity.

All of the theorists agree on some basic points: that the play's presence in the first Folio indicates that the volume's editors believed it to be mainly Shakespeare's work; and that Shakespeare's hand is certainly detectable in many scenes of the play. The differences of opinion reside chiefly in two areas. First, how much of the play is Shakespeare's own work, and how much that of other men? Second, what is the exact relationship between the play and *Parts Two* and *Three*, and when was it written? Among the various theories developed to answer these questions, two main positions are discernible:

1. There was a play in existence in the years 1589–90 on the subject of the reign of Henry VI written by Robert Greene, possibly in collaboration with Thomas Nashe and George Peele. This concerned itself with the Joan of Arc events of the French wars; the Gloucester–Winchester rivalry after the death of Henry V and its influence on the course of the wars; the arrangement of the fictitious peace and the marriage of Henry VI with Margaret of Anjou. Shakespeare is seen as writing a two-part planned sequence to this play (*Henry VI, Parts Two* and *Three*) and making a revision of Greene's work so that it constituted the first part of a three-unit composition. His major revisions are supposed to have comprised the Talbot scenes, which would make the play topical in 1591; the Temple Garden and Vernon and Basset scenes, which show the beginnings of the Roses rivalry, the implications of which are dealt with in *Parts Two* and *Three*; the scenes charting the emergence of the Duke of York and his claims to the throne, also an important issue in *Part Two*; and the origin of the Suffolk–Margaret alliance, which figures prominently in the later play. In short, Shakespeare is believed to be responsible for those scenes which have no basis in the

chronicles, but which prepare the ground for the events dealt with in *Parts Two* and *Three*; and for tinkering with the scenes Greene wrote in an effort to make them fit in with his own additions.

2. The second theory argues that Shakespeare planned a complete trilogy on the reign of Henry VI, in which he intended to deal with the English fortunes in France and the emergence of internal dissension in *Part One*; the domestic implications of this dissension and the Wars of the Roses in *Part Two*; the later battles in the York–Lancaster conflict and the growing power of Richard Duke of Gloucester (later Richard III) in *Part Three*. The unevenness of the writing and the inconsistency in the handling of characters and source material are claimed to be the results of the young Shakespeare's inexpertise and his composing under the influence of established dramatists as he gradually developed his own style during the course of the plays' composition. Some believers of this theory also suggest a revision of *Part One* after *Parts Two* and *Three* had been completed.

*

One can see why *1 Henry VI* has been the subject of so much theorizing. For example, the way in which the events are handled has struck many readers as being neither worthy nor typical of Shakespeare's work as a whole. It is obviously dangerous to deduce from his complete plays anything resembling a fixed method of composition; but, for the history plays, it is generally true to say that his usual practice was to follow with some accuracy a sequence of events that he found in one or more of the chronicles, changing some details, and inventing or adapting new materials to suit his dramatic purposes. The method of working adopted in *1 Henry VI* is so different from this that one critic has called it 'not so much a Chronicle play as a fantasia on historical themes'.

The chief sources are Edward Hall's *The Union of the Two Noble and Illustre Families of Lancaster and York* (1548–50) and Raphael Holinshed's *The Chronicles of England, Scotland, and Ireland* (1587 edition). Some use was also made of Robert Fabyan's *The New Chronicles of England and France* (1516); possibly of Richard Grafton's *A Chronicle at Large* (1569); and of Geoffrey of Monmouth's *Historia Regum Britanniae* and John Stowe's *Chronicles of England* (1580) for special details. When one compares the order and content of the play's scenes with the relevant passages in these sources, it is clear that the drama is a strange mixture of fact and fiction which demonstrates no real sense of accurate historical chronology. Each act deals with its materials in a different way, and the following summary may help the reader to see just how saltatory is the method of construction.

In the opening scene Henry V's funeral, which took place in 1422, is disrupted by a quarrel between the Bishop of Winchester and the Duke of Gloucester, which was at its height in 1426. The audience's interest in this is deflected by a series of messengers announcing the losses of various French towns (two of which were never in English hands), which occurred over a period of time stretching from 1429 to 1451. The coronation of Charles V, which is also announced, did in fact coincide with Henry's death; but the capture of the Earl of Talbot and the cowardly behaviour of Falstaff happened some seven years later. For the remainder of Act I the same sort of time-hopping is evident. The defeat of the Dauphin as it is depicted in the second scene is fictitious. Joan of Arc's introduction to him occurred in 1429. The confrontation between Gloucester and Winchester at the Tower of London (I.3) took place in 1424. Scene 4 deals with the celebration of Talbot's release (1431) and Salisbury's death (1428); and the two final scenes dramatize events in the French camp based on actions that happened in 1429.

Act II does not so much play havoc with historical fact as ignore it altogether. Talbot's recapture of Orleans is distantly based on an incident at Le Mans in 1428, but otherwise it has no factual basis; nor have the encounter between Talbot and the Countess of Auvergne (II.3) and the dispute in the Temple Garden (II.4). The historical Sir John Mortimer did die in captivity in 1424 after urging his cousin Edmund Mortimer's claim to the throne, but there is no evidence for a visit to him by Richard Plantagenet (II.5). Shakespeare also confuses this character with the third Earl of March, who while in captivity in Wales married the daughter of Owen Glendower.

There is a larger debt to the chronicles in the third act, though little accurate chronology. Henry VI rather than the Duke of Bedford is made the peacemaker in the Winchester–Gloucester quarrel of 1426 (III.1). The recapture of Rouen (III.2) is based on the siege of Cornhill in 1441, with the detail of the use of the torch as a signal being inspired by an incident at the Battle of Le Mans in 1428. The death of Bedford, which actually occurred under quite different circumstances in 1435, is given extended dramatic treatment in scene 2. Joan's demonic powers are displayed in scene 3 by showing her able to provoke Burgundy's defection from the English cause, an event which took place in 1434–5, four years after her death. Talbot's services are rewarded with an earldom (which he was granted historically in 1442); and Act III ends with a fictitious dispute between Vernon and Basset.

Apart from the invented incidents of Talbot's rescue of his son (IV.6), a second instalment of the Vernon–Basset enmity (IV.1), and the differences between York and Somerset, the fourth act is based on historical fact. But once again time is telescoped: Henry VI's coronation in France was in 1431, the disgrace of Falstaff in 1429, and the delivery of Burgundy's letter in 1435. York was appointed Regent of France in 1441; the deaths of Talbot and his son occurred in 1453 at Castillon rather than Bordeaux, and they were not the result of the division in the army command depicted in the play.

The play ends with a roughly equal mixture of truth and invention. York's capture of Joan and Suffolk's seizure of Margaret of Anjou (V.3) are both fictitious. Henry VI's betrothal to Margaret (V.5) was arranged in 1443–4; and the English loss of Paris (V.2) and Joan's trial and execution (V.4) both took place in 1431.

*

The impression, gained from the way the sources are handled, that what we have is a rough scissor-and-paste job of play-making is reinforced by the wide range of quality in the poetic and dramatic skills found in it. In many scenes the verse is so flat and uninspired that bardolatrous critics have been loath to believe that even an inexperienced Shakespeare could have had any hand in it. Although such lines can be found throughout the play, they appear in concentrated form in Act I. The writing here is characterized by banal vocabulary, tautology, and circumlocution. There is a good deal of mechanical grammatical inversion in order to make the verse scan, and a tendency to drag in learned allusions for their own sake. What conciseness of expression can be found appears hurried and careless rather than the result of artistic intention. At certain points this drab poetry is combined with lines which strongly suggest the influence of Christopher Marlowe, most noticeably in the opening scenes; for example:

> *Comets, importing change of time and states,*
> *Brandish your crystal tresses in the sky,*
> *And with them scourge the bad revolting stars*
> *That have consented unto Henry's death. . . .*

> *His brandished sword did blind men with his beams;*
> *His arms spread wider than a dragon's wings;*
> *His sparkling eyes, replete with wrathful fire,*
> *More dazzled and drove back his enemies*
> *Than midday sun fierce bent against their faces.*
>
> I.1.2–5, 10–14

A second kind of poetry, no less artificial perhaps, but more successful and striking us as typical of Shakespeare's early manner, occurs mainly in later scenes. Here the wording is specific and elaborate and the imagery obtrusive. Its most sustained exercise is found in the scene between Margaret and Suffolk (V.3), with its conventional, artificial, playful exchanges and its ingenious metaphors imposed upon the sense rather than an integral part of it:

> *Be not offended, nature's miracle;*
> *Thou art allotted to be ta'en by me.*
> *So doth the swan her downy cygnets save,*
> *Keeping them prisoner underneath her wings. . . .*
>
> *As plays the sun upon the glassy streams,*
> *Twinkling another counterfeited beam,*
> *So seems this gorgeous beauty to mine eyes.*
>
> V.3.54–7, 62–4

Equally artificial and mannered, though more distinguished, are the scenes between Talbot and his son before Bordeaux (IV.5–7). The imagery is much richer than elsewhere in the play, the elements of allegorization and classical personification are stronger, and the extensive use of compound and double-barrelled epithets has the effect of formalizing the heroic deaths of Henry V's spiritual heirs:

> *But when my angry guardant stood alone,*
> *Tendering my ruin and assailed of none,*

Dizzy-eyed fury and great rage of heart
Suddenly made him from my side to start
Into the clustering battle of the French;
And in that sea of blood my boy did drench
His over-mounting spirit; and there died
My Icarus, my blossom, in his pride.

IV.7.9–16

There are some scenes in which the poetry is palpably superior to both the artificial-conventional and the plain dull. They include the strong straightforward narrative writing of the scene between Mortimer and Richard Plantagenet in the Tower (II.5); and, more remarkably, the scene in the Temple Garden (II.4). Shakespeare's elaborate artificial manner is certainly present in the latter scene in such lines as those of Warwick:

Between two hawks, which flies the higher pitch;
Between two dogs, which hath the deeper mouth;
Between two blades, which bears the better temper;
Between two horses, which doth bear him best;
Between two girls, which hath the merriest eye,
I have perhaps some shallow spirit of judgement.

II.4.11–16

But the complete scene, founded on the basic imagery of flowers and the garden of state, has a poetic effectiveness and coherence found elsewhere only in single striking lines:

RICHARD
Now, Somerset, where is your argument?
SOMERSET
Here in my scabbard, meditating that
Shall dye your white rose in a bloody red.
RICHARD
Meantime your cheeks do counterfeit our roses;

> *For pale they look with fear, as witnessing*
> *The truth on our side.*
>
> SOMERSET   *No, Plantagenet,*
> *'Tis not for fear, but anger, that thy cheeks*
> *Blush for pure shame to counterfeit our roses,*
> *And yet thy tongue will not confess thy error.*
>
> RICHARD
> *Hath not thy rose a canker Somerset?*
>
> SOMERSET
> *Hath not thy rose a thorn, Plantagenet?*
>
> RICHARD
> *Ay, sharp and piercing, to maintain his truth,*
> *Whiles thy consuming canker eats his falsehood.*
>
> II.4.59–71

*

Despite the variety of styles and the apparently haphazard mingling of historical fact with fiction, it is clear that in the play as we have it there is an organizing imagination at work shaping the historical materials. Further, this unifying force has produced a vision of man the political animal as he is simultaneously the instigator and victim of events in time.

The play has a single theme: the deterioration of England as a national unit and as an influential international power. We witness the double pressure exercised by division and internal weakness that erode government, and the sequence of partial success and incremental failure that characterize the country's adventures abroad. The dramatic method adopted to project this vision of collapse is not a linear narrative recounting of events, but tableau-like repetitive alignments of characters, situations, and visual arrangements. We do not find at work Shakespeare's more usual technique of initial presentation of an action followed by the gradual poetic and dramatic exploration of its deepening implications. The effect is more of a theatrical montage in which simply what scenes and characters are constitutes the comment and qualification they make on similar scenes and figures at other points in the play.

The spectacle of disintegration that is the play's central concern is set against the memory of former national glory personified by Henry V – Holinshed's ideal of puissance and magnanimity, the two qualities which in the course of the play are seen to be eschewed or defeated. It is significant that Act I, scene 1, opens not with praise of Henry V's deeds, but with a lament that they have ceased with his death. This rhetorical setpiece is frustrated by the flare-up of personal enmity between Gloucester and Winchester. As Bedford attempts to get the funeral back on to its proper course, the pattern of frustration is repeated by the interruptions of the messengers announcing the loss of the French towns, Charles V's coronation, and Talbot's capture. This news serves to bring the courtiers to a sense of national duty – the 'oaths to Henry sworn' – and a semblance of unity appears in the concerted decision to act immediately in France. As the scene ends, this unity in its turn is qualified by Winchester's plan to gain control of the young King Henry VI and so 'sit at chiefest stern of public weal' (I.1.177).

This pattern of well-established values being threatened by the immediate pressures of personal ambition is repeated at other moments of symbolic importance. For example, Act III, scene 1, begins with a similar formal entry of the King and his court into the Parliament House. The dispute between Gloucester and Winchester assumes physical proportions in the struggle over the posting of the bill. Somerset and Warwick take sides, and it is the young King who verbalizes for the audience the implications of what they are witnessing:

> *O, what a scandal is it to our crown*
> *That two such noble peers as ye should jar!*
> *Believe me, lords, my tender years can tell*
> *Civil dissension is a viperous worm*
> *That gnaws the bowels of the commonwealth.*
>
> III.1.69–73

This very point is illustrated by stage action as the servants of the two noblemen enter and the Mayor of London depicts how civil strife seeps down from the court into the lower reaches of society. The King patches up a truce between his advisers, his elevation of York to a dukedom draws an expression of hatred from Somerset in an aside, and Exeter is left to utter the true state of affairs behind the concord:

> *This late dissension grown betwixt the peers*
> *Burns under feignèd ashes of forged love ...*
>
> III.1.191–2

and to underline the contrast between this and the former reign.

More significant still, because by its location it links the internal dissension with foreign affairs, is the coronation scene in Paris (IV.1). The opening depicts verbally and visually an oath of loyalty; but disruption is seen at various levels. Personal defection is displayed in Falstaff's cowardice and national defection in the letter from Burgundy. The extended treatment of the squabble between Vernon and Basset is a reflection of the more central division of the Temple Garden; and Henry's efforts at reconciliation are undercut by his choosing to wear Somerset's red rose and by York's half-spoken threat. Once again it is Exeter who acts as the chorus figure to set these actions in the context of their known outcome:

But howsoe'er, no simple man that sees
This jarring discord of nobility . . .
But that it doth presage some ill event.
'Tis much when sceptres are in children's hands;
But more when envy breeds unkind division.
There comes the ruin, there begins confusion.

IV.1.187-8, 191-4

In each of these three scenes, the structure as well as the content serves to convey the central idea, as tenuous surface agreement is shattered by threat, vituperation, physical violence, or explicitly drawn conclusions about inevitable future chaos.

The ideal state of unity and foreign success from which the nation is slipping is kept continually before the audience by both allusion and dramatic demonstration. Its chief representative is Henry V, whose spirit not only dominates the opening scene but is invoked by characters of very different kinds throughout the play. In the main action, Henry's surrogates are the older generation of soldiers – Bedford, Salisbury, and Talbot. All three captains are not only linked verbally with the dead King; they are examples of the traditional English martial virtues that even the French acknowledge:

Froissart, a countryman of ours, records
England all Olivers and Rolands bred
During the time Edward the Third did reign.
More truly now may this be verified;
For none but Samsons and Goliases
It sendeth forth to skirmish.   I.2.29-34

Yet for all the heroism and self-sacrifice displayed in the battle scenes, it is with the deaths of these leaders that English successes are linked. Salisbury falls by a French trick at Orleans; and Talbot's subsequent achievement in recapturing the town is viewed almost totally as an act of revenge which ensures that Salisbury's obsequies may be observed in 'The middle centre of this cursèd town' and that he attain eternal fame by means of

> *A tomb, wherein his corpse shall be interred;*
> *Upon the which, that everyone may read,*
> *Shall be engraved the sack of Orleans,*
> *The treacherous manner of his mournful death,*
> *And what a terror he had been to France.*
>
> II.2.13–17

The same connexion between English loss and success is repeated at the siege of Rouen. As Salisbury's body was placed at centre stage, so Bedford in his invalid chair watches the French defeat and dies happy. His funeral rites are briefer, but they too are performed in a retaken French town that 'hangs her head for grief' (III.2.124).

It is, however, Talbot that is the leading member of the trio and whose character and conduct most nearly represent all that Henry V stood for. He attracts to himself unanimous praise as the ideal warrior who prevails by main force, character, dedication, and reputation – a soldier of the pre-gunpowder age of warfare, whose adherence to the old standards of honour and aristocratic virtues is absolute. His first lines, for example, are a complaint that while he was in captivity the French offered to exchange him for 'a baser man-of-arms' than 'the brave Lord Ponton de Santrailles'. Not only did he refuse but 'cravèd death' rather than accept the insult to his nobility.

Under Talbot's command the English fight by the chivalric textbook. When the French are content to revile the English from the safety of their city walls, Talbot's sense of rightness is outraged: 'Dare ye come forth and meet us in the field?' he asks before Rouen; 'Will ye, like soldiers, come and fight it out?' The lack of proper

martial standards in the French violates all his notions of
the heroic ideal, birth, and fame:

> *Base muleteers of France!*
> *Like peasant footboys do they keep the walls*
> *And dare not take up arms like gentlemen.*
>
> III.2.68–70

Each English military success is seen therefore not only as
an act of revenge for a fallen captain, but also as a punishment for French violations of the chivalric code of war:
the 'base Walloon' who, 'to win the Dauphin's grace, |
Thrust Talbot with a spear into the back' (I.1.137–8); the
'hellish mischief' used to capture Rouen (III.2.39); the
'scoffs and scorns and contumelious taunts' that the captured Talbot suffers in being made a public spectacle in
the French market-place (I.4.39); the dastardly treachery
that takes Salisbury's life (I.4); and the 'false dissembling
guile' of Burgundy (IV.1.63).

It is in the role of Talbot that we see worked out the
implications of this code of honour and its compensations
of great name. The immortality of earthly fame is connected quite explicitly with the deaths of Henry V, Bedford, and Salisbury in the speeches delivered over their
corpses. In Talbot's case the issue is raised during his last
hours and is thus dramatically rather than elegiacally
treated. His instinctive order to his son states the norm as
he has practised it on behalf of others: 'Fly, to revenge
my death if I be slain' (IV.5.18). But young Talbot poses
the dilemma entailed:

> *Surely, by all the glory you have won,*
> *An if I fly, I am not Talbot's son.*
>
> IV.6.50–51

As Talbot himself has made clear at the exequies for
Salisbury, 'name' is the permanent record of heroic ser-

vice. The English soldiers who charge the French with the cry 'À Talbot! À Talbot!' are simply translating this idea into practical terms, as is the soldier who finds that 'The cry of "Talbot" serves me for a sword' (II.1.79). In normal times, this 'name' is the possession that Talbot would leave to his posterity. However, because the play traces the fading of such ideals, we see this posterity with him at his death in the person of young Talbot. As the young man bears the name he does and is his father's son, he must remain and fight; but with the inevitable result that the father realizes:

> In thee thy mother dies, our household's name,
> My death's revenge, thy youth, and England's fame.
>
> IV.6.38–9

Appropriately Talbot and his son are depicted in death almost as a tomb and monument to dead chivalry, an effect that is helped by Sir Thomas Lucy's recital of Talbot's honours taken from his actual tomb in the Cathedral of Rouen (IV.7.61–71). It is noticeable, however, that, even while thus freezing the English hero's death into a historical occasion, Shakespeare also provides his audience with a second view of it. If a fifteenth-century tomb is indeed conjured up by the verse and the arrangement of the figures on the stage, so too is the reminder of the rotten corpse that lies beneath its splendid exterior in Joan's reply to Lucy:

> Him that thou magnifiest with all these titles
> Stinking and flyblown lies here at our feet.
>
> IV.7.75–6

*

In strong contrast to the English adherence to old chivalric ideals is the extreme practicality that governs the French camp. For Charles and his followers, textbook soldiering holds no attraction: Rouen is recaptured by soldiers disguised as peasants, who sneak into the city and admit their forces with covert signals; and English captains are shot by waiting gunners at Orleans. Yet this strategy works; for whereas English success is linked with loss and leads ultimately to the waste of Talbot, the French move from each set-back with increasing confidence until they are able to conclude an advantageous peace despite the loss of their heroine.

At the centre of the French scenes stands Joan la Pucelle, who is thus Talbot's dramatic opposite. Shakespeare has frequently been criticized for his portrayal of her; but much of the disapproval is based on the twentieth century's sentimentalization of this most peculiar saint in the calendar, who typically stimulated the imagination of George Bernard Shaw. The contrast she furnishes with Talbot is carefully worked out. Whereas his ideals are heroic, old-fashioned, aristocratic, his service that naturally expected of noble birth, Joan's tricky expediency is viewed as the product of her base origins. She is appropriately introduced to the Dauphin by the Bastard of Orleans, and was herself illegitimately conceived (according to her father's evidence at her trial). Furthermore, in her attempts to escape death she claims to have conceived a bastard by one or other of the French nobles; and, in strong contrast with young John Talbot, she is ready to deny her father and her family name.

In the chronicles Shakespeare found two versions of her career: a 'French' one, which stressed the idea of the 'damsel divine', and an 'English' one, which claimed her to be a 'damnable sorcerer suborned by Satan'. For the bulk of the play her character is built upon the ironic juxtaposition of both these attitudes. Much of what is said about her is deliberately equivocal, so that even the highest praise of her is combined with some kind of debasing commentary, thus developing the quibble possible in her name: 'Pucelle' (virgin) and 'pussel' (harlot). The scene of her introduction to the Dauphin is typical of the method of characterization adopted. The Bastard of Orleans introduces her, with no irony, as a saint:

> Be not dismayed, for succour is at hand.
> A holy maid hither with me I bring,
> Which, by a vision sent to her from heaven,
> Ordainèd is to raise this tedious siege
> And drive the English forth the bounds of France.
> The spirit of deep prophecy she hath,
> Exceeding the nine sibyls of old Rome.

I.2.50–56

This is immediately followed by Joan's own claims to specifically Christian powers:

> Heaven and Our Lady gracious hath it pleased
> To shine on my contemptible estate.
> Lo, whilst I waited on my tender lambs ...
> God's Mother deignèd to appear to me,
> And in a vision full of majesty
> Willed me to leave my base vocation
> And free my country from calamity.

I.2.74–6, 78–81

However, once she is alone with the Dauphin, their exchanges are shot through with bawdy *double entendres*, as Charles falls into the idiom of the conventional lover:

> Impatiently I burn with thy desire;
> My heart and hands thou hast at once subdued.
> Excellent Pucelle, if thy name be so,
> Let me thy servant and not sovereign be ...

I.2.108–11

and Joan repels his advances with what is clearly only a temporary refusal:

26

> *I must not yield to any rites of love,*
> *For my profession's sacred from above.*
> *When I have chasèd all thy foes from hence,*
> *Then I will think upon a recompense.*

I.2.113–16

The watching courtiers also indulge in sexual innuendo as they comment upstage on the form the encounter takes.

The same method of qualification appears later, after the English attack on Orleans, when a possible liaison between Joan and Charles is ambiguously suggested (II.2.28–31); and even Charles, when making a conscious effort to elevate Joan to superhuman stature, tends to mingle pagan with Christian allusion in the Marlovian manner:

> *'Tis Joan, not we, by whom the day is won;*
> *For which I will divide my crown with her,*
> *And all the priests and friars in my realm*
> *Shall in procession sing her endless praise.*
> *A statelier pyramis to her I'll rear*
> *Than Rhodope's of Memphis ever was.*
> *In memory of her, when she is dead,*
> *Her ashes, in an urn more precious*
> *Than the rich-jewelled coffer of Darius,*
> *Transported shall be at high festivals*
> *Before the kings and queens of France.*
> *No longer on Saint Denis will we cry,*
> *But Joan la Pucelle shall be France's saint.*

I.6.17–29

On the English side there emerges a similar doubleness of view. For example, Burgundy at Orleans seems in no doubt that Joan is the Dauphin's trull (II.2.28); but later he is the bewildered subject of her inexplicable powers of persuasion and personality (III.3.44–84). Talbot too, while convinced of her base birth, witchcraft, and trickery, pays tribute to her extraordinary powers:

> *My thoughts are whirlèd like a potter's wheel;*
> *I know not where I am nor what I do.*
> *A witch by fear, not force, like Hannibal,*
> *Drives back our troops and conquers as she lists.*

I.5.19–22

Even Joan herself seems in two minds about her mission. While she can speak like the divinely inspired maid of legend, she more often emerges as a confident, blunt-spoken, successful exponent of military pragmatism, who can be the eloquent voice of French patriotism as she addresses Burgundy, but is simultaneously the ironic commentator on her own success in effecting the Duke's desertion of the English cause:

> *Done like a Frenchman – (aside) turn and turn again.*

III.3.85

Her spectacular degeneration in the fifth act is merely a display of the lack of true saintliness that has been implicit in the presentation of her character in the previous scenes. Her conjuring of the demons (V.3) supports the earlier accusations of witchcraft; but its positioning immediately before her capture by York and the actual ineffectiveness of her familiars serve only to support the prevailing impression of her character. In her final appearance (V.4) the 'English' view of Joan is seen to dominate; yet even here some attempt is made to utilize the associations of the Pucelle/pussel dichotomy that lies at the basis of her portrayal.

Although she is the central figure in the French party, Joan is also one element in some larger patterns in the play. In opposition to Talbot, she obviously represents expediency, self-interest, base designs, and personal desires which characterize the behaviour of the divided English nobles as well. And her easy success as the manipulator of the Bastard, Charles, and Burgundy is set alongside two parallel scenes which illustrate contrasting English responses to similar female temptation or guile.

The first of these concerns the Countess of Auvergne's attempt to trick Talbot by her proffered hospitality into becoming her prisoner. She clearly has pretensions to being another heroine of France and she speaks of herself in the vein of Marlovian pastiche that the Dauphin applies to Joan:

> *if all things fall out right,*
> *I shall as famous be by this exploit*
> *As Scythian Tomyris by Cyrus' death.*
>
> II.3.4–6

Her invitation to Talbot is to the core of his heroic code:

> *To visit her poor castle where she lies,*
> *That she may boast she hath beheld the man*
> *Whose glory fills the world with loud report.*
>
> II.2.41–3

As the scene of their encounter unfolds, there emerges the familiar Elizabethan fascination with the ideas of shadow and substance, which is to reappear at Talbot's death with its twin realities of his stinking flyblown corpse and his time-transcending fame (IV.7). The Countess mistakenly believes there to be an exact congruity between the magnitude of Talbot's achievement and his physical being: that 'the scourge of France', 'so much feared abroad', must necessarily be

> *some Hercules,*
> *A second Hector, for his grim aspect*
> *And large proportion of his strong-knit limbs.*
>
> II.3.18–20

Her plot fails because the 'weak and writhled shrimp' that stands before her is fully aware that the physical man is but the shadow, the 'least proportion of humanity', whose 'substance, sinews, arms, and strength' lie in the army which is the physical reality of his military code.

A more successful, if less deliberately conniving, Frenchwoman, who also parallels Joan in her Delilah-like role, is Margaret of Anjou. The scene between her and Suffolk towards the end of the play is often claimed by scholars to be merely a preparatory link with *Henry VI, Part Two*; but it requires no such justification. The scene is palpably designed to weld together the themes of war and internal dissension. Up to this point Suffolk has had no role of any importance; but it is noticeable that he alone in the Temple Garden chooses the red rose with Somerset, and also expresses his Machiavellian principles in lines which anticipate his motives in the marriage negotiations:

> *Faith, I have been a truant in the law*
> *And never yet could frame my will to it;*
> *And therefore frame the law unto my will.*

II.4.7–9

It is this same Suffolk that we see depicted in the final battle scene as ambitious politician, unfaithful husband, and pseudo–Petrarchan lover of a French prisoner, and who is so obviously contrasted with Talbot, the ultimate self-sacrifice of whom we have witnessed just three scenes previously. Suffolk's erotic clichés are a measure of the distance English ideals have fallen, even as his success in persuading King Henry to break his contract with the Earl of Armagnac's daughter concentrates into a specific action the self-interest which now prevails in the realm. The 'fame' that Talbot so prized and which struck terror into England's enemies is now contrasted with the 'breath of . . . renown' of a French princess which produces in

England's ruler a lust that is like the 'rigour of tempestuous gusts' driving him

> *Either to suffer shipwreck or arrive*
> *Where I may have fruition of her love.*
>
> V.5.8–9

Just how great this shipwreck is to be is underlined by Suffolk, as he links himself with the Trojan Paris:

> *Thus Suffolk hath prevailed; and thus he goes,*
> *As did the youthful Paris once to Greece,*
> *With hope to find the like event in love.*
>
> V.5.103–5

Margaret's role in the affair is much less active than Suffolk's; but only a scanty knowledge of the Wars of the Roses on the part of Shakespeare's audience would be necessary for them to detect in her a successful version of the Countess of Auvergne and a second Joan of Arc whose full mischief is yet in the womb of time.

*

The national disintegration charted in the French battle scenes is complemented by the happenings at the English court. These deal not with a number of secondary themes, as is often argued, but with diverse aspects of the same one. The enmity between Winchester and Gloucester, the York–Suffolk rivalry, the quarrel in the Temple Garden and its offshoot between Vernon and Basset, York's dynastic claims to the crown, Suffolk's personal ambitions, the ineffectiveness of King Henry, and even Falstaff's and Burgundy's treachery all work together with the war scenes to give a complete picture of England's decline. The relationship between internal and international events is made at many points in the play, as Shakespeare takes his cue from the chronicles and brings into relationship the facts that 'some cities by fraudulent practices, other-some by martial prowess, were recovered by the French' and that the 'devilish division that reigned in England so encombered the heads of the noblemen there that the honour of the realm was clearly forgotten'. The opening scene links the disasters in France with the dispute between Gloucester and Winchester. This is then given extended treatment in the third scene, which illustrates how the personally motivated squabbles between powerful men can spread to physical violence and civil broils among the commons, which can be stopped not by the instigators themselves but by official outside intervention only.

The quarrel flares up again later and its development may serve to show how Shakespeare treats the issue of internal strife as a whole. Even within the limits of the immature character portrayal that prevails in the play, some distinction is made between the natures and motivations of the participants. Gloucester is obviously over-aware of his position and authority, that 'There's none Protector of the realm but I' (I.3.12); and one feels that it is the affront to his personal pride that prompts his attack on Winchester's retainers (I.3) rather than any genuine fear that the Cardinal's ambitions pose a threat to the unity of the nation. Nevertheless, at the King's request Gloucester is seen to be willing to swallow his pride in order to come to terms with the Cardinal in the interests of the national good when these are pointed out to him (III.1). His adversary Winchester is depicted almost totally in negative terms. Shakespeare's audience would certainly have reacted adversely to this 'Peeled priest' of Rome with his political pretensions and the taint of moral decadence. He has no interest in the national welfare; pride and ambition are the mainsprings of his actions. At both moments in the play when the English peers agree on concerted action, it is Winchester who remains behind on

32

stage to soliloquize about his future plans, in which there is no doubt as to whose interest is paramount. At I.1.173–7:

> *Each hath his place and function to attend;*
> *I am left out; for me nothing remains.*
> *But long I will not be Jack out of office.*
> *The King from Eltham I intend to steal*
> *And sit at chiefest stern of public weal.*

And at V.1.58–62 his alternatives are made even plainer:

> *Humphrey of Gloucester, thou shalt well perceive*
> *That neither in birth or for authority*
> *The Bishop will be overborne by thee.*
> *I'll either make thee stoop and bend thy knee*
> *Or sack this country with a mutiny.*

It matters little that the play shows no outcome of all Winchester's plottings; they are merely a part of the keenly felt animosity and repetitive scheming that are endemic at the court and that make future chaos inevitable.

Parallel to this dispute is that between Somerset and York. Like Winchester, Somerset eschews patriotic self-abnegation and acts in accordance with the dictates of his pride. In the Temple Garden (II.4) he submits to majority decision; but when it goes against him, he erupts into threats and recriminations. Later, when York is restored to his dukedom, his is the lone voice which mars the tone of apparent accord (III.1). It is significant that he alone utters the only English condemnation of Talbot the play contains:

> *This expedition was by York and Talbot*
> *Too rashly plotted. . . .*
>   *The over-daring Talbot*
> *Hath sullied all his gloss of former honour*
> *By this unheedful, desperate, wild adventure.*
>
>   IV.4.2–3, 5–7

This attitude to Talbot's feats is found appropriately in the mouth of the man whose prickly self-regard and personal vendetta with York lead directly to the death of the last of the great English leaders.

York, like Gloucester, is portrayed with greater sympathy. He is the less culpable in the breach of military etiquette that leads to Talbot's death; and it is he who assumes Talbot's role in restoring English self-respect in the later scenes of the play. His voice is raised against the proposed truce with France; he is the captor of Joan; and in general he stands among the more constructive elements in the court scenes. However, York's personal differences with Somerset are seen to have more far-reaching effects than Gloucester's with Winchester. This is because York is the leading figure in the Temple Garden scene, which is generally agreed to be the most effective in the play. The other scenes dealing with the internal conflict show how courtly decorum may be shattered by personal feud; but this scene alone demonstrates just how brittle is even the façade of agreement and social cohesion in England. It is noteworthy that we never know what it is that prompts the quarrel: we are simply told it is 'a case of truth'. What is important is that the real issues raised are feudal enmity and personal ambition. It is ironical that the form the quarrel takes is a concern with honour, birth, and fame – those concepts which in Talbot and his son were fully identified with the English cause in France. But for the squabbling courtiers what matters are 'nice sharp quillets of the law', taunts of a father's ill-fame, and histrionic gestures in response to a schoolboy 'dare' about the man who is 'a true-born gentleman/And stands upon the honour of his birth'.

Everything about the scene serves to prove that Shakespeare's imagination was sparked. The slackness and periphrasis found elsewhere in the verse are here replaced by succinctness and economy and fluency. Even the stylized rhetoric and flower imagery effectively convey a courtly polish barely concealing bitter personal and political conflict. The strong visual stage effects entailed in the plucking and wearing of the red and white roses work closely with the verbal quibbling on the ideas of garden and state, red and blood, white and shame; and together they must have made an irresistible appeal to an audience who knew the bitter fruits this seed was to produce in English history. The scenes involving Vernon and Basset indicate briefly but vividly the way the effects of the dispute spread quickly into the fabric of the nation and out of any effective control of its initiators.

York also constitutes a threat to national peace unconnected with the other courtiers in that he is the heir to the Yorkist claim to the crown itself. The scene with Mortimer in the Tower (II.5) treats at length, in serviceable and sometimes memorable blank verse, the historical background to this claim, and serves as a prologue to the emergence of York as yet another ambitious riser competing with Winchester and Suffolk. But although he assures us he intends

> Either to be restorèd to my blood
> Or make my ill th' advantage of my good ...
>
> II.5.128–9

the later scenes find him suppressing his anger at the King's show of partiality to Somerset's side; submerging his personal ambition for the benefit of the nation; and assuming Talbot's mantle so as to provide a strong patriotic note for the war scenes to end on:

> Then swear allegiance to his majesty:
> As thou art knight, never to disobey
> Nor be rebellious to the crown of England –
> Thou, nor thy nobles, to the crown of England.
>
> V.4.169–72

There is one final source of national weakness – Henry VI himself. He is first called a child; but by Act III he is shown displaying some grasp of the responsibilities of his royal position as he plays the orator in making a temporary peace between the red and white rose factions and persuades Winchester and Gloucester to at least a show of reconciliation. Behind these demonstrations, however, there lies the worrying Elizabethan commonplace voiced by Exeter:

> *'Tis much when sceptres are in children's hands;*
> *But more when envy breeds unkind division.*
> *There comes the ruin, there begins confusion.*

IV.1.192–4

A state with a ruler in his minority is bad enough, even when he is guided by a wise nobility; but when this nobility is in 'jarring discord', even good advice can be nullified by the pressures of another faction. This is what is worked out in the scenes devoted to the marriage contract with which the play ends. Although Henry's first reaction to the suggestion of marriage is all demur and submission to Gloucester, under Suffolk's influence he gives way to lustful imaginings. It is made clear that his decision to marry Margaret of Anjou is wrong in every sense. His breaking of his earlier agreement with the Earl of Armagnac degrades his honour; Margaret is beneath him in rank; she brings him no political alliance of any note; and her father's poverty encourages Henry to levy punitive taxes on his own subjects. This marriage to an unsuitable Frenchwoman is the final stage in the degeneration of the English court and simultaneously crowns the 'effeminate peace' which is an unsatisfactory end to the wars that caused

> *the slaughter of so many peers,*
> *So many captains, gentlemen, and soldiers,*

That in this quarrel have been overthrown
And sold their bodies for their country's benefit.

V.4.103–6

*

Many of the features of *1 Henry VI* that are seen as unsatisfactory, and are habitually excused on the supposition
of the badness of the Folio text or multiple layers of composition or composite authorship, are in fact basic to the
intention and design of the play. For the vision of history
it embodies is not so very different in its fundamentals
from that of Shakespeare's mature historical works – even
though the degree of poetic and dramatic skill displayed
in it is markedly inferior to theirs.

All Shakespeare's histories are concerned with man's
attempted management of events in the context of his
society. All depict actions which are the result of an idea,
or belief, or conviction, or of drives deeply rooted in a
particular human personality. All explore with growing
profundity how men are at once the agents and victims of
their attempts to manipulate time. In *1 Henry VI* Shakespeare takes advantage of his audience's familiarity with
the dramatic materials and their known outcome in history
in order to create his characteristic double view, which
combines the theatrical immediacy of events as they
appeared to the participants and the recorded knowledge
of their consequences. Talbot, Bedford, and Salisbury live
by and through their heroic ideals; but they are seen to
operate in a world where such conduct can have little but
temporary success in the new conditions represented by
Joan and the French. The English nobles are committed
to their narrow personal ambitions; and all are convinced
that they can predict the outcome of their actions. The
play suggests that such confidence is as unfounded as
Talbot's; and so it is shot through with Winchester's

mutterings against Gloucester, York's prophecies that his quarrel with Somerset will drench English soil with blood, Suffolk's certainties about his control of the crown through Margaret, Gloucester's vague forebodings of civil chaos, and Exeter's warnings based on proven political truths. None of these threats and promises is seen to come to anything during the course of the play. Rather what we witness is the way in which the pressing personal demands of small men, in pursuit of their own instead of a greater good, blossom to become historical fact under the influence of factors outside their control or remain as still-born testimony to the depressing pervasiveness of such activity in the play as in life itself.

The inconclusiveness of the ending may certainly be viewed as preparation for the other two parts; but it is also the natural outcome of the deliberately planned inconclusiveness of much that the play contains. At this early point in his career, Shakespeare already knew that the history play by its very nature is a piece of shaped incompleteness, that it is a patterned swatch of time dramatized in the full knowledge of prior event and sequent outcome. For all its weaknesses, *1 Henry VI* is an example of that art which the mature Shakespeare perfected and which Edmund Spenser described to Walter Raleigh in this way:

> *The method of a poet historical is not such as of an historiographer. For an historiographer discourseth of affairs orderly as they were, accounting as well the times as the actions; but a poet thrusteth into the midst, even where it most concerneth him, and there recoursing to things forepast, and divining of things to come, maketh a pleasing analysis of all.*

(Letter appended to *The Faerie Queene*)

FURTHER READING

GOOD surveys of scholarly and critical work done on the play are those by Harold Jenkins in *Shakespeare Survey 6* (Cambridge, 1953); by Ronald Berman in *A Reader's Guide to Shakespeare's Plays* (second edition, New York, 1973); and by A. R. Humphreys in *Shakespeare: Select Bibliographical Guides*, edited by Stanley Wells (Oxford, 1974).

Text, Date, and Authorship

The best reproduction of the text in the first Folio is in *The Norton Facsimile: The First Folio of Shakespeare*, prepared by Charlton Hinman (New York, 1968), and the most detailed analyses of it are in the same scholar's *The Printing and Proof-reading of the First Folio of Shakespeare* (2 volumes, Oxford, 1963), in W. W. Greg's *The Shakespeare First Folio* (Oxford, 1955), and in Andrew S. Cairncross's edition for the new Arden Shakespeare (London, 1962). In the eighteenth century most critics doubted that Shakespeare was the sole author of the play, and Edmond Malone presented the first reasoned examination of the evidence in 1787. In the late nineteenth century the play was first divided among possible authors, and later H. C. Hart in his old Arden Shakespeare edition (London, 1909), Allison Gaw in *The Origin and Development of '1 Henry VI'* (Los Angeles, 1926), and Dover Wilson in his edition for the New Cambridge Shakespeare (Cambridge, 1952) apportioned various parts of the play among Robert Greene, Thomas Nashe, and George Peele. Dr Johnson had believed that the play was Shakespeare's and the three parts written in sequence; and in 1903 W. J. Courthope argued that only Shakespeare was capable of planning the whole drama (*A History of English Poetry*, Volume IV (London, 1903), Appendix). Peter Alexander's *Shakespeare's 'Henry VI' and 'Richard III'* (Cambridge, 1929) convinced most scholars that Shakespeare was the author; and his conclusions received support from Hereward T. Price in his *Construction in Shakespeare* (East Lansing, Michigan, 1951) and Leo Kirschbaum in 'The Authorship of *1 Henry VI*', *Publications of the Modern Language Association of America* 67 (1952), 809–22. More recently Marco Mincoff has argued on stylistic grounds that the play was Shakespeare's first composition and that he revised it in 1594 ('The Composition of *Henry VI*, Part 1', *Shakespeare Quarterly* 16 (1965), 279–87); Clifford Leech suggested that a two-part play was equipped with a fore-piece (*Part One*) later revised to strengthen its connexion with the previously written *Parts Two* and *Three* ('The Two-Part Play. Marlowe and the Early Shakespeare', *Shakespeare Jahrbuch* 94 (1958), 90–106). Most of these studies discuss the date, which is placed variously between 1589 and 1592, with possible revision around 1594.

Sources

The chronicles of Edward Hall, Raphael Holinshed, Robert Fabyan, and Richard Grafton are available in early nineteenth-century reprints; the details are given at the head of the Commentary. It is still disputable whether Hall or Holinshed was the principal source. There is a good general article on the use of the chronicles in all three parts of the play by R. A. Law in *Texas Studies in English* 33 (1955), 13–32. Geoffrey Bullough's introduction to his source selections in Volume III (London, 1960) of his *Narrative and Dramatic Sources of Shakespeare* is an invaluable essay.

Criticism

A number of useful books supply accounts of Elizabethan attitudes to history. E. M. W. Tillyard's influential *The Elizabethan World Picture* (London, 1943) gives a summary of the official theory of government, and there are full studies of the history plays of the period in Irving Ribner's *The English History Play in the Age of Shakespeare* (Princeton, N.J., 1957; revised edition London, 1965) and David M. Bevington's

Tudor Drama and Politics: A Critical Approach to Topical Meaning (Cambridge, Mass., 1968).

Among studies of the history plays which see them as reflecting orthodox Elizabethan political beliefs are Tillyard's *Shakespeare's History Plays* (London, 1944), Lily B. Campbell's *Shakespeare's 'Histories': Mirrors of Elizabethan Policy* (San Marino, California, 1947), M. M. Reese's *The Cease of Majesty: A Study of Shakespeare's History Plays* (London, 1961), and S. C. Sen Gupta's *Shakespeare's Historical Plays* (Oxford, 1964). Recent critics have tended to find the plays less conservative in their political ideas. For example, Henry A. Kelly, in his *Divine Providence in the England of Shakespeare's Histories* (Cambridge, Mass., 1970), worked out freshly how Shakespeare treated the ideas he found in the chronicles; and Michael Manheim's *The Weak King Dilemma in the Shakespearean History Play* (Syracuse, N.Y., 1973) contains a penetrating sympathetic analysis of Henry VI as king and man.

There have been a number of full studies of the *Henry VI* sequence. R. B. Pierce examines the family–state correspondences in *Shakespeare's History Plays: The Family and the State* (Columbus, Ohio, 1971); E. W. Talbert's *Elizabethan Drama and Shakespeare's Early Plays* (Chapel Hill, North Carolina, 1963) shows a fine awareness of the problems of dramatizing history; David Riggs has some good comment on how the characters reflect political beliefs in *Shakespeare's Heroical Histories: 'Henry VI' and Its Literary Tradition* (Cambridge, Mass., 1971). Various studies emphasize particular aspects of the plays: Don M. Ricks in *Shakespeare's Emergent Form* (Logan, Utah, 1968) examines the structural principles; Robert Ornstein is perspicacious on character and style in *A Kingdom for a Stage: The Achievement of Shakespeare's History Plays* (Cambridge, Mass., 1972); Edward I. Berry's *Patterns of Decay: Shakespeare's Early Histories* (Charlottesville, Virginia, 1975) is a well-written exploration of the way central themes are embodied; and Robert Y. Turner's *Shakespeare's Apprenticeship* (Chicago, 1974) contains a subtle appreciation of aspects of the plays' dramaturgy. The most stimulating shorter essays on the sequence are J. P. Brockbank's in

Early Shakespeare (Stratford-upon-Avon Studies No. 3), edited by J. R. Brown and Bernard Harris (London, 1961), and A. C. Hamilton's in his *The Early Shakespeare* (San Marino, California, 1967). Among writings on particular aspects of the play are Sigurd Burckhardt's analysis of the Countess of Auvergne scene in *Shakespearean Meanings* (Princeton, N.J., 1968); H. D. F. Kitto's examination of the Temple Garden scene in *More Talking of Shakespeare*, edited by John Garrett (London, 1959); and C. M. Kay's imagery study in *Studies in the Literary Imagination* 1 (1972), 1–26.

Accounts of how the plays have fared on the stage can be found in C. B. Young's notes in Dover Wilson's editions and in Arthur Colby Sprague's *Shakespeare's Histories: Plays for the Stage* (London, 1964). Particular productions are discussed in Sir Barry Jackson's 'On Producing *Henry VI*', *Shakespeare Survey 6* (1953), and John Russell Brown's analysis of Peter Hall's and John Barton's version, *The Wars of the Roses*, in *Shakespeare's Plays in Performance* (London, 1966).

THE FIRST PART OF
KING HENRY THE SIXTH

THE CHARACTERS IN THE PLAY

KING HENRY THE SIXTH

DUKE OF GLOUCESTER, Lord Protector and uncle of the King

DUKE OF BEDFORD, Regent of France and uncle of the King

DUKE OF EXETER, Thomas Beaufort, great-uncle of the King

BISHOP OF WINCHESTER, Henry Beaufort, great-uncle of the King, later a Cardinal

DUKE OF SOMERSET, John Beaufort, formerly Earl of Somerset

RICHARD PLANTAGENET, later Duke of York and Regent of France

EARL OF WARWICK

EARL OF SALISBURY

William de la Pole, EARL OF SUFFOLK

LORD TALBOT, later Earl of Shrewsbury

JOHN TALBOT, his son

EDMUND MORTIMER, Earl of March

SIR WILLIAM GLANSDALE

SIR THOMAS GARGRAVE

SIR JOHN FALSTAFF

SIR WILLIAM LUCY

WOODVILLE, Lieutenant of the Tower of London

MAYOR OF LONDON

VERNON

BASSET

A LAWYER of the Temple

A PAPAL LEGATE

THE CHARACTERS IN THE PLAY

MESSENGERS
WARDERS of the Tower of London
SERVINGMEN
An OFFICER
A SOLDIER
CAPTAINS
A GAOLER
WATCH

CHARLES, Dauphin and later King of France
REIGNIER, Duke of Anjou and titular King of Naples
DUKE OF ALENÇON
BASTARD OF ORLEANS
DUKE OF BURGUNDY
GENERAL of the French army at Bordeaux
MASTER GUNNER of Orleans
A BOY, son of the Master Gunner
SHEPHERD, father of Joan la Pucelle
JOAN LA PUCELLE, Joan of Arc
MARGARET, daughter of Reignier
COUNTESS OF AUVERGNE
PORTER of the Countess of Auvergne
French SERGEANT
French SENTINEL
French SOLDIER
French SCOUT

English and French heralds, soldiers, servants, officers, sentinels, gentlemen, gaolers, attendants, courtiers, the Governor of Paris, ambassadors, fiends (Joan la Pucelle's familiars)

Dead march. Enter the funeral of King Henry the **I.1**
Fifth, attended on by the Duke of Bedford, Regent of
France; the Duke of Gloucester, Protector; the Duke
of Exeter; the Earl of Warwick; the Bishop of
Winchester; and the Duke of Somerset; with heralds

BEDFORD
  Hung be the heavens with black, yield day to night!
  Comets, importing change of times and states,
  Brandish your crystal tresses in the sky,
  And with them scourge the bad revolting stars
  That have consented unto Henry's death –
  King Henry the Fifth, too famous to live long!
  England ne'er lost a king of so much worth.

GLOUCESTER
  England ne'er had a king until his time.
  Virtue he had, deserving to command;
  His brandished sword did blind men with his beams;   10
  His arms spread wider than a dragon's wings;
  His sparkling eyes, replete with wrathful fire,
  More dazzled and drove back his enemies
  Than midday sun fierce bent against their faces.
  What should I say? His deeds exceed all speech;
  He ne'er lift up his hand but conquerèd.

EXETER
  We mourn in black; why mourn we not in blood?
  Henry is dead and never shall revive.
  Upon a wooden coffin we attend;
  And death's dishonourable victory   20
  We with our stately presence glorify,

Like captives bound to a triumphant car.
What? Shall we curse the planets of mishap
That plotted thus our glory's overthrow?
Or shall we think the subtle-witted French
Conjurers and sorcerers, that, afraid of him,
By magic verses have contrived his end?

WINCHESTER

He was a king blessed of the King of Kings.
Unto the French the dreadful Judgement Day
30 So dreadful will not be as was his sight.
The battles of the Lord of Hosts he fought;
The Church's prayers made him so prosperous.

GLOUCESTER

The Church? Where is it? Had not churchmen prayed,
His thread of life had not so soon decayed.
None do you like but an effeminate prince,
Whom like a schoolboy you may overawe.

WINCHESTER

Gloucester, whate'er we like, thou art Protector
And lookest to command the Prince and realm.
Thy wife is proud; she holdeth thee in awe
40 More than God or religious churchmen may.

GLOUCESTER

Name not religion, for thou lovest the flesh;
And ne'er throughout the year to church thou goest,
Except it be to pray against thy foes.

BEDFORD

Cease, cease these jars, and rest your minds in peace;
Let's to the altar. Heralds, wait on us.   *Exeunt heralds*
Instead of gold, we'll offer up our arms,
Since arms avail not, now that Henry's dead.
Posterity, await for wretched years,
When at their mothers' moistened eyes babes shall suck,
50 Our isle be made a nourish of salt tears,
And none but women left to wail the dead.

Henry the Fifth, thy ghost I invocate;
Prosper this realm, keep it from civil broils;
Combat with adverse planets in the heavens!
A far more glorious star thy soul will make
Than Julius Caesar or bright –
   Enter First Messenger

FIRST MESSENGER

My honourable lords, health to you all!
Sad tidings bring I to you out of France,
Of loss, of slaughter, and discomfiture:
Guienne, Champaigne, Rheims, Rouen, Orleans,   60
Paris, Gisors, Poitiers, are all quite lost.

BEDFORD

What sayest thou, man, before dead Henry's corse?
Speak softly, or the loss of those great towns
Will make him burst his lead and rise from death.

GLOUCESTER

Is Paris lost? Is Rouen yielded up?
If Henry were recalled to life again,
These news would cause him once more yield the ghost.

EXETER

How were they lost? What treachery was used?

FIRST MESSENGER

No treachery, but want of men and money.
Amongst the soldiers this is mutterèd,   70
That here you maintain several factions;
And whilst a field should be dispatched and fought,
You are disputing of your generals.
One would have lingering wars with little cost;
Another would fly swift, but wanteth wings;
A third thinks, without expense at all,
By guileful fair words peace may be obtained.
Awake, awake, English nobility!
Let not sloth dim your honours new-begot.
Cropped are the flower-de-luces in your arms;   80

Of England's coat one half is cut away. *Exit*

EXETER

Were our tears wanting to this funeral,
These tidings would call forth her flowing tides.

BEDFORD

Me they concern; Regent I am of France.
Give me my steelèd coat; I'll fight for France.
Away with these disgraceful wailing robes!
Wounds will I lend the French instead of eyes,
To weep their intermissive miseries.

Enter to them another Messenger

SECOND MESSENGER

Lords, view these letters full of bad mischance.
90 France is revolted from the English quite,
Except some petty towns of no import.
The Dauphin Charles is crownèd king in Rheims;
The Bastard of Orleans with him is joined;
Reignier, Duke of Anjou, doth take his part;
The Duke of Alençon flieth to his side. *Exit*

EXETER

The Dauphin crownèd king? All fly to him?
O, whither shall we fly from this reproach?

GLOUCESTER

We will not fly but to our enemies' throats.
Bedford, if thou be slack, I'll fight it out.

BEDFORD

100 Gloucester, why doubtest thou of my forwardness?
An army have I mustered in my thoughts,
Wherewith already France is overrun.

Enter another Messenger

THIRD MESSENGER

My gracious lords, to add to your laments,
Wherewith you now bedew King Henry's hearse,
I must inform you of a dismal fight
Betwixt the stout Lord Talbot and the French.

WINCHESTER
  What? Wherein Talbot overcame, is't so?
THIRD MESSENGER
  O, no; wherein Lord Talbot was o'erthrown.
  The circumstance I'll tell you more at large.
  The tenth of August last this dreadful lord,   110
  Retiring from the siege of Orleans,
  Having full scarce six thousand in his troop,
  By three and twenty thousand of the French
  Was round encompassèd and set upon.
  No leisure had he to enrank his men;
  He wanted pikes to set before his archers;
  Instead whereof, sharp stakes plucked out of hedges
  They pitchèd in the ground confusedly
  To keep the horsemen off from breaking in.
  More than three hours the fight continuèd,   120
  Where valiant Talbot, above human thought,
  Enacted wonders with his sword and lance.
  Hundreds he sent to hell, and none durst stand him;
  Here, there, and everywhere enragèd he slew.
  The French exclaimed the devil was in arms;
  All the whole army stood agazed on him.
  His soldiers, spying his undaunted spirit,
  'À Talbot! À Talbot!' crièd out amain,
  And rushed into the bowels of the battle.
  Here had the conquest fully been sealed up   130
  If Sir John Falstaff had not played the coward.
  He, being in the vaward, placed behind
  With purpose to relieve and follow them,
  Cowardly fled, not having struck one stroke.
  Hence grew the general wrack and massacre;
  Enclosèd were they with their enemies.
  A base Walloon, to win the Dauphin's grace,
  Thrust Talbot with a spear into the back,
  Whom all France, with their chief assembled strength,

140   Durst not presume to look once in the face.

BEDFORD

Is Talbot slain? Then I will slay myself,
For living idly here in pomp and ease,
Whilst such a worthy leader, wanting aid,
Unto his dastard foemen is betrayed.

THIRD MESSENGER

O, no, he lives, but is took prisoner,
And Lord Scales with him, and Lord Hungerford;
Most of the rest slaughtered or took likewise.

BEDFORD

His ransom there is none but I shall pay.
I'll hale the Dauphin headlong from his throne;
150   His crown shall be the ransom of my friend;
Four of their lords I'll change for one of ours.
Farewell, my masters; to my task will I.
Bonfires in France forthwith I am to make
To keep our great Saint George's feast withal.
Ten thousand soldiers with me I will take,
Whose bloody deeds shall make all Europe quake.

THIRD MESSENGER

So you had need, for Orleans is besieged;
The English army is grown weak and faint;
The Earl of Salisbury craveth supply
160   And hardly keeps his men from mutiny,
Since they, so few, watch such a multitude.   *Exit*

EXETER

Remember, lords, your oaths to Henry sworn,
Either to quell the Dauphin utterly
Or bring him in obedience to your yoke.

BEDFORD

I do remember it, and here take my leave
To go about my preparation.   *Exit*

GLOUCESTER

I'll to the Tower with all the haste I can

To view th'artillery and munition,
And then I will proclaim young Henry king.   *Exit*

EXETER

To Eltham will I, where the young King is,   170
Being ordained his special governor,
And for his safety there I'll best devise.

> *Exeunt all but Winchester*

WINCHESTER

Each hath his place and function to attend;
I am left out; for me nothing remains.
But long I will not be Jack out of office.
The King from Eltham I intend to steal
And sit at chiefest stern of public weal.   *Exit*

> *Sound a flourish. Enter Charles the Dauphin, the* I.2
> *Duke of Alençon, and Reignier, marching with drum*
> *and soldiers*

CHARLES

Mars his true moving, even as in the heavens
So in the earth, to this day is not known.
Late did he shine upon the English side;
Now we are victors, upon us he smiles.
What towns of any moment but we have?
At pleasure here we lie, near Orleans;
Otherwhiles the famished English, like pale ghosts,
Faintly besiege us one hour in a month.

ALENÇON

They want their porridge and their fat bull-beeves.
Either they must be dieted like mules   10
And have their provender tied to their mouths,
Or piteous they will look, like drownèd mice.

REIGNIER

Let's raise the siege. Why live we idly here?
Talbot is taken, whom we wont to fear.

Remaineth none but mad-brained Salisbury,
And he may well in fretting spend his gall;
Nor men nor money hath he to make war.

CHARLES

Sound, sound alarum; we will rush on them.
Now for the honour of the forlorn French!
20 Him I forgive my death that killeth me
When he sees me go back one foot or fly.   *Exeunt*
   Here alarum. They are beaten back by the English
   with great loss. Enter Charles, Alençon, and
   Reignier

CHARLES

Who ever saw the like? What men have I!
Dogs! Cowards! Dastards! I would ne'er have fled
But that they left me 'midst my enemies.

REIGNIER

Salisbury is a desperate homicide;
He fighteth as one weary of his life.
The other lords, like lions wanting food,
Do rush upon us as their hungry prey.

ALENÇON

Froissart, a countryman of ours, records
30 England all Olivers and Rolands bred
During the time Edward the Third did reign.
More truly now may this be verified;
For none but Samsons and Goliases
It sendeth forth to skirmish. One to ten!
Lean raw-boned rascals! Who would e'er suppose
They had such courage and audacity?

CHARLES

Let's leave this town; for they are hare-brained slaves,
And hunger will enforce them to be more eager.
Of old I know them; rather with their teeth
40 The walls they'll tear down than forsake the siege.

REIGNIER

I think by some odd gimmers or device

Their arms are set like clocks, still to strike on;
Else ne'er could they hold out so as they do.
By my consent, we'll even let them alone.

ALENÇON
Be it so.

Enter the Bastard of Orleans

BASTARD
Where's the Prince Dauphin? I have news for him.

CHARLES
Bastard of Orleans, thrice welcome to us.

BASTARD
Methinks your looks are sad, your cheer appalled.
Hath the late overthrow wrought this offence?
Be not dismayed, for succour is at hand.   50
A holy maid hither with me I bring,
Which, by a vision sent to her from heaven,
Ordainèd is to raise this tedious siege
And drive the English forth the bounds of France.
The spirit of deep prophecy she hath,
Exceeding the nine sibyls of old Rome:
What's past and what's to come she can descry.
Speak, shall I call her in? Believe my words,
For they are certain and unfallible.

CHARLES
Go, call her in.   *Exit Bastard*
                But first, to try her skill,   60
Reignier, stand thou as Dauphin in my place;
Question her proudly, let thy looks be stern;
By this means shall we sound what skill she hath.

Enter Joan la Pucelle and the Bastard

REIGNIER
Fair maid, is't thou wilt do these wondrous feats?

PUCELLE
Reignier, is't thou that thinkest to beguile me?
Where is the Dauphin? Come, come from behind;
I know thee well, though never seen before.

Be not amazed, there's nothing hid from me.
In private will I talk with thee apart.
70 Stand back, you lords, and give us leave awhile.

REIGNIER
She takes upon her bravely at first dash.

PUCELLE
Dauphin, I am by birth a shepherd's daughter,
My wit untrained in any kind of art.
Heaven and Our Lady gracious hath it pleased
To shine on my contemptible estate.
Lo, whilst I waited on my tender lambs
And to sun's parching heat displayed my cheeks,
God's Mother deignèd to appear to me,
And in a vision full of majesty
80 Willed me to leave my base vocation
And free my country from calamity;
Her aid she promised and assured success.
In complete glory she revealed herself;
And whereas I was black and swart before,
With those clear rays which she infused on me
That beauty am I blessed with which you may see.
Ask me what question thou canst possible,
And I will answer unpremeditated.
My courage try by combat, if thou darest,
90 And thou shalt find that I exceed my sex.
Resolve on this: thou shalt be fortunate
If thou receive me for thy warlike mate.

CHARLES
Thou hast astonished me with thy high terms.
Only this proof I'll of thy valour make:
In single combat thou shalt buckle with me,
And if thou vanquishest, thy words are true;
Otherwise I renounce all confidence.

PUCELLE
I am prepared; here is my keen-edged sword,
Decked with five flower-de-luces on each side,

The which at Touraine, in Saint Katherine's churchyard, 100
Out of a great deal of old iron I chose forth.

CHARLES

Then come, a God's name; I fear no woman.

PUCELLE

And while I live, I'll ne'er fly from a man.

Here they fight, and Joan la Pucelle overcomes

CHARLES

Stay, stay thy hands; thou art an Amazon,
And fightest with the sword of Deborah.

PUCELLE

Christ's Mother helps me, else I were too weak.

CHARLES

Whoe'er helps thee, 'tis thou that must help me.
Impatiently I burn with thy desire;
My heart and hands thou hast at once subdued.
Excellent Pucelle, if thy name be so, 110
Let me thy servant and not sovereign be;
'Tis the French Dauphin sueth to thee thus.

PUCELLE

I must not yield to any rites of love,
For my profession's sacred from above.
When I have chasèd all thy foes from hence,
Then will I think upon a recompense.

CHARLES

Meantime look gracious on thy prostrate thrall.

REIGNIER

My lord, methinks, is very long in talk.

ALENÇON

Doubtless he shrives this woman to her smock;
Else ne'er could he so long protract his speech. 120

REIGNIER

Shall we disturb him, since he keeps no mean?

ALENÇON

He may mean more than we poor men do know;
These women are shrewd tempters with their tongues.

REIGNIER

My lord, where are you? What devise you on?
Shall we give o'er Orleans or no?

PUCELLE

Why, no, I say; distrustful recreants,
Fight till the last gasp; I'll be your guard.

CHARLES

What she says, I'll confirm; we'll fight it out.

PUCELLE

Assigned am I to be the English scourge.
130 This night the siege assuredly I'll raise.
Expect Saint Martin's summer, halcyon days,
Since I have enterèd into these wars.
Glory is like a circle in the water,
Which never ceaseth to enlarge itself
Till by broad spreading it disperse to naught.
With Henry's death the English circle ends;
Dispersèd are the glories it included.
Now am I like that proud insulting ship
Which Caesar and his fortune bare at once.

CHARLES

140 Was Mahomet inspirèd with a dove?
Thou with an eagle art inspirèd then.
Helen, the mother of great Constantine,
Nor yet Saint Philip's daughters were like thee.
Bright star of Venus, fallen down on the earth,
How may I reverently worship thee enough?

ALENÇON

Leave off delays, and let us raise the siege.

REIGNIER

Woman, do what thou canst to save our honours;
Drive them from Orleans and be immortalized.

CHARLES

Presently we'll try. Come, let's away about it.
150 No prophet will I trust if she prove false. *Exeunt*

58

Enter Gloucester, with his servingmen in blue coats

GLOUCESTER
I am come to survey the Tower this day;
Since Henry's death, I fear, there is conveyance.
Where be these warders that they wait not here?
Open the gates! 'Tis Gloucester that calls.
      Servingmen knock

FIRST WARDER (*within*)
Who's there that knocks so imperiously?

FIRST SERVINGMAN
It is the noble Duke of Gloucester.

SECOND WARDER (*within*)
Whoe'er he be, you may not be let in.

FIRST SERVINGMAN
Villains, answer you so the Lord Protector?

FIRST WARDER (*within*)
The Lord protect him! So we answer him.
We do no otherwise than we are willed.   10

GLOUCESTER
Who willèd you? Or whose will stands but mine?
There's none Protector of the realm but I.
Break up the gates; I'll be your warrantize.
Shall I be flouted thus by dunghill grooms?
      Gloucester's men rush at the Tower gates, and Wood-
      ville the Lieutenant speaks within

WOODVILLE (*within*)
What noise is this? What traitors have we here?

GLOUCESTER
Lieutenant, is it you whose voice I hear?
Open the gates; here's Gloucester that would enter.

WOODVILLE (*within*)
Have patience, noble Duke; I may not open;
The Cardinal of Winchester forbids.
From him I have express commandment   20
That thou nor none of thine shall be let in.

GLOUCESTER

Faint-hearted Woodville, prizest him 'fore me?
Arrogant Winchester, that haughty prelate,
Whom Henry, our late sovereign, ne'er could brook?
Thou art no friend to God or to the King.
Open the gates, or I'll shut thee out shortly.

SERVINGMEN

Open the gates unto the Lord Protector,
Or we'll burst them open if that you come not quickly.
Enter to the Protector at the Tower gates Winchester
and his men in tawny coats

WINCHESTER

How now, ambitious Humphrey, what means this?

GLOUCESTER

30   Peeled priest, dost thou command me to be shut out?

WINCHESTER

I do, thou most usurping proditor,
And not Protector of the King or realm.

GLOUCESTER

Stand back, thou manifest conspirator,
Thou that contrived'st to murder our dead lord;
Thou that givest whores indulgences to sin.
I'll canvass thee in thy broad cardinal's hat
If thou proceed in this thy insolence.

WINCHESTER

Nay, stand thou back; I will not budge a foot.
This be Damascus; be thou cursèd Cain,
40   To slay thy brother Abel, if thou wilt.

GLOUCESTER

I will not slay thee, but I'll drive thee back.
Thy scarlet robes as a child's bearing-cloth
I'll use to carry thee out of this place.

WINCHESTER

Do what thou darest; I beard thee to thy face.

GLOUCESTER

What? Am I dared and bearded to my face?

Draw, men, for all this privilegèd place;
Blue coats to tawny coats! Priest, beware your beard;
I mean to tug it and to cuff you soundly.
Under my feet I stamp thy cardinal's hat;
In spite of Pope or dignities of Church,   50
Here by the cheeks I'll drag thee up and down.

WINCHESTER
Gloucester, thou wilt answer this before the Pope.

GLOUCESTER
Winchester goose! I cry a rope, a rope!
Now beat them hence; why do you let them stay?
Thee I'll chase hence, thou wolf in sheep's array.
Out, tawny coats! Out, scarlet hypocrite!

> *Here Gloucester's men beat out the Cardinal's men,
> and enter in the hurly-burly the Mayor of London,
> and his officers*

MAYOR
Fie, lords, that you, being supreme magistrates,
Thus contumeliously should break the peace!

GLOUCESTER
Peace, Mayor, thou knowest little of my wrongs:
Here's Beaufort, that regards nor God nor King,   60
Hath here distrained the Tower to his use.

WINCHESTER
Here's Gloucester, a foe to citizens;
One that still motions war and never peace,
O'ercharging your free purses with large fines;
That seeks to overthrow religion,
Because he is Protector of the realm,
And would have armour here out of the Tower,
To crown himself king and suppress the Prince.

GLOUCESTER
I will not answer thee with words, but blows.

> *Here they skirmish again*

MAYOR
Naught rests for me in this tumultuous strife   70

61

But to make open proclamation.
Come, officer, as loud as e'er thou canst,
Cry.

OFFICER All manner of men assembled here in arms this
day against God's peace and the King's, we charge and
command you, in his highness' name, to repair to your
several dwelling-places, and not to wear, handle, or use
any sword, weapon, or dagger henceforward, upon pain
of death.

GLOUCESTER

80 Cardinal, I'll be no breaker of the law;
But we shall meet and break our minds at large.

WINCHESTER

Gloucester, we'll meet to thy cost, be sure;
Thy heart-blood I will have for this day's work.

MAYOR

I'll call for clubs if you will not away.
This Cardinal's more haughty than the devil.

GLOUCESTER

Mayor, farewell; thou dost but what thou mayst.

WINCHESTER

Abominable Gloucester, guard thy head;
For I intend to have it ere long.

Exeunt Gloucester and
Winchester with their servingmen

MAYOR

See the coast cleared, and then we will depart.

90 Good God, these nobles should such stomachs bear!
I myself fight not once in forty year.   *Exeunt*

I.4   *Enter the Master Gunner of Orleans and his Boy*

MASTER GUNNER

Sirrah, thou knowest how Orleans is besieged
And how the English have the suburbs won.

BOY

Father, I know; and oft have shot at them,
Howe'er unfortunate I missed my aim.

MASTER GUNNER

But now thou shalt not. Be thou ruled by me.
Chief master gunner am I of this town;
Something I must do to procure me grace.
The Prince's espials have informèd me
How the English, in the suburbs close intrenched,
Wont through a secret grate of iron bars   10
In yonder tower to overpeer the city,
And thence discover how with most advantage
They may vex us with shot or with assault.
To intercept this inconvenience,
A piece of ordnance 'gainst it I have placed;
And even these three days have I watched
If I could see them. Now do thou watch,
For I can stay no longer.
If thou spyest any, run and bring me word,
And thou shalt find me at the Governor's.   *Exit* 20

BOY

Father, I warrant you; take you no care;
I'll never trouble you if I may spy them.   *Exit*
    Enter the Earl of Salisbury and Lord Talbot on the
    turrets with Sir William Glansdale, Sir Thomas
    Gargrave, and other soldiers

SALISBURY

Talbot, my life, my joy, again returned?
How wert thou handled being prisoner?
Or by what means got'st thou to be released?
Discourse, I prithee, on this turret's top.

TALBOT

The Duke of Bedford had a prisoner
Called the brave Lord Ponton de Santrailles;
For him was I exchanged and ransomèd.

63

30 But with a baser man-of-arms by far
   Once, in contempt, they would have bartered me;
   Which I, disdaining, scorned, and cravèd death
   Rather than I would be so pilled esteemed.
   In fine, redeemed I was as I desired.
   But, O, the treacherous Falstaff wounds my heart;
   Whom with my bare fists I would execute,
   If I now had him brought into my power.

SALISBURY

   Yet tellest thou not how thou wert entertained.

TALBOT

   With scoffs and scorns and contumelious taunts;
40 In open market-place produced they me
   To be a public spectacle to all.
   'Here', said they, 'is the terror of the French,
   The scarecrow that affrights our children so.'
   Then broke I from the officers that led me,
   And with my nails digged stones out of the ground
   To hurl at the beholders of my shame.
   My grisly countenance made others fly;
   None durst come near for fear of sudden death.
   In iron walls they deemed me not secure;
50 So great fear of my name 'mongst them were spread
   That they supposed I could rend bars of steel
   And spurn in pieces posts of adamant;
   Wherefore a guard of chosen shot I had
   That walked about me every minute while;
   And if I did but stir out of my bed,
   Ready they were to shoot me to the heart.
        Enter the Boy with a linstock and exit

SALISBURY

   I grieve to hear what torments you endured;
   But we will be revenged sufficiently.
   Now it is supper-time in Orleans;
60 Here, through this grate, I count each one

And view the Frenchmen how they fortify.
Let us look in; the sight will much delight thee.
Sir Thomas Gargrave and Sir William Glansdale,
Let me have your express opinions
Where is best place to make our battery next.

GARGRAVE

I think at the north gate; for there stands lords.

GLANSDALE

And I here, at the bulwark of the bridge.

TALBOT

For aught I see, this city must be famished
Or with light skirmishes enfeeblèd.

*Here they shoot, and Salisbury and Gargrave fall
down*

SALISBURY

O Lord, have mercy on us, wretched sinners!   70

GARGRAVE

O Lord, have mercy on me, woeful man!

TALBOT

What chance is this that suddenly hath crossed us?
Speak, Salisbury; at least, if thou canst, speak.
How farest thou, mirror of all martial men?
One of thy eyes and thy cheek's side struck off?
Accursèd tower! Accursèd fatal hand
That hath contrived this woeful tragedy!
In thirteen battles Salisbury o'ercame;
Henry the Fifth he first trained to the wars.
Whilst any trump did sound or drum struck up,   80
His sword did ne'er leave striking in the field.
Yet livest thou, Salisbury? Though thy speech doth fail,
One eye thou hast to look to heaven for grace;
The sun with one eye vieweth all the world.
Heaven, be thou gracious to none alive
If Salisbury wants mercy at thy hands!
Sir Thomas Gargrave, hast thou any life?

Speak unto Talbot. Nay, look up to him.
Bear hence his body; I will help to bury it.

Exeunt attendants with Gargrave's body

90 Salisbury, cheer thy spirit with this comfort,
Thou shalt not die whiles –
He beckons with his hand and smiles on me,
As who should say 'When I am dead and gone,
Remember to avenge me on the French.'
Plantagenet, I will; and like thee, Nero,
Play on the lute, beholding the towns burn.
Wretched shall France be only in my name.

Here an alarum, and it thunders and lightens

What stir is this? What tumult's in the heavens?
Whence cometh this alarum and the noise?

Enter a Messenger

MESSENGER

100 My lord, my lord, the French have gathered head.
The Dauphin, with one Joan la Pucelle joined,
A holy prophetess new risen up,
Is come with a great power to raise the siege.

Here Salisbury lifteth himself up and groans

TALBOT

Hear, hear how dying Salisbury doth groan.
It irks his heart he cannot be revenged.
Frenchmen, I'll be a Salisbury to you.
Pucelle or pussel, Dolphin or dogfish,
Your hearts I'll stamp out with my horse's heels
And make a quagmire of your mingled brains.

110 Convey me Salisbury into his tent,
And then we'll try what these dastard Frenchmen dare.

Alarum. Exeunt with Salisbury's body

I.5   *Here an alarum again, and Talbot pursueth Charles
           the Dauphin and driveth him. Then enter Joan la*

Pucelle, driving Englishmen before her, and exeunt.
Then enter Talbot

TALBOT

Where is my strength, my valour, and my force?
Our English troops retire, I cannot stay them;
A woman clad in armour chaseth them.
        Enter Joan la Pucelle
Here, here she comes. (*To Pucelle*) I'll have a bout with
        thee.
Devil or devil's dam, I'll conjure thee.
Blood will I draw on thee – thou art a witch –
And straightway give thy soul to him thou servest.

PUCELLE

Come, come, 'tis only I that must disgrace thee.
        Here they fight

TALBOT

Heavens, can you suffer hell so to prevail?
My breast I'll burst with straining of my courage,   10
And from my shoulders crack my arms asunder,
But I will chastise this high-minded strumpet.
        They fight again

PUCELLE

Talbot, farewell; thy hour is not yet come.
I must go victual Orleans forthwith.
        A short alarum. Then she enters the town with
        soldiers
O'ertake me if thou canst; I scorn thy strength.
Go, go, cheer up thy hungry-starvèd men;
Help Salisbury to make his testament.
This day is ours, as many more shall be.   *Exit*

TALBOT

My thoughts are whirlèd like a potter's wheel;
I know not where I am nor what I do.   20
A witch by fear, not force, like Hannibal,
Drives back our troops and conquers as she lists.

So bees with smoke and doves with noisome stench
Are from their hives and houses driven away.
They called us, for our fierceness, English dogs;
Now, like to whelps, we crying run away.

A short alarum

Hark, countrymen! Either renew the fight
Or tear the lions out of England's coat;
Renounce your soil, give sheep in lions' stead.
30   Sheep run not half so treacherous from the wolf,
Or horse or oxen from the leopard,
As you fly from your oft-subduèd slaves.

Alarum. Here another skirmish

It will not be. Retire into your trenches.
You all consented unto Salisbury's death,
For none would strike a stroke in his revenge.
Pucelle is entered into Orleans
In spite of us or aught that we could do.
O, would I were to die with Salisbury!
The shame hereof will make me hide my head.

Exit Talbot. Alarum. Retreat

I.6   *Flourish. Enter, on the walls, Joan la Pucelle, Charles,*
     Reignier, Alençon, and soldiers

PUCELLE

Advance our waving colours on the walls;
Rescued is Orleans from the English.
Thus Joan la Pucelle hath performed her word.

CHARLES

Divinest creature, Astraea's daughter,
How shall I honour thee for this success?
Thy promises are like Adonis' garden,
That one day bloomed and fruitful were the next.
France, triumph in thy glorious prophetess!

68

Recovered is the town of Orleans.
More blessèd hap did ne'er befall our state. 10

REIGNIER

Why ring not out the bells aloud throughout the town?
Dauphin, command the citizens make bonfires
And feast and banquet in the open streets
To celebrate the joy that God hath given us.

ALENÇON

All France will be replete with mirth and joy
When they shall hear how we have played the men.

CHARLES

'Tis Joan, not we, by whom the day is won;
For which I will divide my crown with her,
And all the priests and friars in my realm
Shall in procession sing her endless praise. 20
A statelier pyramis to her I'll rear
Than Rhodope's of Memphis ever was.
In memory of her, when she is dead,
Her ashes, in an urn more precious
Than the rich-jewelled coffer of Darius,
Transported shall be at high festivals
Before the kings and queens of France.
No longer on Saint Denis will we cry,
But Joan la Pucelle shall be France's saint.
Come in, and let us banquet royally 30
After this golden day of victory. *Flourish. Exeunt*

*

Enter a French Sergeant of a Band, with two II.1
Sentinels, on the walls

SERGEANT

Sirs, take your places and be vigilant.
If any noise or soldier you perceive

II.1

Near to the walls, by some apparent sign
Let us have knowledge at the court of guard.

SENTINEL

Sergeant, you shall. *Exit Sergeant*
            Thus are poor servitors,
When others sleep upon their quiet beds,
Constrained to watch in darkness, rain, and cold.

Enter Talbot, Bedford, Burgundy, and soldiers, with
scaling-ladders

TALBOT

Lord Regent, and redoubted Burgundy,
By whose approach the regions of Artois,
10 Walloon, and Picardy are friends to us,
This happy night the Frenchmen are secure,
Having all day caroused and banqueted;
Embrace we then this opportunity,
As fitting best to quittance their deceit,
Contrived by art and baleful sorcery.

BEDFORD

Coward of France! How much he wrongs his fame,
Despairing of his own arm's fortitude,
To join with witches and the help of hell!

BURGUNDY

Traitors have never other company.
20 But what's that Pucelle whom they term so pure?

TALBOT

A maid, they say.

BEDFORD   A maid? and be so martial?

BURGUNDY

Pray God she prove not masculine ere long,
If underneath the standard of the French
She carry armour as she hath begun.

TALBOT

Well, let them practise and converse with spirits.

70

God is our fortress, in whose conquering name
Let us resolve to scale their flinty bulwarks.

BEDFORD

Ascend, brave Talbot; we will follow thee.

TALBOT

Not all together; better far, I guess,
That we do make our entrance several ways; 30
That, if it chance the one of us do fail,
The other yet may rise against their force.

BEDFORD

Agreed; I'll to yond corner.

BURGUNDY   And I to this.

TALBOT

And here will Talbot mount, or make his grave.
Now, Salisbury, for thee, and for the right
Of English Henry, shall this night appear
How much in duty I am bound to both.

FIRST SENTINEL

Arm, arm! The enemy doth make assault!

The English scale the walls, cry 'Saint George!
À Talbot!', *and exeunt*
The French leap over the walls in their shirts. Enter,
several ways, the Bastard, Alençon, Reignier, half
ready and half unready

ALENÇON

How now, my lords? What, all unready so?

BASTARD

Unready? Ay, and glad we 'scaped so well. 40

REIGNIER

'Twas time, I trow, to wake and leave our beds,
Hearing alarums at our chamber doors.

ALENÇON

Of all exploits since first I followed arms
Ne'er heard I of a warlike enterprise

More venturous or desperate than this.

BASTARD
    I think this Talbot be a fiend of hell.

REIGNIER
    If not of hell, the heavens sure favour him.

ALENÇON
    Here cometh Charles. I marvel how he sped.
        Enter Charles and Joan la Pucelle

BASTARD
    Tut, holy Joan was his defensive guard.

CHARLES
50   Is this thy cunning, thou deceitful dame?
    Didst thou at first, to flatter us withal,
    Make us partakers of a little gain
    That now our loss might be ten times so much?

PUCELLE
    Wherefore is Charles impatient with his friend?
    At all times will you have my power alike?
    Sleeping or waking must I still prevail,
    Or will you blame and lay the fault on me?
    Improvident soldiers! Had your watch been good,
    This sudden mischief never could have fallen.

CHARLES
60   Duke of Alençon, this was your default
    That, being captain of the watch tonight,
    Did look no better to that weighty charge.

ALENÇON
    Had all your quarters been as safely kept
    As that whereof I had the government,
    We had not been thus shamefully surprised.

BASTARD
    Mine was secure.

REIGNIER   And so was mine, my lord.

CHARLES
    And for myself, most part of all this night

Within her quarter and mine own precinct
I was employed in passing to and fro
About relieving of the sentinels.   70
Then how or which way should they first break in?

PUCELLE
Question, my lords, no further of the case,
How or which way; 'tis sure they found some place
But weakly guarded, where the breach was made.
And now there rests no other shift but this:
To gather our soldiers, scattered and dispersed,
And lay new platforms to endamage them.

>   *Alarum. Enter an English Soldier, crying* 'À Talbot!
>   À Talbot!' *They fly, leaving their clothes behind*

SOLDIER
I'll be so bold to take what they have left.
The cry of 'Talbot' serves me for a sword;
For I have loaden me with many spoils,   80
Using no other weapon but his name.   *Exit*

>   *Enter Talbot, Bedford, Burgundy, a Captain, and* II.2
>   *soldiers*

BEDFORD
The day begins to break and night is fled,
Whose pitchy mantle overveiled the earth.
Here sound retreat and cease our hot pursuit.
>   *Retreat sounded*

TALBOT
Bring forth the body of old Salisbury
And here advance it in the market-place,
The middle centre of this cursèd town.

>   *Enter a funeral procession with Salisbury's body,*
>   *their drums beating a dead march*

Now have I paid my vow unto his soul;
For every drop of blood was drawn from him
There hath at least five Frenchmen died tonight.
₁₀ And that hereafter ages may behold
What ruin happened in revenge of him,
Within their chiefest temple I'll erect
A tomb, wherein his corpse shall be interred;
Upon the which, that everyone may read,
Shall be engraved the sack of Orleans,
The treacherous manner of his mournful death,
And what a terror he had been to France.

> *Exit funeral procession*

But, lords, in all our bloody massacre,
I muse we met not with the Dauphin's grace,
₂₀ His new-come champion, virtuous Joan of Arc,
Nor any of his false confederates.

BEDFORD

'Tis thought, Lord Talbot, when the fight began,
Roused on the sudden from their drowsy beds,
They did amongst the troops of armèd men
Leap o'er the walls for refuge in the field.

BURGUNDY

Myself, as far as I could well discern
For smoke and dusky vapours of the night,
Am sure I scared the Dauphin and his trull,
When arm in arm they both came swiftly running,
₃₀ Like to a pair of loving turtle-doves
That could not live asunder day or night.
After that things are set in order here,
We'll follow them with all the power we have.

> *Enter a Messenger*

MESSENGER

All hail, my lords! Which of this princely train
Call ye the warlike Talbot, for his acts

74

So much applauded through the realm of France?

TALBOT

Here is the Talbot; who would speak with him?

MESSENGER

The virtuous lady, Countess of Auvergne,
With modesty admiring thy renown,
By me entreats, great lord, thou wouldst vouchsafe   40
To visit her poor castle where she lies,
That she may boast she hath beheld the man
Whose glory fills the world with loud report.

BURGUNDY

Is it even so? Nay, then I see our wars
Will turn unto a peaceful comic sport,
When ladies crave to be encountered with.
You may not, my lord, despise her gentle suit.

TALBOT

Ne'er trust me then; for when a world of men
Could not prevail with all their oratory,
Yet hath a woman's kindness overruled;   50
And therefore tell her I return great thanks
And in submission will attend on her.
Will not your honours bear me company?

BEDFORD

No, truly, 'tis more than manners will;
And I have heard it said unbidden guests
Are often welcomest when they are gone.

TALBOT

Well, then, alone, since there's no remedy,
I mean to prove this lady's courtesy.
Come hither, captain. (*He whispers*) You perceive my
          mind?

CAPTAIN

I do, my lord, and mean accordingly.

Exeunt 60

75

COUNTESS

Porter, remember what I gave in charge,
And when you have done so, bring the keys to me.

PORTER

Madam, I will.   *Exit*

COUNTESS

The plot is laid; if all things fall out right,
I shall as famous be by this exploit
As Scythian Tomyris by Cyrus' death.
Great is the rumour of this dreadful knight,
And his achievements of no less account.
Fain would mine eyes be witness with mine ears,
10   To give their censure of these rare reports.

Enter the Messenger and Talbot

MESSENGER

Madam, according as your ladyship desired,
By message craved, so is Lord Talbot come.

COUNTESS

And he is welcome. What? Is this the man?

MESSENGER

Madam, it is.

COUNTESS   Is this the scourge of France?
Is this the Talbot so much feared abroad
That with his name the mothers still their babes?
I see report is fabulous and false.
I thought I should have seen some Hercules,
A second Hector, for his grim aspect
20   And large proportion of his strong-knit limbs.
Alas, this is a child, a silly dwarf!
It cannot be this weak and writhled shrimp
Should strike such terror to his enemies.

TALBOT

Madam, I have been bold to trouble you;
But since your ladyship is not at leisure,

I'll sort some other time to visit you.

He starts to leave

COUNTESS

What means he now? Go ask him whither he goes.

MESSENGER

Stay, my Lord Talbot; for my lady craves
To know the cause of your abrupt departure.

TALBOT

Marry, for that she's in a wrong belief,   30
I go to certify her Talbot's here.

Enter the Porter with keys

COUNTESS

If thou be he, then art thou prisoner.

TALBOT

Prisoner? To whom?

COUNTESS   To me, blood-thirsty lord;
And for that cause I trained thee to my house.
Long time thy shadow hath been thrall to me,
For in my gallery thy picture hangs;
But now the substance shall endure the like,
And I will chain these legs and arms of thine
That hast by tyranny these many years
Wasted our country, slain our citizens,   40
And sent our sons and husbands captivate.

TALBOT

Ha, ha, ha!

COUNTESS

Laughest thou, wretch? Thy mirth shall turn to moan.

TALBOT

I laugh to see your ladyship so fond
To think that you have aught but Talbot's shadow
Whereon to practise your severity.

COUNTESS

Why, art thou not the man?

TALBOT   I am indeed.

COUNTESS

Then have I substance too.

TALBOT

No, no, I am but shadow of myself.

50 You are deceived. My substance is not here;
For what you see is but the smallest part
And least proportion of humanity.
I tell you, madam, were the whole frame here,
It is of such a spacious lofty pitch
Your roof were not sufficient to contain't.

COUNTESS

This is a riddling merchant for the nonce;
He will be here, and yet he is not here.
How can these contrarieties agree?

TALBOT

That will I show you presently.

He winds his horn. Drums strike up. A peal of ordnance. Enter soldiers

60 How say you, madam? Are you now persuaded
That Talbot is but shadow of himself?
These are his substance, sinews, arms, and strength,
With which he yoketh your rebellious necks,
Razeth your cities, and subverts your towns
And in a moment makes them desolate.

COUNTESS

Victorious Talbot, pardon my abuse.
I find thou art no less than fame hath bruited,
And more than may be gathered by thy shape.
Let my presumption not provoke thy wrath,
70 For I am sorry that with reverence
I did not entertain thee as thou art.

TALBOT

Be not dismayed, fair lady, nor misconster
The mind of Talbot as you did mistake
The outward composition of his body.

What you have done hath not offended me;
Nor other satisfaction do I crave
But only, with your patience, that we may
Taste of your wine and see what cates you have;
For soldiers' stomachs always serve them well.

COUNTESS
With all my heart, and think me honourèd   80
To feast so great a warrior in my house.   *Exeunt*

Enter Richard Plantagenet, Warwick, Somerset, II.4
Suffolk, Vernon, a Lawyer, and other gentlemen

RICHARD
Great lords and gentlemen, what means this silence?
Dare no man answer in a case of truth?

SUFFOLK
Within the Temple Hall we were too loud;
The garden here is more convenient.

RICHARD
Then say at once if I maintained the truth;
Or else was wrangling Somerset in th'error?

SUFFOLK
Faith, I have been a truant in the law
And never yet could frame my will to it;
And therefore frame the law unto my will.

SOMERSET
Judge you, my lord of Warwick, then between us.   10

WARWICK
Between two hawks, which flies the higher pitch;
Between two dogs, which hath the deeper mouth;
Between two blades, which bears the better temper;
Between two horses, which doth bear him best;
Between two girls, which hath the merriest eye,
I have perhaps some shallow spirit of judgement;
But in these nice sharp quillets of the law,

Good faith, I am no wiser than a daw.

RICHARD

Tut, tut, here is a mannerly forbearance.

20 The truth appears so naked on my side

That any purblind eye may find it out.

SOMERSET

And on my side it is so well apparelled,

So clear, so shining, and so evident,

That it will glimmer through a blind man's eye.

RICHARD

Since you are tongue-tied and so loath to speak,

In dumb significants proclaim your thoughts.

Let him that is a true-born gentleman

And stands upon the honour of his birth,

If he suppose that I have pleaded truth,

30 From off this briar pluck a white rose with me.

SOMERSET

Let him that is no coward nor no flatterer,

But dare maintain the party of the truth,

Pluck a red rose from off this thorn with me.

WARWICK

I love no colours; and, without all colour

Of base insinuating flattery,

I pluck this white rose with Plantagenet.

SUFFOLK

I pluck this red rose with young Somerset,

And say withal I think he held the right.

VERNON

Stay, lords and gentlemen, and pluck no more

40 Till you conclude that he upon whose side

The fewest roses are cropped from the tree

Shall yield the other in the right opinion.

SOMERSET

Good Master Vernon, it is well objected;

If I have fewest, I subscribe in silence.

RICHARD

  And I.

VERNON

  Then, for the truth and plainness of the case,
  I pluck this pale and maiden blossom here,
  Giving my verdict on the white rose side.

SOMERSET

  Prick not your finger as you pluck it off,
  Lest, bleeding, you do paint the white rose red,   50
  And fall on my side so against your will.

VERNON

  If I, my lord, for my opinion bleed,
  Opinion shall be surgeon to my hurt
  And keep me on the side where still I am.

SOMERSET

  Well, well, come on; who else?

LAWYER (to Somerset)

  Unless my study and my books be false,
  The argument you held was wrong in you;
  In sign whereof I pluck a white rose too.

RICHARD

  Now, Somerset, where is your argument?

SOMERSET

  Here in my scabbard, meditating that   60
  Shall dye your white rose in a bloody red.

RICHARD

  Meantime your cheeks do counterfeit our roses;
  For pale they look with fear, as witnessing
  The truth on our side.

SOMERSET   No, Plantagenet,
  'Tis not for fear, but anger, that thy cheeks
  Blush for pure shame to counterfeit our roses,
  And yet thy tongue will not confess thy error.

RICHARD

  Hath not thy rose a canker, Somerset?

SOMERSET

Hath not thy rose a thorn, Plantagenet?

RICHARD

70   Ay, sharp and piercing, to maintain his truth,
Whiles thy consuming canker eats his falsehood.

SOMERSET

Well, I'll find friends to wear my bleeding roses,
That shall maintain what I have said is true
Where false Plantagenet dare not be seen.

RICHARD

Now, by this maiden blossom in my hand,
I scorn thee and thy fashion, peevish boy.

SUFFOLK

Turn not thy scorns this way, Plantagenet.

RICHARD

Proud Pole, I will, and scorn both him and thee.

SUFFOLK

I'll turn my part thereof into thy throat.

SOMERSET

80   Away, away, good William de la Pole!
We grace the yeoman by conversing with him.

WARWICK

Now, by God's will, thou wrongest him, Somerset;
His grandfather was Lionel Duke of Clarence,
Third son to the third Edward, King of England.
Spring crestless yeomen from so deep a root?

RICHARD

He bears him on the place's privilege,
Or durst not for his craven heart say thus.

SOMERSET

By Him that made me, I'll maintain my words
On any plot of ground in Christendom.
90   Was not thy father, Richard Earl of Cambridge,
For treason executed in our late king's days?
And by his treason standest not thou attainted,

Corrupted, and exempt from ancient gentry?
His trespass yet lives guilty in thy blood,
And till thou be restored thou art a yeoman.

RICHARD

My father was attachèd, not attainted,
Condemned to die for treason, but no traitor;
And that I'll prove on better men than Somerset,
Were growing time once ripened to my will.
For your partaker Pole, and you yourself,   100
I'll note you in my book of memory
To scourge you for this apprehension.
Look to it well and say you are well warned.

SOMERSET

Ah, thou shalt find us ready for thee still;
And know us by these colours for thy foes,
For these my friends in spite of thee shall wear.

RICHARD

And, by my soul, this pale and angry rose,
As cognizance of my blood-drinking hate,
Will I for ever, and my faction, wear
Until it wither with me to my grave,   110
Or flourish to the height of my degree.

SUFFOLK

Go forward, and be choked with thy ambition!
And so farewell until I meet thee next.   *Exit*

SOMERSET

Have with thee, Pole. Farewell, ambitious Richard. *Exit*

RICHARD

How I am braved and must perforce endure it!

WARWICK

This blot that they object against your house
Shall be wiped out in the next parliament,
Called for the truce of Winchester and Gloucester;
And if thou be not then created York,
I will not live to be accounted Warwick.   120

Meantime, in signal of my love to thee,
Against proud Somerset and William Pole,
Will I upon thy party wear this rose;
And here I prophesy: this brawl today,
Grown to this faction in the Temple garden,
Shall send between the red rose and the white
A thousand souls to death and deadly night.

RICHARD

Good Master Vernon, I am bound to you
That you on my behalf would pluck a flower.

VERNON

130 In your behalf still will I wear the same.

LAWYER

And so will I.

RICHARD

Thanks, gentle sir.
Come, let us four to dinner. I dare say
This quarrel will drink blood another day.   *Exeunt*

II.5   *Enter Mortimer, brought in a chair, and Gaolers*

MORTIMER

Kind keepers of my weak decaying age,
Let dying Mortimer here rest himself.
Even like a man new halèd from the rack,
So fare my limbs with long imprisonment;
And these grey locks, the pursuivants of Death,
Nestor-like agèd in an age of care,
Argue the end of Edmund Mortimer.
These eyes, like lamps whose wasting oil is spent,
Wax dim, as drawing to their exigent;
10 Weak shoulders, overborne with burdening grief,
And pithless arms, like to a withered vine
That droops his sapless branches to the ground.
Yet are these feet, whose strengthless stay is numb,

Unable to support this lump of clay,
Swift-wingèd with desire to get a grave,
As witting I no other comfort have.
But tell me, keeper, will my nephew come?

GAOLER

Richard Plantagenet, my lord, will come.
We sent unto the Temple, unto his chamber;
And answer was returned that he will come.   20

MORTIMER

Enough; my soul shall then be satisfied.
Poor gentleman, his wrong doth equal mine.
Since Henry Monmouth first began to reign,
Before whose glory I was great in arms,
This loathsome sequestration have I had;
And even since then hath Richard been obscured,
Deprived of honour and inheritance.
But now the arbitrator of despairs,
Just Death, kind umpire of men's miseries,
With sweet enlargement doth dismiss me hence.   30
I would his troubles likewise were expired,
That so he might recover what was lost.

Enter Richard Plantagenet

GAOLER

My lord, your loving nephew now is come.

MORTIMER

Richard Plantagenet, my friend, is he come?

RICHARD

Ay, noble uncle, thus ignobly used,
Your nephew, late despisèd Richard, comes.

MORTIMER

Direct mine arms I may embrace his neck
And in his bosom spend my latter gasp.
O, tell me when my lips do touch his cheeks,
That I may kindly give one fainting kiss.   40
And now declare, sweet stem from York's great stock,

Why didst thou say of late thou wert despised?

RICHARD

First, lean thine agèd back against mine arm,
And in that ease I'll tell thee my disease.
This day an argument upon a case
Some words there grew 'twixt Somerset and me;
Among which terms he used his lavish tongue
And did upbraid me with my father's death;
Which obloquy set bars before my tongue,
50 Else with the like I had requited him.
Therefore, good uncle, for my father's sake,
In honour of a true Plantagenet,
And for alliance' sake, declare the cause
My father, Earl of Cambridge, lost his head.

MORTIMER

That cause, fair nephew, that imprisoned me
And hath detained me all my flowering youth
Within a loathsome dungeon, there to pine,
Was cursèd instrument of his decease.

RICHARD

Discover more at large what cause that was,
60 For I am ignorant and cannot guess.

MORTIMER

I will, if that my fading breath permit
And death approach not ere my tale be done.
Henry the Fourth, grandfather to this king,
Deposed his nephew Richard, Edward's son,
The first-begotten and the lawful heir
Of Edward king, the third of that descent;
During whose reign the Percys of the north,
Finding his usurpation most unjust,
Endeavoured my advancement to the throne.
70 The reason moved these warlike lords to this
Was for that – young Richard thus removed,

Leaving no heir begotten of his body –
I was the next by birth and parentage;
For by my mother I derivèd am
From Lionel Duke of Clarence, third son
To King Edward the Third; whereas he
From John of Gaunt doth bring his pedigree,
Being but fourth of that heroic line.
But mark: as in this haughty great attempt
They labourèd to plant the rightful heir,　　　80
I lost my liberty, and they their lives.
Long after this, when Henry the Fifth,
Succeeding his father Bolingbroke, did reign,
Thy father, Earl of Cambridge then, derived
From famous Edmund Langley, Duke of York,
Marrying my sister that thy mother was,
Again, in pity of my hard distress,
Levied an army, weening to redeem
And have installed me in the diadem;
But, as the rest, so fell that noble earl,　　　90
And was beheaded. Thus the Mortimers,
In whom the title rested, were suppressed.

RICHARD

Of which, my lord, your honour is the last.

MORTIMER

True, and thou seest that I no issue have,
And that my fainting words do warrant death.
Thou art my heir. The rest I wish thee gather;
But yet be wary in thy studious care.

RICHARD

Thy grave admonishments prevail with me.
But yet methinks my father's execution
Was nothing less than bloody tyranny.　　　100

MORTIMER

With silence, nephew, be thou politic.

Strong fixèd is the house of Lancaster
And like a mountain, not to be removed.
But now thy uncle is removing hence,
As princes do their courts when they are cloyed
With long continuance in a settled place.

RICHARD

O uncle, would some part of my young years
Might but redeem the passage of your age!

MORTIMER

Thou dost then wrong me, as that slaughterer doth
110 Which giveth many wounds when one will kill.
Mourn not, except thou sorrow for my good;
Only give order for my funeral.
And so farewell, and fair be all thy hopes,
And prosperous be thy life in peace and war! *He dies*

RICHARD

And peace, no war, befall thy parting soul!
In prison hast thou spent a pilgrimage,
And like a hermit overpassed thy days.
Well, I will lock his counsel in my breast;
And what I do imagine, let that rest.
120 Keepers, convey him hence, and I myself
Will see his burial better than his life.

                    Exeunt Gaolers, with Mortimer's body
Here dies the dusky torch of Mortimer,
Choked with ambition of the meaner sort;
And for those wrongs, those bitter injuries,
Which Somerset hath offered to my house,
I doubt not but with honour to redress;
And therefore haste I to the parliament,
Either to be restorèd to my blood
Or make my ill th'advantage of my good.   *Exit*

✳

Flourish. Enter the King, Exeter, Gloucester, Win-
chester, Warwick, Somerset, Suffolk, Richard Plan-
tagenet, and others. Gloucester offers to put up a bill.
Winchester snatches it, tears it

WINCHESTER
Comest thou with deep premeditated lines?
With written pamphlets studiously devised?
Humphrey of Gloucester, if thou canst accuse
Or aught intendest to lay unto my charge,
Do it without invention, suddenly;
As I with sudden and extemporal speech
Purpose to answer what thou canst object.

GLOUCESTER
Presumptuous priest, this place commands my patience,
Or thou shouldst find thou hast dishonoured me.
Think not, although in writing I preferred   10
The manner of thy vile outrageous crimes,
That therefore I have forged, or am not able
Verbatim to rehearse the method of my pen.
No, prelate; such is thy audacious wickedness,
Thy lewd, pestiferous, and dissentious pranks,
As very infants prattle of thy pride.
Thou art a most pernicious usurer;
Froward by nature, enemy to peace,
Lascivious, wanton, more than well beseems
A man of thy profession and degree.   20
And for thy treachery, what's more manifest,
In that thou laidest a trap to take my life,
As well at London Bridge as at the Tower?
Besides, I fear me, if thy thoughts were sifted,
The King, thy sovereign, is not quite exempt
From envious malice of thy swelling heart.

WINCHESTER
Gloucester, I do defy thee. Lords, vouchsafe

To give me hearing what I shall reply.
If I were covetous, ambitious, or perverse,
30 As he will have me, how am I so poor?
Or how haps it I seek not to advance
Or raise myself, but keep my wonted calling?
And for dissension, who preferreth peace
More than I do, except I be provoked?
No, my good lords, it is not that offends;
It is not that that hath incensed the Duke:
It is because no one should sway but he,
No one but he should be about the King;
And that engenders thunder in his breast
40 And makes him roar these accusations forth.
But he shall know I am as good –

GLOUCESTER   As good?
Thou bastard of my grandfather!

WINCHESTER
Ay, lordly sir; for what are you, I pray,
But one imperious in another's throne?

GLOUCESTER
Am I not Protector, saucy priest?

WINCHESTER
And am not I a prelate of the Church?

GLOUCESTER
Yes, as an outlaw in a castle keeps,
And useth it to patronage his theft.

WINCHESTER
Unreverent Gloucester!

GLOUCESTER   Thou art reverend
50 Touching thy spiritual function, not thy life.

WINCHESTER
Rome shall remedy this.

WARWICK   Roam thither then.

SOMERSET (*to Warwick*)
My lord, it were your duty to forbear.

WARWICK

Ay, see the Bishop be not overborne.

SOMERSET

Methinks my lord should be religious,
And know the office that belongs to such.

WARWICK

Methinks his lordship should be humbler;
It fitteth not a prelate so to plead.

SOMERSET

Yes, when his holy state is touched so near.

WARWICK

State holy or unhallowed, what of that?
Is not his grace Protector to the King?   60

RICHARD (*aside*)

Plantagenet, I see, must hold his tongue,
Lest it be said 'Speak, sirrah, when you should;
Must your bold verdict enter talk with lords?'
Else would I have a fling at Winchester.

KING

Uncles of Gloucester and of Winchester,
The special watchmen of our English weal,
I would prevail, if prayers might prevail,
To join your hearts in love and amity.
O, what a scandal is it to our crown
That two such noble peers as ye should jar!   70
Believe me, lords, my tender years can tell
Civil dissension is a viperous worm
That gnaws the bowels of the commonwealth.

    A noise within: 'Down with the tawny coats!'
What tumult's this?

WARWICK   An uproar, I dare warrant,
Begun through malice of the Bishop's men.

    A noise again: 'Stones! Stones!' *Enter the Mayor*

MAYOR

O my good lords, and virtuous Henry,

Pity the city of London, pity us!
The Bishop and the Duke of Gloucester's men,
Forbidden late to carry any weapon,
80 Have filled their pockets full of pebble stones
And, banding themselves in contrary parts,
Do pelt so fast at one another's pate
That many have their giddy brains knocked out.
Our windows are broke down in every street
And we, for fear, compelled to shut our shops.

> *Enter Servingmen of Gloucester and Winchester in skirmish with bloody pates*

KING
We charge you, on allegiance to ourself,
To hold your slaughtering hands and keep the peace.
Pray, uncle Gloucester, mitigate this strife.

FIRST SERVINGMAN Nay, if we be forbidden stones,
90 we'll fall to it with our teeth.

SECOND SERVINGMAN
Do what ye dare, we are as resolute.

> *Skirmish again*

GLOUCESTER
You of my household, leave this peevish broil
And set this unaccustomed fight aside.

THIRD SERVINGMAN
My lord, we know your grace to be a man
Just and upright, and for your royal birth
Inferior to none but to his majesty;
And ere that we will suffer such a prince,
So kind a father of the commonweal,
To be disgracèd by an inkhorn mate,
100 We and our wives and children all will fight
And have our bodies slaughtered by thy foes.

FIRST SERVINGMAN Ay, and the very parings of our nails
shall pitch a field when we are dead.

> *They begin to skirmish again*

GLOUCESTER

Stay, stay, I say!
And if you love me, as you say you do,
Let me persuade you to forbear awhile.

KING

O, how this discord doth afflict my soul!
Can you, my lord of Winchester, behold
My sighs and tears and will not once relent?
Who should be pitiful if you be not?   110
Or who should study to prefer a peace
If holy churchmen take delight in broils?

WARWICK

Yield, my Lord Protector, yield, Winchester,
Except you mean with obstinate repulse
To slay your sovereign and destroy the realm.
You see what mischief, and what murder too,
Hath been enacted through your enmity.
Then be at peace, except ye thirst for blood.

WINCHESTER

He shall submit, or I will never yield.

GLOUCESTER

Compassion on the King commands me stoop,   120
Or I would see his heart out ere the priest
Should ever get that privilege of me.

WARWICK

Behold, my lord of Winchester, the Duke
Hath banished moody discontented fury,
As by his smoothèd brows it doth appear;
Why look you still so stern and tragical?

GLOUCESTER

Here, Winchester, I offer thee my hand.

KING

Fie, uncle Beaufort, I have heard you preach
That malice was a great and grievous sin;
And will not you maintain the thing you teach,   130

93

But prove a chief offender in the same?

WARWICK

Sweet King! The Bishop hath a kindly gird.
For shame, my lord of Winchester, relent;
What, shall a child instruct you what to do?

WINCHESTER

Well, Duke of Gloucester, I will yield to thee.
Love for thy love and hand for hand I give.

GLOUCESTER (*aside*)

Ay, but, I fear me, with a hollow heart.
(*To them*) See here, my friends and loving countrymen:
This token serveth for a flag of truce

140 Betwixt ourselves and all our followers.
So help me God, as I dissemble not.

WINCHESTER

So help me God – (*aside*) as I intend it not.

KING

O loving uncle, kind Duke of Gloucester,
How joyful am I made by this contract!
Away, my masters! Trouble us no more,
But join in friendship, as your lords have done.

FIRST SERVINGMAN Content; I'll to the surgeon's.

SECOND SERVINGMAN And so will I.

THIRD SERVINGMAN And I will see what physic the
150 tavern affords.   *Exeunt Servingmen and Mayor*

WARWICK

Accept this scroll, most gracious sovereign,
Which in the right of Richard Plantagenet
We do exhibit to your majesty.

GLOUCESTER

Well urged, my Lord of Warwick; for, sweet prince,
An if your grace mark every circumstance,
You have great reason to do Richard right,
Especially for those occasions
At Eltham Place I told your majesty.

KING

    And those occasions, uncle, were of force;
    Therefore, my loving lords, our pleasure is   160
    That Richard be restorèd to his blood.

WARWICK

    Let Richard be restorèd to his blood;
    So shall his father's wrongs be recompensed.

WINCHESTER

    As will the rest, so willeth Winchester.

KING

    If Richard will be true, not that alone
    But all the whole inheritance I give
    That doth belong unto the House of York,
    From whence you spring by lineal descent.

RICHARD

    Thy humble servant vows obedience
    And humble service till the point of death.   170

KING

    Stoop then and set your knee against my foot;
    And in reguerdon of that duty done
    I girt thee with the valiant sword of York.
    Rise, Richard, like a true Plantagenet,
    And rise created princely Duke of York.

RICHARD

    And so thrive Richard as thy foes may fall!
    And as my duty springs, so perish they
    That grudge one thought against your majesty!

ALL

    Welcome, high prince, the mighty Duke of York!

SOMERSET (*aside*)

    Perish, base prince, ignoble Duke of York!   180

GLOUCESTER

    Now will it best avail your majesty
    To cross the seas and to be crowned in France.
    The presence of a king engenders love

Amongst his subjects and his loyal friends,
As it disanimates his enemies.

KING

When Gloucester says the word, King Henry goes;
For friendly counsel cuts off many foes.

GLOUCESTER

Your ships already are in readiness.

                              Sennet. Flourish. Exeunt all but Exeter

EXETER

Ay, we may march in England or in France,
190   Not seeing what is likely to ensue.
This late dissension grown betwixt the peers
Burns under feignèd ashes of forged love
And will at last break out into a flame.
As festered members rot but by degree
Till bones and flesh and sinews fall away,
So will this base and envious discord breed.
And now I fear that fatal prophecy
Which in the time of Henry named the Fifth
Was in the mouth of every sucking babe:
200   That Henry born at Monmouth should win all
And Henry born at Windsor should lose all;
Which is so plain that Exeter doth wish
His days may finish ere that hapless time.   *Exit*

III.2   *Enter Joan la Pucelle disguised, with four soldiers
             dressed like countrymen with sacks upon their backs*

PUCELLE

These are the city gates, the gates of Rouen,
Through which our policy must make a breach.
Take heed, be wary how you place your words;
Talk like the vulgar sort of market-men
That come to gather money for their corn.
If we have entrance, as I hope we shall,
And that we find the slothful watch but weak,

I'll by a sign give notice to our friends,
That Charles the Dauphin may encounter them.

FIRST SOLDIER

Our sacks shall be a mean to sack the city, 10
And we be lords and rulers over Rouen.
Therefore we'll knock.
They knock

WATCH (*within*)
Qui là?

PUCELLE
Paysans, la pauvre gent de France,
Poor market folks that come to sell their corn.

WATCH (*opening the gates*)
Enter, go in; the market bell is rung.

PUCELLE
Now, Rouen, I'll shake thy bulwarks to the ground.
Exeunt into the city
*Enter Charles, the Bastard, Alençon, Reignier, and
soldiers*

CHARLES
Saint Denis bless this happy stratagem,
And once again we'll sleep secure in Rouen.

BASTARD
Here entered Pucelle and her practisants. 20
Now she is there, how will she specify
Here is the best and safest passage in?

REIGNIER
By thrusting out a torch from yonder tower,
Which, once discerned, shows that her meaning is:
No way to that, for weakness, which she entered.
*Enter Joan la Pucelle on the top, thrusting out a torch
burning*

PUCELLE
Behold, this is the happy wedding torch
That joineth Rouen unto her countrymen,
But burning fatal to the Talbotites. *Exit*

BASTARD

See, noble Charles, the beacon of our friend;
30   The burning torch in yonder turret stands.

CHARLES

Now shine it like a comet of revenge,
A prophet to the fall of all our foes!

REIGNIER

Defer no time; delays have dangerous ends.
Enter and cry 'The Dauphin!' presently,
And then do execution on the watch.

           Alarum. They storm the gates and exeunt
           An alarum. Enter Talbot in an excursion from within
           the town

TALBOT

France, thou shalt rue this treason with thy tears,
If Talbot but survive thy treachery.
Pucelle, that witch, that damnèd sorceress,
Hath wrought this hellish mischief unawares,
40   That hardly we escaped the pride of France.   *Exit*
           An alarum. Excursions. Bedford brought in sick in a
           chair
           Enter Talbot and Burgundy without; within, Joan la
           Pucelle, Charles, the Bastard, Alençon, and Reignier
           on the walls

PUCELLE

Good morrow, gallants, want ye corn for bread?
I think the Duke of Burgundy will fast
Before he'll buy again at such a rate.
'Twas full of darnel; do you like the taste?

BURGUNDY

Scoff on, vile fiend and shameless courtesan!
I trust ere long to choke thee with thine own,
And make thee curse the harvest of that corn.

CHARLES

Your grace may starve, perhaps, before that time.

BEDFORD

  O, let no words, but deeds, revenge this treason!

PUCELLE

  What will you do, good greybeard? Break a lance,   50
  And run a-tilt at death within a chair?

TALBOT

  Foul fiend of France and hag of all despite,
  Encompassed with thy lustful paramours,
  Becomes it thee to taunt his valiant age
  And twit with cowardice a man half dead?
  Damsel, I'll have a bout with you again,
  Or else let Talbot perish with this shame.

PUCELLE

  Are ye so hot, sir? Yet, Pucelle, hold thy peace.
  If Talbot do but thunder, rain will follow.
    The English whisper together in counsel
  God speed the parliament; who shall be the Speaker?   60

TALBOT

  Dare ye come forth and meet us in the field?

PUCELLE

  Belike your lordship takes us then for fools,
  To try if that our own be ours or no.

TALBOT

  I speak not to that railing Hecate,
  But unto thee, Alençon, and the rest.
  Will ye, like soldiers, come and fight it out?

ALENÇON

  Signor, no.

TALBOT

  Signor, hang! Base muleteers of France!
  Like peasant footboys do they keep the walls
  And dare not take up arms like gentlemen.   70

PUCELLE

  Away, captains! Let's get us from the walls,
  For Talbot means no goodness by his looks.

God bye, my lord; we came but to tell you
That we are here.   *Exeunt from the walls*

TALBOT

And there will we be too ere it be long,
Or else reproach be Talbot's greatest fame!
Vow, Burgundy, by honour of thy house,
Pricked on by public wrongs sustained in France,
Either to get the town again or die;

80 And I, as sure as English Henry lives
And as his father here was conqueror,
As sure as in this late betrayèd town
Great Coeur-de-lion's heart was burièd,
So sure I swear to get the town or die.

BURGUNDY

My vows are equal partners with thy vows.

TALBOT

But, ere we go, regard this dying prince,
The valiant Duke of Bedford. Come, my lord,
We will bestow you in some better place,
Fitter for sickness and for crazy age.

BEDFORD

90 Lord Talbot, do not so dishonour me;
Here will I sit, before the walls of Rouen,
And will be partner of your weal or woe.

BURGUNDY

Courageous Bedford, let us now persuade you.

BEDFORD

Not to be gone from hence; for once I read
That stout Pendragon in his litter sick
Came to the field and vanquishèd his foes.
Methinks I should revive the soldiers' hearts,
Because I ever found them as myself.

TALBOT

Undaunted spirit in a dying breast!
100 Then be it so. Heavens keep old Bedford safe!

And now no more ado, brave Burgundy,
But gather we our forces out of hand
And set upon our boasting enemy.

Exeunt all but Bedford and attendants
An alarum. Excursions. Enter Sir John Falstaff and
a Captain

CAPTAIN
Whither away, Sir John Falstaff, in such haste?

FALSTAFF
Whither away? To save myself by flight.
We are like to have the overthrow again.

CAPTAIN
What, will you fly and leave Lord Talbot?

FALSTAFF   Ay,
All the Talbots in the world, to save my life.   *Exit*

CAPTAIN
Cowardly knight, ill fortune follow thee!   *Exit*
Retreat. Excursions. Pucelle, Alençon, and Charles
enter from the town and fly

BEDFORD
Now, quiet soul, depart when heaven please,   110
For I have seen our enemies' overthrow.
What is the trust or strength of foolish man?
They that of late were daring with their scoffs
Are glad and fain by flight to save themselves.

Bedford dies and is carried in by
two attendants in his chair
An alarum. Enter Talbot, Burgundy, and the rest of
the English soldiers

TALBOT
Lost and recovered in a day again!
This is a double honour, Burgundy.
Yet heavens have glory for this victory!

BURGUNDY
Warlike and martial Talbot, Burgundy

Enshrines thee in his heart and there erects
120   Thy noble deeds as valour's monuments.

TALBOT

Thanks, gentle Duke. But where is Pucelle now?
I think her old familiar is asleep.
Now where's the Bastard's braves and Charles his gleeks?
What, all amort? Rouen hangs her head for grief
That such a valiant company are fled.
Now will we take some order in the town,
Placing therein some expert officers,
And then depart to Paris to the King,
For there young Henry with his nobles lie.

BURGUNDY

130   What wills Lord Talbot pleaseth Burgundy.

TALBOT

But yet, before we go, let's not forget
The noble Duke of Bedford, late deceased,
But see his exequies fulfilled in Rouen.
A braver soldier never couchèd lance;
A gentler heart did never sway in court.
But kings and mightiest potentates must die,
For that's the end of human misery.   *Exeunt*

III.3   *Enter Charles, the Bastard, Alençon, Joan la Pucelle,*
        and soldiers

PUCELLE

Dismay not, princes, at this accident,
Nor grieve that Rouen is so recoverèd.
Care is no cure, but rather corrosive,
For things that are not to be remedied.
Let frantic Talbot triumph for a while
And like a peacock sweep along his tail;
We'll pull his plumes and take away his train,
If Dauphin and the rest will be but ruled.

CHARLES

    We have been guided by thee hitherto,

    And of thy cunning had no diffidence;   10

    One sudden foil shall never breed distrust.

BASTARD

    Search out thy wit for secret policies,

    And we will make thee famous through the world.

ALENÇON

    We'll set thy statue in some holy place,

    And have thee reverenced like a blessèd saint.

    Employ thee then, sweet virgin, for our good.

PUCELLE

    Then thus it must be; this doth Joan devise:

    By fair persuasions, mixed with sugared words,

    We will entice the Duke of Burgundy

    To leave the Talbot and to follow us.   20

CHARLES

    Ay, marry, sweeting, if we could do that,

    France were no place for Henry's warriors,

    Nor should that nation boast it so with us,

    But be extirpèd from our provinces.

ALENÇON

    For ever should they be expulsed from France,

    And not have title of an earldom here.

PUCELLE

    Your honours shall perceive how I will work

    To bring this matter to the wishèd end.

       Drum sounds afar off

    Hark, by the sound of drum you may perceive

    Their powers are marching unto Paris-ward.   30

       Here sound an English march

    There goes the Talbot with his colours spread,

    And all the troops of English after him.

       Here sound a French march

    Now in the rearward comes the Duke and his;

Fortune in favour makes him lag behind.
Summon a parley; we will talk with him.
Trumpets sound a parley

CHARLES

A parley with the Duke of Burgundy!
Enter Burgundy and troops

BURGUNDY

Who craves a parley with the Burgundy?

PUCELLE

The princely Charles of France, thy countryman.

BURGUNDY

What sayest thou, Charles? for I am marching hence.

CHARLES

40 Speak, Pucelle, and enchant him with thy words.

PUCELLE

Brave Burgundy, undoubted hope of France,
Stay, let thy humble handmaid speak to thee.

BURGUNDY

Speak on; but be not over-tedious.

PUCELLE

Look on thy country, look on fertile France,
And see the cities and the towns defaced
By wasting ruin of the cruel foe;
As looks the mother on her lowly babe
When death does close his tender-dying eyes,
See, see the pining malady of France;
50 Behold the wounds, the most unnatural wounds,
Which thou thyself hast given her woeful breast.
O, turn thy edgèd sword another way;
Strike those that hurt, and hurt not those that help!
One drop of blood drawn from thy country's bosom
Should grieve thee more than streams of foreign gore.
Return thee therefore with a flood of tears,
And wash away thy country's stainèd spots.

BURGUNDY *(aside)*

Either she hath bewitched me with her words,

Or nature makes me suddenly relent.

PUCELLE

Besides, all French and France exclaims on thee,　　60
Doubting thy birth and lawful progeny.
Who joinest thou with but with a lordly nation
That will not trust thee but for profit's sake?
When Talbot hath set footing once in France,
And fashioned thee that instrument of ill,
Who then but English Henry will be lord,
And thou be thrust out like a fugitive?
Call we to mind, and mark but this for proof:
Was not the Duke of Orleans thy foe?
And was he not in England prisoner?　　70
But when they heard he was thine enemy,
They set him free without his ransom paid,
In spite of Burgundy and all his friends.
See then, thou fightest against thy countrymen,
And joinest with them will be thy slaughtermen.
Come, come, return; return, thou wandering lord;
Charles and the rest will take thee in their arms.

BURGUNDY (aside)

I am vanquished. These haughty words of hers
Have battered me like roaring cannon-shot
And made me almost yield upon my knees.　　80
(To them) Forgive me, country, and sweet countrymen!
And, lords, accept this hearty kind embrace.
My forces and my power of men are yours.
So farewell, Talbot; I'll no longer trust thee.

PUCELLE

Done like a Frenchman – (aside) turn and turn again.

CHARLES

Welcome, brave Duke. Thy friendship makes us fresh.

BASTARD

And doth beget new courage in our breasts.

ALENÇON

Pucelle hath bravely played her part in this,

And doth deserve a coronet of gold.

CHARLES

90 Now let us on, my lords, and join our powers,
And seek how we may prejudice the foe.   *Exeunt*

III.4   *Enter the King, Gloucester, Winchester, Richard*
            Duke of York, Suffolk, Somerset, Warwick, Exeter,
            Vernon, Basset, and other courtiers. To them, with
            his soldiers, Talbot

TALBOT

My gracious prince, and honourable peers,
Hearing of your arrival in this realm,
I have awhile given truce unto my wars
To do my duty to my sovereign;
In sign whereof this arm that hath reclaimed
To your obedience fifty fortresses,
Twelve cities, and seven wallèd towns of strength,
Beside five hundred prisoners of esteem,
Lets fall his sword before your highness' feet,
      (*He kneels*)
10 And with submissive loyalty of heart
Ascribes the glory of his conquest got
First to my God and next unto your grace.

KING

Is this the Lord Talbot, uncle Gloucester,
That hath so long been resident in France?

GLOUCESTER

Yes, if it please your majesty, my liege.

KING

Welcome, brave captain and victorious lord!
When I was young – as yet I am not old –
I do remember how my father said
A stouter champion never handled sword.
20 Long since we were resolvèd of your truth,
Your faithful service, and your toil in war;

Yet never have you tasted our reward
Or been reguerdoned with so much as thanks,
Because till now we never saw your face.
Therefore stand up, and for these good deserts
We here create you Earl of Shrewsbury;
And in our coronation take your place.

Sennet. Flourish. Exeunt all but Vernon
and Basset

VERNON

Now, sir, to you, that were so hot at sea,
Disgracing of these colours that I wear
In honour of my noble lord of York,   30
Darest thou maintain the former words thou spakest?

BASSET

Yes, sir, as well as you dare patronage
The envious barking of your saucy tongue
Against my lord the Duke of Somerset.

VERNON

Sirrah, thy lord I honour as he is.

BASSET

Why, what is he? As good a man as York.

VERNON

Hark ye, not so. In witness take ye that.
He strikes him

BASSET

Villain, thou knowest the law of arms is such
That whoso draws a sword 'tis present death,
Or else this blow should broach thy dearest blood.   40
But I'll unto his majesty and crave
I may have liberty to venge this wrong,
When thou shalt see I'll meet thee to thy cost.

VERNON

Well, miscreant, I'll be there as soon as you,
And after meet you sooner than you would.   *Exeunt*

✳

Enter the King, Gloucester, Winchester, Richard Duke of York, Suffolk, Somerset, Warwick, Talbot, Exeter, the Governor of Paris, and others

GLOUCESTER

Lord Bishop, set the crown upon his head.

WINCHESTER

God save King Henry, of that name the sixth!

GLOUCESTER

Now, Governor of Paris, take your oath:
    (*The Governor kneels*)
That you elect no other king but him,
Esteem none friends but such as are his friends,
And none your foes but such as shall pretend
Malicious practices against his state.
This shall ye do, so help you righteous God.

                           Exeunt Governor and his train

    Enter Falstaff

FALSTAFF

My gracious sovereign, as I rode from Calais
10   To haste unto your coronation,
A letter was delivered to my hands,
Writ to your grace from th'Duke of Burgundy.

TALBOT

Shame to the Duke of Burgundy and thee!
I vowed, base knight, when I did meet thee next
To tear the Garter from thy craven's leg,
    (*He plucks it off*)
Which I have done, because unworthily
Thou wast installèd in that high degree.
Pardon me, princely Henry, and the rest:
This dastard, at the Battle of Patay,
20   When, but in all, I was six thousand strong,
And that the French were almost ten to one,
Before we met or that a stroke was given,
Like to a trusty squire did run away;

In which assault we lost twelve hundred men.
Myself and divers gentlemen beside
Were there surprised and taken prisoners.
Then judge, great lords, if I have done amiss,
Or whether that such cowards ought to wear
This ornament of knighthood, yea or no!

GLOUCESTER

To say the truth, this fact was infamous,   30
And ill beseeming any common man,
Much more a knight, a captain, and a leader.

TALBOT

When first this Order was ordained, my lords,
Knights of the Garter were of noble birth,
Valiant and virtuous, full of haughty courage,
Such as were grown to credit by the wars;
Not fearing death nor shrinking for distress,
But always resolute in most extremes.
He then that is not furnished in this sort
Doth but usurp the sacred name of knight,   40
Profaning this most honourable order,
And should, if I were worthy to be judge,
Be quite degraded, like a hedge-born swain
That doth presume to boast of gentle blood.

KING

Stain to thy countrymen, thou hearest thy doom.
Be packing therefore, thou that wast a knight;
Henceforth we banish thee on pain of death.

Exit Falstaff

And now, Lord Protector, view the letter
Sent from our uncle Duke of Burgundy.

GLOUCESTER (*looking at the outside of the letter*)

What means his grace that he hath changed his style?   50
No more but plain and bluntly 'To the King'?
Hath he forgot he is his sovereign?
Or doth this churlish superscription

Pretend some alteration in good will?
What's here? (*He reads*) *I have, upon especial cause,*
Moved with compassion of my country's wrack,
Together with the pitiful complaints
Of such as your oppression feeds upon,
Forsaken your pernicious faction,
60 *And joined with Charles, the rightful King of France.*
O, monstrous treachery! Can this be so?
That in alliance, amity, and oaths
There should be found such false dissembling guile?

KING

What? Doth my uncle Burgundy revolt?

GLOUCESTER

He doth, my lord, and is become your foe.

KING

Is that the worst this letter doth contain?

GLOUCESTER

It is the worst, and all, my lord, he writes.

KING

Why then, Lord Talbot there shall talk with him
And give him chastisement for this abuse.
70 How say you, my lord; are you not content?

TALBOT

Content, my liege? Yes; but that I am prevented,
I should have begged I might have been employed.

KING

Then gather strength and march unto him straight;
Let him perceive how ill we brook his treason,
And what offence it is to flout his friends.

TALBOT

I go, my lord, in heart desiring still
You may behold confusion of your foes.   *Exit*

    Enter Vernon and Basset

VERNON

Grant me the combat. gracious sovereign.

BASSET

And me, my lord, grant me the combat too.

RICHARD

This is my servant; hear him, noble prince.   80

SOMERSET

And this is mine; sweet Henry, favour him.

KING

Be patient, lords, and give them leave to speak.

Say, gentlemen, what makes you thus exclaim,

And wherefore crave you combat, or with whom?

VERNON

With him, my lord, for he hath done me wrong.

BASSET

And I with him, for he hath done me wrong.

KING

What is that wrong whereof you both complain?

First let me know, and then I'll answer you.

BASSET

Crossing the sea from England into France,

This fellow here with envious carping tongue   90

Upbraided me about the rose I wear,

Saying the sanguine colour of the leaves

Did represent my master's blushing cheeks

When stubbornly he did repugn the truth

About a certain question in the law

Argued betwixt the Duke of York and him;

With other vile and ignominious terms.

In confutation of which rude reproach,

And in defence of my lord's worthiness,

I crave the benefit of law of arms.   100

VERNON

And that is my petition, noble lord;

For though he seem with forgèd quaint conceit

To set a gloss upon his bold intent,

Yet know, my lord, I was provoked by him,

And he first took exceptions at this badge,
Pronouncing that the paleness of this flower
Bewrayed the faintness of my master's heart.

RICHARD

Will not this malice, Somerset, be left?

SOMERSET

Your private grudge, my lord of York, will out,
110 Though ne'er so cunningly you smother it.

KING

Good Lord, what madness rules in brainsick men,
When for so slight and frivolous a cause
Such factious emulations shall arise!
Good cousins both, of York and Somerset,
Quiet yourselves, I pray, and be at peace.

RICHARD

Let his dissension first be tried by fight,
And then your highness shall command a peace.

SOMERSET

The quarrel toucheth none but us alone;
Betwixt ourselves let us decide it then.

RICHARD

120 There is my pledge; accept it, Somerset.

VERNON

Nay, let it rest where it began at first.

BASSET

Confirm it so, mine honourable lord.

GLOUCESTER

Confirm it so? Confounded be your strife,
And perish ye with your audacious prate!
Presumptuous vassals, are you not ashamed
With this immodest clamorous outrage
To trouble and disturb the King and us?
And you, my lords, methinks you do not well
To bear with their perverse objections,
130 Much less to take occasion from their mouths

To raise a mutiny betwixt yourselves.
Let me persuade you take a better course.

EXETER

It grieves his highness. Good my lords, be friends.

KING

Come hither, you that would be combatants.
Henceforth I charge you, as you love our favour,
Quite to forget this quarrel and the cause.
And you, my lords, remember where we are –
In France, amongst a fickle, wavering nation;
If they perceive dissension in our looks
And that within ourselves we disagree,   140
How will their grudging stomachs be provoked
To wilful disobedience, and rebel!
Beside, what infamy will there arise
When foreign princes shall be certified
That for a toy, a thing of no regard,
King Henry's peers and chief nobility
Destroyed themselves and lost the realm of France!
O, think upon the conquest of my father,
My tender years, and let us not forgo
That for a trifle that was bought with blood!   150
Let me be umpire in this doubtful strife.
I see no reason, if I wear this rose,
    (*He puts on a red rose*)
That anyone should therefore be suspicious
I more incline to Somerset than York;
Both are my kinsmen, and I love them both.
As well they may upbraid me with my crown
Because, forsooth, the King of Scots is crowned.
But your discretions better can persuade
Than I am able to instruct or teach;
And, therefore, as we hither came in peace,   160
So let us still continue peace and love.
Cousin of York, we institute your grace

To be our Regent in these parts of France;
And, good my lord of Somerset, unite
Your troops of horsemen with his bands of foot;
And like true subjects, sons of your progenitors,
Go cheerfully together and digest
Your angry choler on your enemies.
Ourself, my Lord Protector, and the rest
170 After some respite will return to Calais;
From thence to England, where I hope ere long
To be presented, by your victories,
With Charles, Alençon, and that traitorous rout.

Flourish. Exeunt all but Richard Duke of
York, Warwick, Exeter, Vernon

WARWICK

My lord of York, I promise you, the King
Prettily, methought, did play the orator.

RICHARD

And so he did; but yet I like it not,
In that he wears the badge of Somerset.

WARWICK

Tush, that was but his fancy; blame him not;
I dare presume, sweet prince, he thought no harm.

RICHARD

180 An if I wist he did – but let it rest;
Other affairs must now be managèd.

Exeunt all but Exeter

EXETER

Well didst thou, Richard, to suppress thy voice;
For, had the passions of thy heart burst out,
I fear we should have seen deciphered there
More rancorous spite, more furious raging broils,
Than yet can be imagined or supposed.
But howsoe'er, no simple man that sees
This jarring discord of nobility,
This shouldering of each other in the court,

This factious bandying of their favourites,   190
But that it doth presage some ill event.
'Tis much when sceptres are in children's hands;
But more when envy breeds unkind division.
There comes the ruin, there begins confusion.   *Exit*

Enter Talbot, with trump and drum, before Bordeaux IV.2

TALBOT

Go to the gates of Bordeaux, trumpeter;
Summon their general unto the wall.

Trumpet sounds. Enter the General aloft with his men

English John Talbot, captains, calls you forth,
Servant in arms to Harry King of England;
And thus he would: open your city gates,
Be humble to us, call my sovereign yours
And do him homage as obedient subjects,
And I'll withdraw me and my bloody power;
But if you frown upon this proffered peace,
You tempt the fury of my three attendants,   10
Lean famine, quartering steel, and climbing fire;
Who in a moment even with the earth
Shall lay your stately and air-braving towers,
If you forsake the offer of their love.

GENERAL

Thou ominous and fearful owl of death,
Our nation's terror and their bloody scourge!
The period of thy tyranny approacheth.
On us thou canst not enter but by death;
For I protest we are well fortified,
And strong enough to issue out and fight.   20
If thou retire, the Dauphin, well appointed,
Stands with the snares of war to tangle thee.
On either hand thee there are squadrons pitched
To wall thee from the liberty of flight;

And no way canst thou turn thee for redress
But death doth front thee with apparent spoil
And pale destruction meets thee in the face.
Ten thousand French have ta'en the sacrament
To rive their dangerous artillery
30 Upon no Christian soul but English Talbot.
Lo, there thou standest, a breathing valiant man
Of an invincible unconquered spirit!
This is the latest glory of thy praise
That I, thy enemy, due thee withal;
For ere the glass that now begins to run
Finish the process of his sandy hour,
These eyes that see thee now well colourèd
Shall see thee withered, bloody, pale, and dead.

Drum afar off

Hark, hark! The Dauphin's drum, a warning bell,
40 Sings heavy music to thy timorous soul;
And mine shall ring thy dire departure out.

Exit with his men

TALBOT

He fables not; I hear the enemy.
Out, some light horsemen, and peruse their wings.
O, negligent and heedless discipline!
How are we parked and bounded in a pale –
A little herd of England's timorous deer,
Mazed with a yelping kennel of French curs!
If we be English deer, be then in blood;
Not rascal-like to fall down with a pinch,
50 But rather, moody-mad and desperate stags,
Turn on the bloody hounds with heads of steel
And make the cowards stand aloof at bay.
Sell every man his life as dear as mine,
And they shall find dear deer of us, my friends.
God and Saint George, Talbot and England's right,
Prosper our colours in this dangerous fight! *Exeunt*

Enter Richard Duke of York, with trumpet and many IV.3
soldiers. Enter a Messenger that meets York

RICHARD

Are not the speedy scouts returned again
That dogged the mighty army of the Dauphin?

MESSENGER

They are returned, my lord, and give it out
That he is marched to Bordeaux with his power
To fight with Talbot; as he marched along,
By your espials were discoverèd
Two mightier troops than that the Dauphin led,
Which joined with him and made their march for
    Bordeaux.

RICHARD

A plague upon that villain Somerset,
That thus delays my promisèd supply   10
Of horsemen that were levied for this siege!
Renownèd Talbot doth expect my aid,
And I am louted by a traitor villain
And cannot help the noble chevalier.
God comfort him in this necessity!
If he miscarry, farewell wars in France.
    Enter another messenger, Sir William Lucy

LUCY

Thou princely leader of our English strength,
Never so needful on the earth of France,
Spur to the rescue of the noble Talbot,
Who now is girdled with a waist of iron   20
And hemmed about with grim destruction.
To Bordeaux, warlike Duke! To Bordeaux, York!
Else farewell Talbot, France, and England's honour.

RICHARD

O God, that Somerset, who in proud heart
Doth stop my cornets, were in Talbot's place!
So should we save a valiant gentleman

By forfeiting a traitor and a coward.
Mad ire and wrathful fury makes me weep
That thus we die while remiss traitors sleep.

LUCY

30   O, send some succour to the distressed lord!

RICHARD

He dies, we lose; I break my warlike word;
We mourn, France smiles; we lose, they daily get;
All 'long of this vile traitor Somerset.

LUCY

Then God take mercy on brave Talbot's soul
And on his son, young John, who two hours since
I met in travel toward his warlike father.
This seven years did not Talbot see his son,
And now they meet where both their lives are done.

RICHARD

Alas, what joy shall noble Talbot have
40   To bid his young son welcome to his grave?
Away! Vexation almost stops my breath
That sundered friends greet in the hour of death.
Lucy, farewell; no more my fortune can
But curse the cause I cannot aid the man.
Maine, Blois, Poitiers, and Tours are won away,
'Long all of Somerset and his delay.

Exit with his soldiers

LUCY

Thus, while the vulture of sedition
Feeds in the bosom of such great commanders,
Sleeping neglection doth betray to loss
50   The conquest of our scarce-cold conqueror,
That ever-living man of memory,
Henry the Fifth. Whiles they each other cross,
Lives, honours, lands, and all hurry to loss.   *Exit*

SOMERSET

It is too late; I cannot send them now.
This expedition was by York and Talbot
Too rashly plotted. All our general force
Might with a sally of the very town
Be buckled with. The over-daring Talbot
Hath sullied all his gloss of former honour
By this unheedful, desperate, wild adventure.
York set him on to fight and die in shame,
That, Talbot dead, great York might bear the name.

CAPTAIN

Here is Sir William Lucy, who with me   10
Set from our o'ermatched forces forth for aid.
      Enter Sir William Lucy

SOMERSET

How now, Sir William, whither were you sent?

LUCY

Whither, my lord? From bought and sold Lord Talbot,
Who, ringed about with bold adversity,
Cries out for noble York and Somerset
To beat assailing death from his weak legions;
And whiles the honourable captain there
Drops bloody sweat from his war-wearied limbs,
And, in advantage lingering, looks for rescue,
You, his false hopes, the trust of England's honour,   20
Keep off aloof with worthless emulation.
Let not your private discord keep away
The levied succours that should lend him aid,
While he, renownèd noble gentleman,
Yield up his life unto a world of odds.
Orleans the Bastard, Charles, Burgundy,
Alençon, Reignier compass him about,
And Talbot perisheth by your default.

SOMERSET

York set him on; York should have sent him aid.

LUCY

30 And York as fast upon your grace exclaims,
Swearing that you withhold his levied host,
Collected for this expedition.

SOMERSET

York lies; he might have sent and had the horse.
I owe him little duty, and less love,
And take foul scorn to fawn on him by sending.

LUCY

The fraud of England, not the force of France,
Hath now entrapped the noble-minded Talbot.
Never to England shall he bear his life,
But dies betrayed to fortune by your strife.

SOMERSET

40 Come, go; I will dispatch the horsemen straight;
Within six hours they will be at his aid.

LUCY

Too late comes rescue. He is ta'en or slain;
For fly he could not, if he would have fled;
And fly would Talbot never, though he might.

SOMERSET

If he be dead, brave Talbot, then adieu!

LUCY

His fame lives in the world, his shame in you. *Exeunt*

IV.5   *Enter Talbot and his son*

TALBOT

O young John Talbot, I did send for thee
To tutor thee in stratagems of war,
That Talbot's name might be in thee revived
When sapless age and weak unable limbs

Should bring thy father to his drooping chair.
But, O, malignant and ill-boding stars!
Now thou art come unto a feast of death,
A terrible and unavoided danger.
Therefore, dear boy, mount on my swiftest horse,
And I'll direct thee how thou shalt escape   10
By sudden flight. Come, dally not, be gone.

JOHN

Is my name Talbot, and am I your son?
And shall I fly? O, if you love my mother,
Dishonour not her honourable name
To make a bastard and a slave of me.
The world will say he is not Talbot's blood
That basely fled when noble Talbot stood.

TALBOT

Fly, to revenge my death if I be slain.

JOHN

He that flies so will ne'er return again.

TALBOT

If we both stay, we both are sure to die.   20

JOHN

Then let me stay, and, father, do you fly.
Your loss is great, so your regard should be;
My worth unknown, no loss is known in me.
Upon my death the French can little boast;
In yours they will; in you all hopes are lost.
Flight cannot stain the honour you have won;
But mine it will, that no exploit have done.
You fled for vantage, everyone will swear;
But if I bow, they'll say it was for fear.
There is no hope that ever I will stay   30
If the first hour I shrink and ryn away.
Here on my knee I beg mortality
Rather than life preserved with infamy.

TALBOT

Shall all thy mother's hopes lie in one tomb?

JOHN

Ay, rather than I'll shame my mother's womb.

TALBOT

Upon my blessing I command thee go.

JOHN

To fight I will, but not to fly the foe.

TALBOT

Part of thy father may be saved in thee.

JOHN

No part of him but will be shame in me.

TALBOT

40 Thou never hadst renown, nor canst not lose it.

JOHN

Yes, your renownèd name; shall flight abuse it?

TALBOT

Thy father's charge shall clear thee from that stain.

JOHN

You cannot witness for me being slain.
If death be so apparent, then both fly.

TALBOT

And leave my followers here to fight and die?
My age was never tainted with such shame.

JOHN

And shall my youth be guilty of such blame?
No more can I be severed from your side
Than can yourself yourself in twain divide.

50 Stay, go, do what you will – the like do I;
For live I will not if my father die.

TALBOT

Then here I take my leave of thee, fair son,
Born to eclipse thy life this afternoon.
Come, side by side together live and die,
And soul with soul from France to heaven fly. *Exeunt*

TALBOT

Saint George and victory! Fight, soldiers, fight!
The Regent hath with Talbot broke his word
And left us to the rage of France his sword.
Where is John Talbot? Pause, and take thy breath;
I gave thee life and rescued thee from death.

JOHN

O twice my father, twice am I thy son!
The life thou gavest me first was lost and done
Till with thy warlike sword, despite of fate,
To my determined time thou gavest new date.

TALBOT

When from the Dauphin's crest thy sword struck fire,   10
It warmed thy father's heart with proud desire
Of bold-faced victory. Then leaden age,
Quickened with youthful spleen and warlike rage,
Beat down Alençon, Orleans, Burgundy,
And from the pride of Gallia rescued thee.
The ireful Bastard Orleans, that drew blood
From thee, my boy, and had the maidenhood
Of thy first fight, I soon encounterèd,
And, interchanging blows, I quickly shed
Some of his bastard blood; and in disgrace   20
Bespoke him thus: 'Contaminated, base,
And misbegotten blood I spill of thine,
Mean and right poor, for that pure blood of mine
Which thou didst force from Talbot, my brave boy.'
Here, purposing the Bastard to destroy,
Came in strong rescue. Speak, thy father's care;
Art thou not weary, John? How dost thou fare?
Wilt thou yet leave the battle, boy, and fly,
Now thou art sealed the son of chivalry?
Fly, to revenge my death when I am dead;   30

The help of one stands me in little stead.
O, too much folly is it, well I wot,
To hazard all our lives in one small boat.
If I today die not with Frenchmen's rage,
Tomorrow I shall die with mickle age.
By me they nothing gain an if I stay;
'Tis but the shortening of my life one day.
In thee thy mother dies, our household's name,
My death's revenge, thy youth, and England's fame.
40   All these, and more, we hazard by thy stay;
All these are saved if thou wilt fly away.

JOHN

The sword of Orleans hath not made me smart;
These words of yours draw lifeblood from my heart.
On that advantage, bought with such a shame,
To save a paltry life and slay bright fame,
Before young Talbot from old Talbot fly,
The coward horse that bears me fall and die!
And like me to the peasant boys of France,
To be shame's scorn and subject of mischance!
50   Surely, by all the glory you have won,
An if I fly, I am not Talbot's son;
Then talk no more of flight; it is no boot;
If son to Talbot, die at Talbot's foot.

TALBOT

Then follow thou thy desperate sire of Crete,
Thou Icarus; thy life to me is sweet.
If thou wilt fight, fight by thy father's side;
And, commendable proved, let's die in pride.   *Exeunt*

IV.7   *Alarum. Excursions. Enter old Talbot, led by a Servant*

TALBOT

Where is my other life? Mine own is gone.

O, where's young Talbot? Where is valiant John?
Triumphant Death, smeared with captivity,
Young Talbot's valour makes me smile at thee.
When he perceived me shrink and on my knee,
His bloody sword he brandished over me,
And like a hungry lion did commence
Rough deeds of rage and stern impatience;
But when my angry guardant stood alone,
Tendering my ruin and assailed of none,   10
Dizzy-eyed fury and great rage of heart
Suddenly made him from my side to start
Into the clustering battle of the French;
And in that sea of blood my boy did drench
His over-mounting spirit; and there died
My Icarus, my blossom, in his pride.

    Enter soldiers with John Talbot, borne

SERVANT

O my dear lord, lo where your son is borne!

TALBOT

Thou antic Death, which laughest us here to scorn,
Anon, from thy insulting tyranny,
Coupled in bonds of perpetuity,   20
Two Talbots, wingèd through the lither sky,
In thy despite shall 'scape mortality.
O thou whose wounds become hard-favoured Death,
Speak to thy father ere thou yield thy breath!
Brave Death by speaking, whether he will or no;
Imagine him a Frenchman, and thy foe.
Poor boy! He smiles, methinks, as who should say
'Had Death been French, then Death had died today.'
Come, come, and lay him in his father's arms.
My spirit can no longer bear these harms.   30
Soldiers, adieu! I have what I would have,
Now my old arms are young John Talbot's grave.

    He dies

*Enter Charles, Alençon, Burgundy, the Bastard, and
Joan la Pucelle*

CHARLES

Had York and Somerset brought rescue in,
We should have found a bloody day of this.

BASTARD

How the young whelp of Talbot's, raging wood,
Did flesh his puny sword in Frenchmen's blood!

PUCELLE

Once I encountered him and thus I said:
'Thou maiden youth, be vanquished by a maid.'
But with a proud majestical high scorn

40   He answered thus: 'Young Talbot was not born
To be the pillage of a giglot wench.'
So, rushing in the bowels of the French,
He left me proudly, as unworthy fight.

BURGUNDY

Doubtless he would have made a noble knight.
See where he lies inhearsèd in the arms
Of the most bloody nurser of his harms.

BASTARD

Hew them to pieces, hack their bones asunder,
Whose life was England's glory, Gallia's wonder.

CHARLES

O, no, forbear! For that which we have fled

50   During the life, let us not wrong it dead.

Enter Lucy, accompanied by a French herald

LUCY

Herald, conduct me to the Dauphin's tent,
To know who hath obtained the glory of the day.

CHARLES

On what submissive message art thou sent?

LUCY

Submission, Dauphin? 'Tis a mere French word;

We English warriors wot not what it means.
I come to know what prisoners thou hast ta'en
And to survey the bodies of the dead.

CHARLES

For prisoners askest thou? Hell our prison is.
But tell me whom thou seekest.

LUCY

But where's the great Alcides of the field,   60
Valiant Lord Talbot, Earl of Shrewsbury,
Created for his rare success in arms
Great Earl of Washford, Waterford, and Valence,
Lord Talbot of Goodrig and Urchinfield,
Lord Strange of Blackmere, Lord Verdun of Alton,
Lord Cromwell of Wingfield, Lord Furnival of Sheffield,
The thrice-victorious Lord of Falconbridge,
Knight of the noble Order of Saint George,
Worthy Saint Michael, and the Golden Fleece,
Great Marshal to Henry the Sixth   70
Of all his wars within the realm of France?

PUCELLE

Here's a silly stately style indeed!
The Turk, that two and fifty kingdoms hath,
Writes not so tedious a style as this.
Him that thou magnifiest with all these titles
Stinking and flyblown lies here at our feet.

LUCY

Is Talbot slain, the Frenchmen's only scourge,
Your kingdom's terror and black Nemesis?
O, were mine eyeballs into bullets turned,
That I in rage might shoot them at your faces!   80
O that I could but call these dead to life!
It were enough to fright the realm of France.
Were but his picture left amongst you here,
It would amaze the proudest of you all.

Give me their bodies, that I may bear them hence
And give them burial as beseems their worth.

PUCELLE

I think this upstart is old Talbot's ghost,
He speaks with such a proud commanding spirit.
For God's sake, let him have them; to keep them here,
90   They would but stink and putrefy the air.

CHARLES

Go take their bodies hence.

LUCY

I'll bear them hence; but from their ashes shall be reared
A phoenix that shall make all France afeard.

CHARLES

So we be rid of them, do with them what thou wilt.
And now to Paris in this conquering vein!
All will be ours, now bloody Talbot's slain.   *Exeunt*

*

V.1   *Sennet. Enter the King, Gloucester, and Exeter*

KING

Have you perused the letters from the Pope,
The Emperor, and the Earl of Armagnac?

GLOUCESTER

I have, my lord, and their intent is this:
They humbly sue unto your excellence
To have a godly peace concluded of
Between the realms of England and of France.

KING

How doth your grace affect their motion?

GLOUCESTER

Well, my good lord, and as the only means
To stop effusion of our Christian blood
10   And stablish quietness on every side.

KING

    Ay, marry, uncle; for I always thought
    It was both impious and unnatural
    That such immanity and bloody strife
    Should reign among professors of one faith.

GLOUCESTER

    Beside, my lord, the sooner to effect
    And surer bind this knot of amity,
    The Earl of Armagnac, near knit to Charles,
    A man of great authority in France,
    Proffers his only daughter to your grace
    In marriage, with a large and sumptuous dowry.   20

KING

    Marriage, uncle? Alas, my years are young,
    And fitter is my study and my books
    Than wanton dalliance with a paramour.
    Yet call th'ambassadors; and, as you please,
    So let them have their answers every one.
    I shall be well content with any choice
    Tends to God's glory and my country's weal.

        Enter Winchester, in cardinal's habit, and three
        ambassadors, one a Papal Legate

EXETER (*aside*)

    What, is my lord of Winchester installed,
    And called unto a cardinal's degree?
    Then I perceive that will be verified   30
    Henry the Fifth did sometime prophesy:
    'If once he come to be a cardinal,
    He'll make his cap co-equal with the crown.'

KING

    My Lords Ambassadors, your several suits
    Have been considered and debated on.
    Your purpose is both good and reasonable,
    And therefore are we certainly resolved
    To draw conditions of a friendly peace,

Which by my lord of Winchester we mean

40   Shall be transported presently to France.

GLOUCESTER (*to the Armagnac ambassador*)

And for the proffer of my lord your master,

I have informed his highness so at large

As, liking of the lady's virtuous gifts,

Her beauty, and the value of her dower,

He doth intend she shall be England's Queen.

KING

In argument and proof of which contract,

Bear her this jewel, pledge of my affection.

And so, my Lord Protector, see them guarded

And safely brought to Dover, where inshipped,

50   Commit them to the fortune of the sea.

                  Exeunt all but Winchester and the Legate

WINCHESTER

Stay, my Lord Legate. You shall first receive

The sum of money which I promisèd

Should be delivered to his holiness

For clothing me in these grave ornaments.

LEGATE

I will attend upon your lordship's leisure.

    He steps aside

WINCHESTER

Now Winchester will not submit, I trow,

Or be inferior to the proudest peer.

Humphrey of Gloucester, thou shalt well perceive

That neither in birth or for authority

60   The Bishop will be overborne by thee.

I'll either make thee stoop and bend thy knee

Or sack this country with a mutiny.   *Exeunt*

Enter Charles, Burgundy, Alençon, the Bastard, V.2
Reignier, and Joan la Pucelle

CHARLES

These news, my lords, may cheer our drooping spirits:
'Tis said the stout Parisians do revolt
And turn again unto the warlike French.

ALENÇON

Then march to Paris, royal Charles of France,
And keep not back your powers in dalliance.

PUCELLE

Peace be amongst them if they turn to us;
Else ruin combat with their palaces!

Enter a Scout

SCOUT

Success unto our valiant general,
And happiness to his accomplices!

CHARLES

What tidings send our scouts? I prithee speak.   10

SCOUT

The English army, that divided was
Into two parties, is now conjoined in one,
And means to give you battle presently.

CHARLES

Somewhat too sudden, sirs, the warning is,
But we will presently provide for them.
I trust the ghost of Talbot is not there.

BURGUNDY

Now he is gone, my lord, you need not fear.

PUCELLE

Of all base passions fear is most accursed.
Command the conquest, Charles, it shall be thine,
Let Henry fret and all the world repine.   20

CHARLES

Then on, my lords; and France be fortunate!   *Exeunt*

PUCELLE

The Regent conquers and the Frenchmen fly.
Now help, ye charming spells and periapts;
And ye choice spirits that admonish me,
And give me signs of future accidents;
    (*Thunder*)
You speedy helpers that are substitutes
Under the lordly monarch of the north,
Appear and aid me in this enterprise!
    Enter fiends
This speedy and quick appearance argues proof
Of your accustomed diligence to me.
10   Now, ye familiar spirits that are culled
Out of the powerful legions under earth,
Help me this once, that France may get the field.
    They walk, and speak not
O, hold me not with silence over-long!
Where I was wont to feed you with my blood,
I'll lop a member off and give it you
In earnest of a further benefit,
So you do condescend to help me now.
    They hang their heads
No hope to have redress? My body shall
Pay recompense, if you will grant my suit.
    They shake their heads
20   Cannot my body nor blood-sacrifice
Entreat you to your wonted furtherance?
Then take my soul – my body, soul, and all,
Before that England give the French the foil.
                        They depart
See, they forsake me! Now the time is come
That France must vail her lofty-plumèd crest
And let her head fall into England's lap.
My ancient incantations are too weak,

And hell too strong for me to buckle with.
Now, France, thy glory droopeth to the dust.   *Exit*
    Excursions. Burgundy and Richard Duke of York
    fight hand to hand. York then fights with Joan la
    Pucelle and overcomes her. The French fly

RICHARD

Damsel of France, I think I have you fast.   30
Unchain your spirits now with spelling charms,
And try if they can gain your liberty.
A goodly prize, fit for the devil's grace!
See how the ugly witch doth bend her brows
As if, with Circe, she would change my shape!

PUCELLE

Changed to a worser shape thou canst not be.

RICHARD

O, Charles the Dauphin is a proper man;
No shape but his can please your dainty eye.

PUCELLE

A plaguing mischief light on Charles and thee!
And may ye both be suddenly surprised   40
By bloody hands in sleeping on your beds!

RICHARD

Fell banning hag! Enchantress, hold thy tongue!

PUCELLE

I prithee give me leave to curse awhile.

RICHARD

Curse, miscreant, when thou comest to the stake.
                                     Exeunt
    Alarum. Enter Suffolk, with Margaret in his hand

SUFFOLK

Be what thou wilt, thou art my prisoner.
    He gazes on her
O fairest beauty, do not fear nor fly!
For I will touch thee but with reverent hands;
I kiss these fingers for eternal peace,

And lay them gently on thy tender side.

50 Who art thou? Say, that I may honour thee.

MARGARET

Margaret my name, and daughter to a king,
The King of Naples, whosoe'er thou art.

SUFFOLK

An earl I am and Suffolk am I called.
Be not offended, nature's miracle;
Thou art allotted to be ta'en by me.
So doth the swan her downy cygnets save,
Keeping them prisoner underneath her wings.
Yet, if this servile usage once offend,
Go and be free again as Suffolk's friend.

She is going

60 O, stay! (*Aside*) I have no power to let her pass;
My hand would free her, but my heart says no.
As plays the sun upon the glassy streams,
Twinkling another counterfeited beam,
So seems this gorgeous beauty to mine eyes.
Fain would I woo her, yet I dare not speak.
I'll call for pen and ink, and write my mind.
Fie, de la Pole, disable not thyself.
Hast not a tongue? Is she not here?
Wilt thou be daunted at a woman's sight?

70 Ay, beauty's princely majesty is such
Confounds the tongue and makes the senses rough.

MARGARET

Say, Earl of Suffolk, if thy name be so,
What ransom must I pay before I pass?
For I perceive I am thy prisoner.

SUFFOLK (*aside*)

How canst thou tell she will deny thy suit
Before thou make a trial of her love?

MARGARET

Why speakest thou not? What ransom must I pay?

SUFFOLK (*aside*)

  She's beautiful, and therefore to be wooed;
  She is a woman, therefore to be won.

MARGARET

  Wilt thou accept of ransom, yea or no? 80

SUFFOLK (*aside*)

  Fond man, remember that thou hast a wife.
  Then how can Margaret be thy paramour?

MARGARET

  I were best to leave him, for he will not hear.

SUFFOLK

  There all is marred; there lies a cooling card.

MARGARET

  He talks at random. Sure the man is mad.

SUFFOLK

  And yet a dispensation may be had.

MARGARET

  And yet I would that you would answer me.

SUFFOLK

  I'll win this Lady Margaret. For whom?
  Why, for my king! Tush, that's a wooden thing!

MARGARET

  He talks of wood. It is some carpenter. 90

SUFFOLK (*aside*)

  Yet so my fancy may be satisfied
  And peace establishèd between these realms.
  But there remains a scruple in that too;
  For though her father be the King of Naples,
  Duke of Anjou and Maine, yet is he poor,
  And our nobility will scorn the match.

MARGARET

  Hear ye, captain? Are you not at leisure?

SUFFOLK (*aside*)

  It shall be so, disdain they ne'er so much.
  Henry is youthful and will quickly yield. –

100   (*To her*) Madam, I have a secret to reveal.

MARGARET (*aside*)

    What though I be enthralled? He seems a knight
    And will not any way dishonour me.

SUFFOLK

    Lady, vouchsafe to listen what I say.

MARGARET (*aside*)

    Perhaps I shall be rescued by the French,
    And then I need not crave his courtesy.

SUFFOLK

    Sweet madam, give me hearing in a cause –

MARGARET (*aside*)

    Tush, women have been captivate ere now.

SUFFOLK

    Lady, wherefore talk you so?

MARGARET

    I cry you mercy, 'tis but *quid* for *quo*.

SUFFOLK

110   Say, gentle Princess, would you not suppose
    Your bondage happy, to be made a queen?

MARGARET

    To be a queen in bondage is more vile
    Than is a slave in base servility;
    For princes should be free.

SUFFOLK   And so shall you,

    If happy England's royal King be free.

MARGARET

    Why, what concerns his freedom unto me?

SUFFOLK

    I'll undertake to make thee Henry's queen,
    To put a golden sceptre in thy hand
    And set a precious crown upon thy head,
    If thou wilt condescend to be my –

120 MARGARET   What?

SUFFOLK

    His love.

MARGARET

I am unworthy to be Henry's wife.

SUFFOLK

No, gentle madam; I unworthy am
To woo so fair a dame to be his wife
And have no portion in the choice myself.
How say you, madam? Are ye so content?

MARGARET

An if my father please, I am content.

SUFFOLK

Then call our captains and our colours forth!
And, madam, at your father's castle walls
We'll crave a parley to confer with him.   130

Sound a parley. Enter Reignier on the walls

See, Reignier, see thy daughter prisoner.

REIGNIER

To whom?

SUFFOLK   To me.

REIGNIER   Suffolk, what remedy?

I am a soldier and unapt to weep
Or to exclaim on fortune's fickleness.

SUFFOLK

Yes, there is remedy enough, my lord.
Consent, and for thy honour give consent,
Thy daughter shall be wedded to my king,
Whom I with pain have wooed and won thereto;
And this her easy-held imprisonment
Hath gained thy daughter princely liberty.   140

REIGNIER

Speaks Suffolk as he thinks?

SUFFOLK   Fair Margaret knows

That Suffolk doth not flatter, face, or feign.

REIGNIER

Upon thy princely warrant I descend
To give thee answer of thy just demand.

Exit from the walls

SUFFOLK

And here I will expect thy coming.
Trumpets sound. Enter Reignier below

REIGNIER

Welcome, brave Earl, into our territories;
Command in Anjou what your honour pleases.

SUFFOLK

Thanks, Reignier, happy for so sweet a child,
Fit to be made companion with a king.

150   What answer makes your grace unto my suit?

REIGNIER

Since thou dost deign to woo her little worth
To be the princely bride of such a lord,
Upon condition I may quietly
Enjoy mine own, the country Maine and Anjou,
Free from oppression or the stroke of war,
My daughter shall be Henry's, if he please.

SUFFOLK

That is her ransom. I deliver her,
And those two counties I will undertake
Your grace shall well and quietly enjoy.

REIGNIER

160   And I again, in Henry's royal name,
As deputy unto that gracious king,
Give thee her hand for sign of plighted faith.

SUFFOLK

Reignier of France, I give thee kingly thanks,
Because this is in traffic of a king.
(*Aside*) And yet methinks I could be well content
To be mine own attorney in this case.
(*To them*) I'll over then to England with this news
And make this marriage to be solemnized.
So, farewell, Reignier. Set this diamond safe

170   In golden palaces, as it becomes.

REIGNIER

I do embrace thee as I would embrace

The Christian prince King Henry, were he here.

MARGARET
Farewell, my lord. Good wishes, praise, and prayers
Shall Suffolk ever have of Margaret.

She is going

SUFFOLK
Farewell, sweet madam. But hark you, Margaret –
No princely commendations to my king?

MARGARET
Such commendations as becomes a maid,
A virgin, and his servant, say to him.

SUFFOLK
Words sweetly placed and modestly directed.
But, madam, I must trouble you again –   180
No loving token to his majesty?

MARGARET
Yes, my good lord: a pure unspotted heart,
Never yet taint with love, I send the King.

SUFFOLK
And this withal.

He kisses her

MARGARET
That for thyself. I will not so presume
To send such peevish tokens to a king.

Exeunt Reignier and Margaret

SUFFOLK
O, wert thou for myself! But, Suffolk, stay;
Thou mayst not wander in that labyrinth:
There Minotaurs and ugly treasons lurk.
Solicit Henry with her wondrous praise.   190
Bethink thee on her virtues that surmount,
And natural graces that extinguish art;
Repeat their semblance often on the seas,
That, when thou comest to kneel at Henry's feet,
Thou mayst bereave him of his wits with wonder.

Exit

Enter Richard Duke of York, Warwick, a Shepherd,
and Joan la Pucelle, guarded

RICHARD

Bring forth that sorceress condemned to burn.

SHEPHERD

Ah, Joan, this kills thy father's heart outright.
Have I sought every country far and near,
And, now it is my chance to find thee out,
Must I behold thy timeless cruel death?
Ah, Joan, sweet daughter Joan, I'll die with thee!

PUCELLE

Decrepit miser! Base ignoble wretch!
I am descended of a gentler blood;
Thou art no father nor no friend of mine.

SHEPHERD

10   Out, out! My lords, an please you, 'tis not so.
I did beget her, all the parish knows.
Her mother liveth yet, can testify
She was the first fruit of my bachelorship.

WARWICK

Graceless, wilt thou deny thy parentage?

RICHARD

This argues what her kind of life hath been,
Wicked and vile; and so her death concludes.

SHEPHERD

Fie, Joan, that thou wilt be so obstacle!
God knows thou art a collop of my flesh,
And for thy sake have I shed many a tear.
20   Deny me not, I prithee, gentle Joan.

PUCELLE

Peasant, avaunt! – You have suborned this man
Of purpose to obscure my noble birth.

SHEPHERD

'Tis true, I gave a noble to the priest
The morn that I was wedded to her mother.

Kneel down and take my blessing, good my girl.
Wilt thou not stoop? Now cursèd be the time
Of thy nativity! I would the milk
Thy mother gave thee when thou sucked'st her breast
Had been a little ratsbane for thy sake.
Or else, when thou didst keep my lambs a-field,   30
I wish some ravenous wolf had eaten thee.
Dost thou deny thy father, cursèd drab?
O, burn her, burn her! Hanging is too good.   *Exit*

RICHARD

Take her away; for she hath lived too long,
To fill the world with vicious qualities.

PUCELLE

First let me tell you whom you have condemned:
Not me begotten of a shepherd swain,
But issued from the progeny of kings;
Virtuous and holy, chosen from above
By inspiration of celestial grace   40
To work exceeding miracles on earth.
I never had to do with wicked spirits.
But you, that are polluted with your lusts,
Stained with the guiltless blood of innocents,
Corrupt and tainted with a thousand vices,
Because you want the grace that others have,
You judge it straight a thing impossible
To compass wonders but by help of devils.
No, misconceived! Joan of Arc hath been
A virgin from her tender infancy,   50
Chaste and immaculate in very thought,
Whose maiden blood, thus rigorously effused,
Will cry for vengeance at the gates of heaven.

RICHARD

Ay, ay. Away with her to execution!

WARWICK

And hark ye, sirs; because she is a maid,

Spare for no faggots; let there be enow.
Place barrels of pitch upon the fatal stake,
That so her torture may be shortenèd.

PUCELLE

Will nothing turn your unrelenting hearts?
60 Then, Joan, discover thine infirmity,
That warranteth by law to be thy privilege.
I am with child, ye bloody homicides.
Murder not then the fruit within my womb,
Although ye hale me to a violent death.

RICHARD

Now heaven forfend! The holy maid with child?

WARWICK

The greatest miracle that e'er ye wrought!
Is all your strict preciseness come to this?

RICHARD

She and the Dauphin have been juggling.
I did imagine what would be her refuge.

WARWICK

70 Well, go to; we'll have no bastards live,
Especially since Charles must father it.

PUCELLE

You are deceived; my child is none of his:
It was Alençon that enjoyed my love.

RICHARD

Alençon, that notorious Machiavel?
It dies, an if it had a thousand lives.

PUCELLE

O, give me leave, I have deluded you.
'Twas neither Charles nor yet the Duke I named,
But Reignier, King of Naples, that prevailed.

WARWICK

A married man! That's most intolerable.

RICHARD

80 Why, here's a girl! I think she knows not well,

There were so many, whom she may accuse.

WARWICK

It's sign she hath been liberal and free.

RICHARD

And yet, forsooth, she is a virgin pure!
Strumpet, thy words condemn thy brat and thee.
Use no entreaty, for it is in vain.

PUCELLE

Then lead me hence; with whom I leave my curse:
May never glorious sun reflex his beams
Upon the country where you make abode;
But darkness and the gloomy shade of death
Environ you, till mischief and despair   90
Drive you to break your necks or hang yourselves!

Exit, guarded

RICHARD

Break thou in pieces and consume to ashes,
Thou foul accursèd minister of hell!

Enter Winchester with attendants

WINCHESTER

Lord Regent, I do greet your excellence
With letters of commission from the King.
For know, my lords, the states of Christendom,
Moved with remorse of these outrageous broils,
Have earnestly implored a general peace
Betwixt our nation and the aspiring French;
And here at hand the Dauphin and his train   100
Approacheth, to confer about some matter.

RICHARD

Is all our travail turned to this effect?
After the slaughter of so many peers,
So many captains, gentlemen, and soldiers,
That in this quarrel have been overthrown
And sold their bodies for their country's benefit,
Shall we at last conclude effeminate peace?

Have we not lost most part of all the towns,
By treason, falsehood, and by treachery,
110   Our great progenitors had conquerèd?
O Warwick, Warwick! I foresee with grief
The utter loss of all the realm of France.

WARWICK

Be patient, York. If we conclude a peace,
It shall be with such strict and severe covenants
As little shall the Frenchmen gain thereby.

> *Enter Charles, Alençon, the Bastard, Reignier, and*
> *attendants*

CHARLES

Since, lords of England, it is thus agreed
That peaceful truce shall be proclaimed in France,
We come to be informèd by yourselves
What the conditions of that league must be.

RICHARD

120   Speak, Winchester; for boiling choler chokes
The hollow passage of my poisoned voice,
By sight of these our baleful enemies.

WINCHESTER

Charles, and the rest, it is enacted thus:
That, in regard King Henry gives consent,
Of mere compassion and of lenity,
To ease your country of distressful war
And suffer you to breathe in fruitful peace,
You shall become true liegemen to his crown;
And, Charles, upon condition thou wilt swear
130   To pay him tribute and submit thyself,
Thou shalt be placed as viceroy under him,
And still enjoy thy regal dignity.

ALENÇON

Must he be then as shadow of himself?
Adorn his temples with a coronet,
And yet, in substance and authority,

Retain but privilege of a private man?
This proffer is absurd and reasonless.

CHARLES

'Tis known already that I am possessed
With more than half the Gallian territories,
And therein reverenced for their lawful king.   140
Shall I, for lucre of the rest unvanquished,
Detract so much from that prerogative
As to be called but viceroy of the whole?
No, Lord Ambassador; I'll rather keep
That which I have than, coveting for more,
Be cast from possibility of all.

RICHARD

Insulting Charles, hast thou by secret means
Used intercession to obtain a league,
And, now the matter grows to compromise,
Standest thou aloof upon comparison?   150
Either accept the title thou usurpest,
Of benefit proceeding from our king
And not of any challenge of desert,
Or we will plague thee with incessant wars.

REIGNIER (aside to Charles)

My lord, you do not well in obstinacy
To cavil in the course of this contract.
If once it be neglected, ten to one
We shall not find like opportunity.

ALENÇON (aside to Charles)

To say the truth, it is your policy
To save your subjects from such massacre   160
And ruthless slaughters as are daily seen
By our proceeding in hostility;
And therefore take this compact of a truce,
Although you break it when your pleasure serves.

WARWICK

How sayst thou, Charles? Shall our condition stand?

CHARLES

It shall;
Only reserved you claim no interest
In any of our towns of garrison.

RICHARD

Then swear allegiance to his majesty:
170 As thou art knight, never to disobey
Nor be rebellious to the crown of England –
Thou, nor thy nobles, to the crown of England.

*Charles and the French nobles kneel and acknowledge
the sovereignty of Henry*

So, now dismiss your army when ye please;
Hang up your ensigns, let your drums be still,
For here we entertain a solemn peace.   *Exeunt*

V.5   *Enter Suffolk, in conference with the King, Gloucester,
and Exeter*

KING

Your wondrous rare description, noble Earl,
Of beauteous Margaret hath astonished me.
Her virtues, gracèd with external gifts,
Do breed love's settled passions in my heart;
And like as rigour of tempestuous gusts
Provokes the mightiest hulk against the tide,
So am I driven by breath of her renown
Either to suffer shipwreck or arrive
Where I may have fruition of her love.

SUFFOLK

10 Tush, my good lord, this superficial tale
Is but a preface of her worthy praise.
The chief perfections of that lovely dame,
Had I sufficient skill to utter them,
Would make a volume of enticing lines
Able to ravish any dull conceit;

And, which is more, she is not so divine,
So full replete with choice of all delights,
But with as humble lowliness of mind
She is content to be at your command –
Command, I mean, of virtuous chaste intents, 20
To love and honour Henry as her lord.

KING

And otherwise will Henry ne'er presume.
Therefore, my Lord Protector, give consent
That Margaret may be England's royal Queen.

GLOUCESTER

So should I give consent to flatter sin.
You know, my lord, your highness is betrothed
Unto another lady of esteem.
How shall we then dispense with that contract
And not deface your honour with reproach?

SUFFOLK

As doth a ruler with unlawful oaths, 30
Or one that at a triumph, having vowed
To try his strength, forsaketh yet the lists
By reason of his adversary's odds.
A poor earl's daughter is unequal odds,
And therefore may be broke without offence.

GLOUCESTER

Why, what, I pray, is Margaret more than that?
Her father is no better than an earl,
Although in glorious titles he excel.

SUFFOLK

Yes, my lord, her father is a king,
The King of Naples and Jerusalem, 40
And of such great authority in France
As his alliance will confirm our peace
And keep the Frenchmen in allegiance.

GLOUCESTER

And so the Earl of Armagnac may do,

Because he is near kinsman unto Charles.

EXETER

Beside, his wealth doth warrant a liberal dower,
Where Reignier sooner will receive than give.

SUFFOLK

A dower, my lords? Disgrace not so your king
That he should be so abject, base, and poor
50 To choose for wealth and not for perfect love.
Henry is able to enrich his queen,
And not to seek a queen to make him rich.
So worthless peasants bargain for their wives,
As market-men for oxen, sheep, or horse.
Marriage is a matter of more worth
Than to be dealt in by attorneyship;
Not whom we will, but whom his grace affects,
Must be companion of his nuptial bed.
And therefore, lords, since he affects her most,
60 It most of all these reasons bindeth us
In our opinions she should be preferred.
For what is wedlock forcèd but a hell,
An age of discord and continual strife?
Whereas the contrary bringeth bliss
And is a pattern of celestial peace.
Whom should we match with Henry, being a king,
But Margaret, that is daughter to a king?
Her peerless feature, joinèd with her birth,
Approves her fit for none but for a king;
70 Her valiant courage and undaunted spirit,
More than in women commonly is seen,
Will answer our hope in issue of a king.
For Henry, son unto a conqueror,
Is likely to beget more conquerors,
If with a lady of so high resolve
As is fair Margaret he be linked in love.
Then yield, my lords, and here conclude with me

That Margaret shall be Queen, and none but she.

KING

Whether it be through force of your report,
My noble lord of Suffolk, or for that   80
My tender youth was never yet attaint
With any passion of inflaming love,
I cannot tell; but this I am assured,
I feel such sharp dissension in my breast,
Such fierce alarums both of hope and fear,
As I am sick with working of my thoughts.
Take therefore shipping; post, my lord, to France;
Agree to any covenants, and procure
That Lady Margaret do vouchsafe to come
To cross the seas to England and be crowned   90
King Henry's faithful and anointed queen.
For your expenses and sufficient charge,
Among the people gather up a tenth.
Be gone, I say; for till you do return
I rest perplexèd with a thousand cares.
And you, good uncle, banish all offence:
If you do censure me by what you were,
Not what you are, I know it will excuse
This sudden execution of my will.
And so conduct me where, from company,   100
I may resolve and ruminate my grief.   *Exit*

GLOUCESTER

Ay, grief, I fear me, both at first and last.
                              Exeunt Gloucester and Exeter

SUFFOLK

Thus Suffolk hath prevailed; and thus he goes,
As did the youthful Paris once to Greece,
With hope to find the like event in love
But prosper better than the Trojan did.
Margaret shall now be Queen, and rule the King;
But I will rule both her, the King, and realm.   *Exit*

COMMENTARY

THE chief sources of the play are the chronicles of Edward
Hall, Raphael Holinshed, Robert Fabyan, and perhaps Richard
Grafton. In this Commentary, Hall is quoted where all the
chroniclers agree, Holinshed, Fabyan, and Grafton only where
special use seems to have been made of them. References are
to the following editions: Hall's *The Union of the Two Noble
and Illustre Families of Lancaster and York* (1548–50), the reprint of 1809; Holinshed's *The Chronicles of England, Scotland,
and Ireland* (Volume III, 2nd ed., 1587), the reprint of 1808;
Fabyan's *The New Chronicles of England and France* (1516), the
reprint of 1811; Grafton's *A Chronicle at Large* (1569), the
reprint of 1809. Biblical quotations are from the Bishops'
Bible (1568 etc.), the official English translation of Elizabeth's
reign. Quotations are normally given in modernized spelling
and punctuation, with the exception of those from the first
Folio, 1623 (referred to as 'F').

The Characters in the Play

For the variation in the spelling of the names in F, see the
Account of the Text, page 239; for the family relationships
between the principal characters, see the Genealogical Tables;
and for the regularization of names in this edition, see the Collations, pages 241–4. Biographical facts about each character are
given in the Commentary at his or her first appearance in the
play or mention in the text.

Joan la Pucelle. In F this character is called variously 'La
Pucelle', 'De Pucelle', 'Pucelle', 'Pusel', 'Puzel', 'Ione',
'Ioane'. At II.2.20 she is called 'Ioane of Acre' and at V.4.49
'Ione of Aire'. In the present text these variants have been
regularized to 'La Pucelle' and 'Joan' and 'Joan of Arc'.

I.1   The ceremonial funeral procession of Henry V is an ironical opening for the play, which is to deal with the loss of England's possessions in France, the defeat and death of Lord Talbot (Henry V's spiritual successor in the play), and the division of the English nobles which was to lead to the Wars of the Roses.

According to the chronicles the scene takes place in Westminster Abbey. Shakespeare does not follow historical chronology: Henry V was buried in 1422; of the towns mentioned in lines 60–61, Rheims was lost in 1429, Paris in 1436, Rouen in 1449, and Guienne in 1451; the Dauphin was crowned in 1429; Talbot's capture and Falstaff's cowardice at Patay took place in 1429. The details of the parts of the chronicles used are given in the relevant notes below.

(stage direction) *Bedford*. John of Lancaster (1389–1435), third son of Henry IV, was created Duke in 1414 and on the death of Henry V became Regent of France and Protector of England. He raised the siege of Orleans in 1429, purchased Joan of Arc from her Burgundian captors, and arranged her burning as a witch at Rouen in 1431.

Gloucester. Humphrey of Lancaster (1391–1447), youngest son of Henry IV, was created duke in 1414 and was wounded at Agincourt. He claimed the Regency at the death of Henry V, but was allowed only to act as Bedford's deputy. He constantly opposed the policies of his uncle, Henry Beaufort, Bishop of Winchester; he was Protector in 1427–9, and his influence on Henry VI was strong until 1441.

Exeter. Sir Thomas Beaufort (d. 1427), the son of John of Gaunt by Catherine Swynford, was legitimated in 1397 and created Duke in 1416. He became captain of Rouen and negotiated the Treaty of Troyes in 1420.

Warwick. Richard de Beauchamp (1382–1439) accompanied Henry V to France in 1415 and held important posts in the wars. He arranged the truce preparatory to the Treaty of Troyes and was charged with the education of the infant Henry VI in 1428.

Winchester. Henry Beaufort (d. 1447) was the second illegitimate son of John of Gaunt and Catherine Swynford. He was Chancellor on the accession of Henry V, who on his deathbed named him guardian to Henry VI. He was nominated Cardinal-Priest in 1426. In F there is some inconsistency about his elevation to Cardinal; see the Account of the Text, page 240.

Somerset. John Beaufort, first Duke (1403–44), was the grandson of John of Gaunt and Catherine Swynford and was Captain-General in Aquitaine and Normandy in 1443. He was created Earl in 1419 and Duke in 1443.

1   *Hung be the heavens with black.* The reference is to the practice in the Elizabethan theatre of draping the stage with black hangings when a tragedy was to be played; compare *A Warning for Fair Women* (1599): 'The stage is hung with black, and I perceive | The auditors prepared for tragedy' (*The School of Shakespeare*, edited by R. Simpson, II, 244), and John Marston's *The Insatiate Countess* (*c.* 1610), IV.5.4–5: 'The stage of heaven is hung with solemn black, | A time best fitting to act tragedies'.

heavens. This may be an allusion to the ceiling of the penthouse roof which projected over the rear of the Elizabethan stage and was decorated with astral bodies.

2   *Comets, importing change of times and states.* It was a widespread belief that comets boded evil to states and rulers; compare *King John*, III.4.153–9, and *Julius Caesar*, II.2.30–31. The connexion between comets and Henry V may have been suggested by Hall's phrase describing Henry as 'the blazing comet . . . in his days' (page 113).

importing portending

states (1) circumstances; (2) governments

3   *Brandish* (1) dart forth, scatter; (2) flourish by way of threat

3   *crystal* bright. The adjective was often used to describe astronomical phenomena.

4   *scourge*. The image shifts from viewing the bright tails of the comets as flowing hair to seeing them as hair plaited like whips.

      revolting rebellious

5   *consented unto* conspired together to effect

7–16   *England ne'er . . . .* Hall supplied the traditional picture of Henry V: 'This Henry was a king whose life was immaculate and his living without spot. . . . He had such knowledge in ordering and guiding an army and such a grace in encouraging his people that the Frenchmen said he could not be vanquished in battle. . . . What should I say, he was the blazing comet and apparent lantern in his days, he was the mirror of Christendom and the glory of his country, he was the flower of kings past, and a glass to them that should succeed. . . . No prince had less of his subjects and never king conquered more, whose fame by his death as lively flourisheth as his acts in his life were seen and remembered' (pages 112–13).

9   *Virtue* essential goodness and power

10   *his* its

11–12   *His arms spread wider than a dragon's wings; | His sparkling eyes, replete with wrathful fire.* These lines are probably a recollection of Edmund Spenser's *The Faerie Queene* (I.11.14):

> His blazing eyes, like two bright shining shields,
> Did burn with wrath, and sparkled living fire; . . .
> So flamed his eyne with rage and rancorous ire.

12   *replete with* full of

14   *fierce* fiercely

15   *What should I say?* how can I describe it? The phrase is very common in Hall.

16   *lift* lifted

      but conquerèd without overcoming

17   *We mourn in black.* Hall notes that Henry's coffin was

attended by 'five hundred men of arms, all in black harness and their horses barded black' (page 114).

in blood (that is, by making war in France, the scene of Henry's greatest martial exploits)

19   *wooden.* The quibble is on (1) made of wood; (2) senseless, unfeeling.

21   *stately presence* ceremonial procession

22   *Like captives bound to a triumphant car.* The allusion is probably to a famous scene in Christopher Marlowe's *Tamburlaine, Part 2*, IV.3; compare also Marlowe's *Edward II*, I.1.174: 'With captive kings at his triumphant car'.

23   *of mishap* which cause misfortune (by astrological influence)

25   *subtle-witted* of crafty intelligence

26   *Conjurers* magicians. This looks ahead to Joan la Pucelle's dealings with supernatural agents in V.3.

27   *magic verses* incantations, rhymed spells
    contrived plotted

28   *King of Kings* (Revelation 19.16)

30   *his sight* the sight of him

31   *Lord of Hosts* (Isaiah 9.7). The comparison between Henry V and David implicit in this line is in keeping with the traditional view of Henry as the Christian warrior king; compare also 1 Samuel 25.28: 'because my lord fighteth the battles of the Lord'.

33–43   *Had not . . . thy foes.* Hall records that in 1426–7 there 'fell a great division in the realm of England, which of a sparkle was like to grow to a great flame; for whether the Bishop of Winchester, called Henry Beaufort, . . . envied the authority of Humphrey Duke of Gloucester . . . or whether the Duke had taken disdain at the riches and pompous estate of the Bishop, sure it is that the whole realm was troubled with them and their partakers' (page 130).

33   *Had not churchmen prayed.* Gloucester accuses Winchester of praying against Henry V; compare line 43. *prayed.* There is a possible pun on 'preyed'.

34   *thread of life.* The reference is to the three Parcae (or
      Fates) in classical mythology, who spin, measure, and
      cut the thread of human life.

      decayed been destroyed

35   *effeminate* weak and unmanly

      prince ruler

36   *Whom like a schoolboy you may overawe.* This seems to
      have been suggested by Hall's 'like a young scholar or
      innocent pupil to be governed by the disposition of
      another man' (page 208).

38   *lookest* expectest

39   *Thy wife is proud.* This is the only reference in this
      part of the play to Eleanor Cobham, the second wife of
      Gloucester, whose pride and ambition are developed
      in the Second Part. Hall notes that the marriage caused
      a scandal: 'The Duke of Gloucester, . . . by wanton
      affection blinded, took to his wife Eleanor Cobham,
      daughter to the Lord Cobham, . . . which before (as
      the fame went) was his sovereign lady and paramour,
      to his great slander and reproach' (page 129).

      holdeth thee in awe dominates you

44–56 *Cease, cease . . . bright.* Compare Hall for the years
      1426–7: 'The Duke of Bedford, being sore grieved and
      unquieted with these news, . . . returned again over the
      seas into England. . . . The twenty-fifth day of March,
      after his coming to London, a parliament began at the
      town of Leicester, where the Duke of Bedford openly
      rebuked the lords in general, because that they in the
      time of war, through their privy malice and inward
      grudge, had almost moved the people to war and
      commotion' (page 130).

44   *jars* (literally 'musical discords') quarrels

45   *wait on us* go on ahead

46   *arms* weapons

48–50 *Posterity . . . tears* future generations, expect evil days,
      when mothers shall feed their babes only with their
      tears and England shall nurse her children with tears
      also

50   *nourish.* This is a variant form of 'nourice' (meaning 'nurse'), which, in view of the preceding line, seems to be the sense intended. However, Alexander Pope's suggestion 'marish' (meaning 'saline marsh'), made in his eighteenth-century edition of Shakespeare, is attractive.

52   *ghost* spirit
     invocate call upon

53   *Prosper* make prosperous
     broils conflicts

54   *adverse planets* (sources of evil influence)

55–6 *A far more glorious . . . Julius Caesar.* The allusion is to Ovid's *Metamorphoses*, XV.843–5, where Caesar is seen as turning into a blazing star.

56   *bright –.* Editors have suggested various candidates to be described by this adjective; but F's dash clearly indicates that the Messenger interrupts Bedford in mid-sentence.

60   *Champaigne* Compiègne. Hall and Fabyan spell the word 'Champeigne'.
     Rouen. This addition to the F text seems called for in view of Gloucester's reaction in line 65.
     Orleans. This was pronounced with three syllables.

60, 61 *Orleans . . . Poitiers.* In fact neither of these towns had ever been in English hands.

62   *corse* corpse

64   *lead* (the leaden lining of the wooden coffin). Compare Hall: 'His body was embalmed and closed in lead' (page 113).

67   *These news.* 'News' was often treated as plural in sixteenth-century English.
     yield. Gloucester echoes *yielded* in line 65 to emphasize that Rouen's loss would cause Henry V to die again.

69–79 *No treachery . . . new-begot.* See the note to lines 44–56.

69   *want* lack

71–3 *here . . . generals.* The inability of the English nobles to submerge their differences in the face of a common enemy is heavily stressed in the chronicles.

71   *several* separate

72   *field* (1) battle; (2) combat force
       dispatched organized promptly

73   *of* about

74   *lingering* long-drawn-out

75   *would fly swift, but wanteth wings* (proverbial)
       wanteth lacks

79   *new-begot* recently acquired

80–81   *Cropped . . . away.* By the Treaty of Troyes of 1420,
       Henry V was designated 'heir of France' and was
       ceded the French crown, although Charles VI remained
       nominally king of France. At Henry's death in 1422 his
       titles passed to Henry VI; but Charles died within
       two months of this event and his son, Charles VII, was
       proclaimed king. The loss of the French crown would
       deprive the English king of the right to display the
       fleur-de-lis (the *flower-de-luces*), the national heraldic
       flower of France. Thus one half of England's coat
       (of arms) is cut away.

80   *Cropped* plucked

82, 143 *wanting* lacking

83   *her* (England's)

85   *steelèd* made of steel

87–8   *Wounds will I lend the French, instead of eyes, | To weep*
       I will give the French wounds to shed blood in place
       of eyes to weep tears for

88   *intermissive* temporarily interrupted (by the death of
       Henry V) but now to be resumed

90   *revolted.* The word comes from Holinshed: 'a great
       many of the nobility . . . did now revolt to the Dauphin'
       (page 137).
       quite completely

91   *petty* small
       import significance

92   *The Dauphin Charles is crownèd king in Rheims.* Charles
       VII (1403–61) was actually crowned at Rheims in 1429;
       but he had been crowned as a youth at Poitiers in 1422.
       Dauphin (title of the heir to the French throne)

93   *The Bastard of Orleans.* John Count of Dunois (1403–68) was the illegitimate son of Louis Duke of Orleans, and was first cousin to Charles VII.

94   *Reignier.* René, Duke of Anjou and Lorraine (1409–80), who as son of Louis II of Naples was titular king of Naples, and whose daughter Margaret married Henry VI.

       take his part support him

95   *Alençon.* John, second Duke (1409–76), a leading figure in the French wars.

96   *fly* flock

97   *fly* flee

       reproach shame

98   *fly* spring with violence

104   *bedew* (with tears resulting from lamentation)

105   *dismal fight* disastrous, savage battle (the Battle of Patay, 1429)

106   *stout* valiant, resolute

       Lord Talbot. John, first Earl of Shrewsbury (1388?–1453), was the greatest soldier of his time. His association with the Duke of Bedford's exploits in France after 1427 led to his capture by Joan of Arc in 1429 and his imprisonment for two years. After his release he became an ally of Philip Duke of Burgundy until his death at Castillon (see IV.7).

107   *is't so?* isn't that right?

109   *circumstance* details

       more at large at greater length

110   *The tenth of August last* (historically 18 June, 1429)

       dreadful inspiring fear

112   *full scarce* barely

       six thousand. This is the number Holinshed gives; Hall has five thousand.

114   *round encompassèd* surrounded

115   *enrank* draw up in lines of battle

116–19 *He wanted pikes ... breaking in.* Holinshed notes that 'The Englishmen had not leisure to put themselves in array, after they had put up their stakes before their archers' (page 165). The pikes to protect the archers and foot soldiers from cavalry charges are described by Hall: 'stakes bound with iron sharp at both ends, of the length of five or six foot, to be pitched before the archers and of every side the foot men like an hedge, to the intent that if the barded horses ran rashly upon them they might shortly be gored and destroyed' (page 67).

116   *wanted* lacked

121   *above human thought* beyond the power of human imagination

123   *stand him* stand up against him

124   *slew.* Some editors emend this to 'flew' by reference to a passage in *The Faerie Queene* (III.1.66):

> Wherewith enraged she fiercely at them flew . . .
> Here, there, and everywhere about her swayed
> Her wrathful steel. . . .

As the resemblance between the two passages rests on the cliché *Here, there, and everywhere* and *enraged*, there seems no reason to change F's reading, which makes good sense.

126   *agazed on* astounded at

127   *spying* perceiving, observing

128   *A Talbot.* Some editors take the 'A' to be a definite article; but the meaning is clearly 'rally to Talbot'.
      amain forcefully

130   *sealed up* made perfect

131   *Falstaff.* Historically Sir John Falstaff, or 'Fastolfe' as he is called in the chronicles (and in some editions of the play, to distinguish him from the character in *Henry IV*), was a Norfolk landowner. He lived from *c.* 1378 to 1459, served successfully under Henry V and later the Duke of Bedford, and in 1423 became Governor of Anjou and Maine. Among his contemporaries he was a well respected figure; the view of him as a coward originated in the fifteenth-century *Chronique de Monstrelet*, and was perpetuated by the Tudor

chroniclers, from whom Shakespeare took it over.
Shakespeare was later to use the same name for his
famous character in the Henry IV plays, to whom he
originally gave the name 'Oldcastle'. The reference
here is based very closely on Hall: 'From this battle
departed without any stroke stricken Sir John Fas-
tolffe' (page 150).

132   *vaward* vanguard
132–3   *placed behind | With purpose to relieve and follow them*
following up the vanguard proper as support troops
135   *wrack* disaster
136   *with* by
137   *Walloon*. The reference is presumably to a mercenary
from the border country between what is now southern
Belgium and France.
138   *Thrust Talbot with a spear into the back.* Hall records
only that 'Lord Talbot was sore wounded at the back
and so taken' (page 150).
139   *chief* finest
       strength armed forces
140   *Durst not presume to look once in the face.* This is a
recollection from Hall's account of Talbot's death:
'But his enemies . . . cowardly killed him, lying on the
ground, whom they never durst look in the face while
he stood on his feet' (page 229).
146   *Lord Scales.* Thomas de Scales, seventh Baron (1399?–
1460), took part in many of the battles of the French
wars, serving under the Duke of Bedford.
       Lord Hungerford. Sir Walter, first Baron Hungerford
(d. 1449), fought at Agincourt and at the siege of
Rouen, and was executor of Henry V's will.
148   *His ransom there is none but I shall pay* I shall pay the
only ransom which the French can expect (that is the
acts Bedford threatens in lines 149–51)
149   *hale* drag
151   *change* exchange (kill in retaliation)
153   *am* intend
154   *Saint George's feast* (23 April). Bedford intends to keep

this English feast on French soil. Holinshed (pages 142–3) twice speaks of Saint George in connexion with Bedford's deeds in 1424.

157   *Orleans is besieged.* This contradicts the Messenger's announcement in lines 60–61, unless the meaning is that the English army is besieged in Orleans.

158–61   *The English army ... multitude.* The source is Hall's account of the siege by Salisbury in 1428–9 (pages 143–6).

159   *Salisbury.* Thomas de Montacute (1388–1428), fourth Earl of Salisbury, was one of Henry V's ablest lieutenants and, with Talbot, the most celebrated of the English generals in France after Henry's death. He died while in command of the English forces at the siege of Orleans (see I.4).

supply reinforcements and munitions

160   *hardly* with difficulty

161   *watch* keep under surveillance

162   *your oaths to Henry sworn* the oath each of you swore to Henry. The reference is to the oath by the English nobles to Henry on his deathbed, part of which was 'never make treaty with Charles that calleth himself Dauphin' (Hall, page 112).

163   *quell* destroy

165   *it* (his oath)

167   *the Tower* (of London)

170   *Eltham* (a royal residence from the thirteenth to the sixteenth century, situated nine miles south-east of London on the Canterbury road)

171   *special governor.* In Hall both Exeter and Winchester jointly have the custody of the young Henry VI in 1422; but Shakespeare stresses the limiting of the office to Exeter.

175–7   *But long ... public weal.* In Hall, Gloucester accuses Winchester of this crime in the parliament of 1426: 'my said lord of Winchester, without the advice and assent of my said lord of Gloucester, or of the King's Council, purposed and disposed him to set hand on

the King's person, and to have removed him from
Eltham, the place that he was in, to Windsor, to the
intent to put him in such governance as him list' (page
131).

175   *Jack out of office* (proverbial for someone dismissed
from his appointment)

176   *steal*. Emendation of F's 'send' seems to be called for
on the grounds of both sense and the rhyme of the
final couplet. *Steal* is exactly what Winchester did,
according to Gloucester's accusation in 1426. See the
quotation in the note to lines 175–7.

177   *chiefest stern* position of supreme authority (the helms-
man's position on the ship of state)
     public weal the commonwealth, the state

I.2   The scene is before the city of Orleans, and is based on
Holinshed's account of incidents in the French camp
during John Count of Dunois's attempt to raise the
siege (page 161). Of the other characters listed in the
stage direction, only Alençon was present historically.
Joan's encounter with Charles is chiefly based on
Holinshed (pages 163–4, 171), though Hall's two
accounts are also used; the details are given in the
notes on the relevant lines.
     (stage direction) *flourish* (a fanfare of trumpets)
     Charles ... Alençon ... Reignier. See the notes to
I.1.92–5.
     drum drummer

1–2   *Mars his true ... known.* The planet Mars has an
eccentric orbit, and the variations in the rate of its
orbital motion were not understood until Kepler
published his *De Motibus Stellae Martis* in 1609. The
reference here is also to the favour of the god of war.

1   *Mars his* (the old form of the genitive: 'Mars's')

3   *Late* recently

5   *but we have* are not in our hands. Compare I.1.60–61.

6–8   *At pleasure ... month.* See I.1.158–61.

6   *lie* are encamped

7   *Otherwhiles* at times

8   *Faintly* weakly
    one hour once

9   *porridge and their fat bull-beeves.* These foods were
    reputed to stimulate warmth and courage respec-
    tively.
    porridge (a dish made by stewing meat, vegetables, and
    herbs, thickened with barley)

10   *dieted* fed

12   *like drownèd mice* (proverbial)

13   *raise* end by driving off the besieging forces

14   *Talbot is taken, whom we wont to fear.* Compare I.1.137–
    40.
    wont were accustomed

16   *fretting* impatience, bad temper
    spend his gall expend his irritation

17   *Nor men nor money.* Compare I.1.69.
    Nor neither

18   *alarum* a call to arms

19   *forlorn* who perform their duty at imminent risk of life

25   *homicide* killer of men

27–8 *like lions wanting food, | Do rush upon us as their hungry
    prey.* Compare Psalm 17.12: 'Like as a lion that is
    greedy of his prey'.

27   *wanting* lacking

28   *hungry prey* prey for which they are hungry

29–31 *Froissart ... reign.* Jean Froissart (*c.* 1338–*c.* 1410),
    whose chronicle was translated into English by Lord
    Berners in 1523–5, records that in a victory over the
    French in 1367 every Englishman was 'accounted
    worth a Roland or an Oliver' (Tudor Translations, IV,
    429). The reference is to Charlemagne's two famous
    knights in *La Chanson de Roland* (*c.* 1150).

33   *Goliases* Goliaths

34   *skirmish* (a stronger meaning than the modern one) do
    battle

35   *raw-boned.* Compare line 7.

rascals (literally 'lean, inferior deer', but here used as 'worthless wretches')

37   *hare-brained* mad as hares

     slaves (a term of contempt)

38   *hunger will enforce them to be more eager* (proverbial)

     eager (1) fierce in battle; (2) keen for food

41   *gimmers* gimmals (jointed mechanical parts in machinery for transmitting clockwork motion)

42   *still* continually

44   *consent* advice

     even nothing else but

48   *cheer appalled* countenance made pale with fear

49   *late overthrow* recent defeat

     offence injury, harm

51   *A holy maid.* Joan of Arc was born between 1410 and 1412 at Domrémy, a village in the Vosges partly in Champagne and partly in Lorraine. In 1429 she persuaded Robert de Baudricourt to give her an introduction to the Dauphin, whom she met at Chinon. She led an army of 5,000 men into Orleans and forced the English to raise the siege. After military successes at Jargeau, Beaugency, and Patay, she persuaded the Dauphin to march to Rheims and be crowned King of France in the Cathedral. In 1430 at the defence of Compiègne she was captured while leading an unsuccessful sortie against the Duke of Burgundy. The English bought her from Burgundy and delivered her to the Inquisition in 1431. She was tried as a heretic and a witch and was burnt at Rouen on 30 May 1431. *A holy maid hither with me I bring.* In the chronicles Joan is brought to Charles at Chinon, at the time of the siege of Orleans in March 1429, 'by one Peter Baudricourt, captain of Vaucouleurs' (Holinshed, page 163).

52–4   *Which by a vision ... France.* Compare Holinshed: 'she set out unto him [Charles] the singular feats (forsooth) given her to understand by revelation divine, that in virtue of that sword she should achieve, which were how with honour and victory she would raise the siege at Orleans, set him in state of the crown of France, and drive the English out of the country' (page 164).

54   *forth* out of

56   *nine sibyls.* The sibyls were ten prophetesses of the ancient world. Shakespeare's *nine* is probably due to a confusing of the sibyls themselves with the nine books of the Sibyl of Cumae.

59   *unfallible* (an old form of 'infallible')

60–68   *But first ... from me.* This episode is based on a conflation of the accounts of Holinshed and Hall: 'the Dauphin ... shadowing himself behind, setting other gay lords before him to try her cunning, from all the company with a salutation ... she picked him out alone' (Holinshed, pages 163–4); 'she knew and called him her king whom she never saw before' (Hall, page 148).

63   *sound* penetrate

       (stage direction) *Pucelle* (French for 'maid, virgin')

65   *beguile* deceive

69   *In private will I talk with thee apart.* This is only in Holinshed: '[the Dauphin] had her to the end of the gallery, where she held him an hour in secret and private talk' (pages 163–4).

70   *Stand back.* The lords presumably withdraw to the rear or side of the stage.

71   *takes upon her bravely at first dash* plays her part finely from the beginning

72   *I am by birth a shepherd's daughter.* Compare Holinshed: 'her father, a sorry shepherd, James of Are' (page 163).

73   *wit* intelligence

       untrained. Compare Holinshed: 'brought up poorly in their trade of keeping cattle' (page 163).

       art learning

74   *Our Lady gracious* (the Virgin Mary)

75   *shine on my contemptible estate* show favour to someone in my lowly position

76–8   *Lo, whilst . . . to me.* Compare Holinshed: 'her pastoral bringing up, rude, without any virtuous instruction, her campestral conversation with wicked spirits, whom, in her first salutation to Charles the Dauphin, she uttered to be Our Lady . . . that . . . came and gave her commandments . . . as she kept her father's lambs in the fields' (page 171).

77   *to sun's parching heat displayed my cheeks.* The Elizabethan standard of beauty was fair, and ladies of the time protected their complexions from the sun; compare *The Two Gentlemen of Verona*, IV.4.150.

80   *base* lowly

83   *complete* (accented on the first syllable) perfect

84–6   *whereas . . . may see.* Hall claims that Joan had a 'foul face, that no man would desire it' (page 148). Shakespeare combines this with Holinshed's 'of favour was she counted likesome' (page 163) to produce a miraculous happening.

84   *swart* dark-complexioned, weatherbeaten

85   *With* by virtue of
       infused on poured into

87   *what question . . . possible* what possible question

91   *Resolve on* be certain of

92   *mate* (1) companion; (2) lover. Throughout the rest of this exchange the audience's reaction to Joan as virtuous woman is made ambiguous by means of the bawdy quibbling on the terms used in connexion with her. Compare II.1.22–5, where military terms are used in the same way.

93   *high terms* lofty expression

94   *proof* trial

95   *buckle* grapple in close combat (with a sexual connotation also)

97   *confidence* (1) trust; (2) intimacy

99   *Decked* decorated, engraved
       five. F's 'fine' is probably the result either of the 'u' and 'n' types being mixed up in the printer's boxes or of the compositor's misreading of 'u' as 'n' in the

manuscript. Holinshed notes: 'from Saint Katherine's church of Fierbois in Touraine, where she had never been and knew not, in a secret place there among old iron, appointed she her sword to be sought out and brought her, that with five flower-de-luces was graven on both sides' (page 163).

99   *flower-de-luces.* See the note to I.1.80.

100   *churchyard.* Some editors emend to 'church' on the grounds both of metre and of the evidence of the source (see the second note to line 99).

101   *chose forth* selected

102   *a* in

103   *I'll ne'er fly from a man* (a possible *double entendre*)

104   *Amazon* (one of a mythical race of female warriors)

105   *Deborah* (a Hebrew prophetess, the judge over Israel, and commander of the army which defeated Sisera and the Canaanites; see Judges 4.4–6). The comparison is also made in Holinshed (page 172).

108   *thy desire* desire for thee

110   *so* that

111   *servant* (1) follower; (2) wooer

114   *sacred* consecrated

117   *thrall* slave

118   *very long in talk.* Compare Holinshed: 'she held him an hour in secret and private talk, that of his privy chamber was thought very long, and therefore would have broken it off' (page 164).

119   *shrives* (literally 'hears confession and grants absolution'; here used to mean 'examines closely')
      to her smock (literally 'to her undergarment', with a sexual innuendo here) completely

121   *keeps no mean* (1) observes no moderation; (2) has no sexual self-control

123   *shrewd* cunning, artful

124   *where are you?* what are your intentions?
      devise you on? have you decided?

126   *distrustful recreants* faithless cowards

131   *Saint Martin's summer* (warm weather at the Feast of St Martin, 11 November; an Indian summer)

halcyon days a time of calm (derived from the belief that the kingfish (*halcyon*) builds its nest in the sea in December after the winter roughness has passed)

138–9   *that proud insulting ship | Which Caesar and his fortune bare at once.* According to Plutarch in his *Life of Caesar*, a small ship in which Caesar was travelling down river was beset by such bad weather that the captain attempted to turn back up river; however, Caesar 'taking him by the hand said unto him: "Good fellow, be of good cheer, and forwards hardily; fear not, for thou hast Caesar and his fortune with thee"' (Thomas North's 1579 translation).

140   *Was Mahomet inspirèd with a dove?* There are many Elizabethan allusions to Mahomet teaching a dove to take seed from his ear so that he could persuade his followers that the dove was the Holy Ghost bringing him divine revelation.

  Mahomet (accented on the first and third syllables)

  with by

141   *eagle* (the attribute of St John and symbol of highest inspiration)

142   *Helen.* Saint Helena was reputed to have been led by a vision to discover where the true Cross was buried on Mount Calvary.

  Constantine (Roman emperor, who in A.D. 323 declared the Roman Empire officially Christian)

143   *Saint Philip's daughters.* Compare Acts 21.9: 'four daughters, virgins, which did prophesy'.

149   *Presently* immediately

I.3   The scene takes place before the Tower of London. For the sources, see the Introduction, page 13, and the note to lines 80–81.

  (stage direction) *blue coats.* Line 47 and the stage direction at line 28 suggest that the two parties in the faction are distinguished by blue and tawny coats of livery.

1   *survey* inspect

2   *conveyance* dishonest dealing

3   *warders* guards

10   *willed* commanded

11   *stands* prevails

12   *none* no other

13   *Break up* open with violence

        warrantize surety, authorization

14   *dunghill* (a common term of contempt)

        (stage direction) *Woodville*. Richard Woodville (d. 1441) was a Lancastrian supporter whose descendants were strong supporters of the House of York and became very powerful after Woodville's grand-daughter Elizabeth married Edward IV in 1464.

17   *would* wishes to

19   *Cardinal of Winchester*. See the fifth note to the opening stage direction of I.1. His title is incorrect in this form; he was Cardinal Beaufort, Bishop of Winchester.

21   *of thine* of your followers

22   *prizest* do you esteem

24   *brook* endure, stand

28   *if that* if. ('That' was often added after words such as 'if', 'after', 'when'.)

        (stage direction) *tawny coats*. These were worn by the summoners of the ecclesiastical courts.

30   *Peeled* tonsured

31   *proditor* traitor

34   *contrived'st* plotted, intrigued

        to murder our dead lord. In Hall, Gloucester asserts that a man found hiding in Westminster Palace 'confessed that he was there by the stirring up and procuring of my said Lord of Winchester, ordained to have slain the said Prince there in his bed' (page 131). Henry V was Prince of Wales at the time.

35   *Thou that givest whores indulgences to sin*. The brothels in the London suburb of Southwark were under the jurisdiction of the Bishop of Winchester, who received revenues from them. One of the houses bore the sign of the Cardinal's Hat.

indulgences remission of sins (for payment)

36   *canvass* beat (literally 'toss in a canvas or coarse sheet'; perhaps also with a quibble on the meaning 'investigate thoroughly')

39   *This be* let this be

        Damascus. It was believed that this city was built on the site where Cain killed Abel.

40   *brother* kinsman. Winchester was actually Gloucester's half-uncle; see Table 1 (pages 252–3).

42   *scarlet robes* (cardinal's robes)

        bearing-cloth christening robe

44   *beard* defy

46   *for all this* in spite of this being a

        privilegèd (governed by the ordinance forbidding the drawing of weapons near a royal residence)

48   *tug it.* Tugging the beard was considered an act of defiance and a challenge.

49   *I.* Some editors emend to 'I'll', but Gloucester is simply using the dramatic present tense for effect.

50   *dignities* dignitaries

53   *Winchester goose* (proverbially a swelling in the groin caused by venereal disease; also used of a person so infected or a whore)

        a rope. Gloucester is quibbling on the meaning 'a halter' and the sound a parrot was reputed to make.

55   *wolf in sheep's array* (biblical and proverbial)

56   *scarlet.* See the first note to line 42. There may be a quibble on the 'scarlet woman' of Revelation 17.4.

        (stage direction) *hurly-burly* disorder, confusion

57   *magistrates* (not in the strict legal sense; here simply government leaders)

58   *contumeliously* contemptuously, arrogantly

60   *regards nor* has respect for neither

61   *distrained* seized, confiscated

63   *still* continuously

        motions advocates

64   *O'ercharging* overburdening

        free generous, open

        fines taxes

67   *armour*. The Tower of London was the principal arsenal in the City; compare I.1.167–8.

68   *Prince* (Henry VI)

70   *rests for me* remains for me to do

77   *several* various

80–81   *Cardinal ... at large.* In Hall, Gloucester presents to the parliament at Leicester in 1426–7 accusations against Winchester, the first of which is: 'whereas he, being protector and defender of this land, desired the Tower to be opened to him, and to lodge him therein, Richard Woodville esquire, having at that time the charge of the keeping of the Tower, refused his desire, and kept the same Tower against him, unduly and against reason, by the commandment of my said lord of Winchester' (page 130).

81   *break our minds* (1) express our views; (2) crack heads *at large* at length, in detail

84   *call for clubs* (that is, call for the London apprentices to bring their clubs to put down a civil disorder)

87   *Abominable* inhuman, unnatural

89   *the coast cleared* (proverbial)

90   *these* that these
     such stomachs bear possess such angry tempers. The stomach was regarded as the seat of anger.

91   *year* (a common Elizabethan plural)

I.4   There has been much discussion about the probable staging of this scene in the Elizabethan theatre, which involves speculation about the physical make-up of the staging area. From F's stage directions it seems that the Master Gunner and his son come on to the main stage and have their conversation (lines 1–20), in which the Gunner points out an elevated area, possibly at the rear of the stage, as *yonder tower* (line 11). The Gunner exits, leaving his son to assure the audience of his intention of firing on the English himself should an opportunity occur (lines 21–2). Talbot and the English

172

nobles appear on *the turrets* (line 22, stage direction):
that is, on the elevated area previously indicated by the
Gunner. After the exchanges about Talbot's imprisonment, the Boy enters *with a linstock* (line 56), to remind
the audience of his watching and his intention to fire
the *piece of ordnance* placed opposite the grating of the
turret, and presumably goes out again, although there is
no exit marked in F. The stage direction *Here they
shoot* (line 69), rather than '*Boy shoots*', presumably
calls for gunfire from off stage, and the audience
witnesses the effects of the shot for the remainder of
the scene.

The events used in this scene are drawn from different dates in the chronicles. Joan met the Dauphin,
and Talbot came to Orleans after Salisbury's death, in
October 1428; and Talbot's capture and imprisonment
took place in 1429–31. Talbot's release by exchange
with Ponton de Santrailles is recorded (Hall, page
164), but the details of his incarceration given here are
invented.

1   *Sirrah* (a form of address used for inferiors)

2   *the suburbs won.* The chronicles record that the Bastard
'destroyed the suburbs' and that the English took
the 'bulwark of the bridge ... with a great tower,
standing at the end of the same', which were 'committed to William Glasdale' (Hall, pages 144–5).

4   *Howe'er unfortunate* although unfortunately

7   *grace* honour

8   *espials* spies

10   *Wont* are accustomed

10–17   *through a secret ... see them.* This is taken directly from
the chronicles: 'In the tower that was taken at the
bridge end ... there was a high chamber having a
grate full of bars of iron by the which a man might
look all the length of the bridge into the city, at which
grate many of the chief captains stood diverse times,
viewing the city and devising in what place it was best
assaultable. They within the city perceived well this

toting hole, and laid a piece of ordnance directly against the window' (Hall, page 145).

10　　*grate* latticework (covering a window)

13　　*vex* harass

14　　*inconvenience* mischief, harm

15　　*'gainst* opposite, directed at

16　　*watched* kept under constant surveillance

18–20　*I can ... Governor's.* In the chronicles the master gunner 'was gone down to dinner' (Hall, page 145).

21　　*take you no care* don't you worry

22　　(stage direction) *Glansdale.* In the chronicles he is called 'Glasdale', which name also appears in a list of captains of towns in Normandy in 1417.
　　　Gargrave. Nothing is known of this soldier apart from the mention in the chronicles.

24　　*being* while you were

25　　*got'st thou* did you manage

27　　*Duke.* F reads 'Earle', but there is no doubt about Bedford's rank. Historically he was created duke in 1414.

28　　*the brave Lord Ponton de Santrailles.* Compare Hall: 'the valiant captain, called Ponton of Santrailles' (page 164).

30　　*baser man-of-arms* soldier of lower rank

31　　*in contempt.* To exchange Talbot for a prisoner of lower rank would be an insult to him.

33　　*pilled esteemed* beggarly esteemed. Many editors emend to 'vile esteemed', citing Sonnet 121: 'Vile esteemed'; but F's reading makes good sense.

34　　*In fine* finally
　　　redeemed ransomed

35　　*Falstaff.* See the note to I.1.131.

38　　*entertained* treated

42　　*the terror of the French.* The phrase is from Hall: 'the terror and scourge of the French people' (page 229).

43　　*affrights our children so.* Compare Hall: 'women in France to fear their young children would cry "The Talbot cometh, the Talbot cometh!"' (page 230).

47   *grisly* grim

50   *were.* Some editors emend to 'was', but it was common
     in Elizabethan English for the verb to take the number
     of a near pronoun.

52   *spurn in* kick to
     adamant (a legendary substance which was reputed to
     be impervious to even the greatest force)

53   *chosen shot* outstanding marksmen

54   *every minute while* at minute intervals

56   (stage direction) See the headnote to this scene.
     linstock (a pronged stick, about a metre (three feet)
     long, for holding the gunner's match which ignited the
     fuse of a cannon)

60   *grate* framework of bars

64   *express* carefully considered, definite

65   *battery* assault

67   *bulwark* defence fortification, bastion

69–97 *Here they shoot ... my name.* Compare Hall: 'It so
     chanced that the fifty-ninth day after the siege laid
     before the city, the Earl of Salisbury, Sir Thomas
     Gargrave, and William Glasdale and divers other
     went into the said tower and so into the high chamber
     and looked out at the grate; and within a short space,
     the son of the master gunner perceived men looking
     out at the window, took his match, as his father had
     taught him ... and fired the gun, which brake and
     shivered the iron bars of the grate, whereof one struck
     the Earl so strongly on the head that it struck away one
     of his eyes and the side of his cheek. Sir Thomas
     Gargrave was likewise stricken, so that he died within
     two days' (page 145).

70   *have mercy on us, wretched sinners.* This echoes the
     opening petition of the Litany.

72   *chance* unfortunate event
     crossed afflicted

74   *farest* progressest
     mirror of example to

77   *contrived* plotted

78–9   *In thirteen battles Salisbury o'ercame; | Henry the Fifth he first trained to the wars*. Both of these details appear to be Shakespeare's inventions, as there is no mention of them in the chronicles.

81   *leave* cease from

84   *The sun with one eye vieweth all the world.* Compare Arthur Golding's translation of Ovid's *Metamorphoses* (1567), XIII.1002–3: 'Views not the sun all things from heaven? Yet but one only eye | He hath'.

86   *wants* lacks

87–8   *Sir Thomas Gargrave . . . to him.* In F these lines follow line 89 in this edition. But in view of what follows, line 89 cannot possibly refer to Salisbury's body.

91   *whiles* until

93   *As who* as one who

95   *Plantagenet.* Salisbury's family name was Montacute; but he was descended from Edward I via Alice (great-grand-daughter of Edward I and his wife Margaret), who married Edward, first Lord Montacute.
and like thee, Nero. F omits *Nero*, but it is clear that Talbot sees himself as watching the burning of the French towns he intends to defeat in revenge for Salisbury's death, even as Nero played the lute and sang of the sack of Troy while witnessing the burning of some sections of Rome. The ultimate source for this story is Suetonius, *The Twelve Caesars*; but Grafton has an account of it: 'He commanded the city of Rome to be set on fire, and himself in the mean season with all semblance of joy, sitting in an high tower to behold the same, played upon the harp and sang the destruction of Troy' (I.61).

97   *only in* at the mere sound of
(stage direction) *it thunders and lightens.* This detail is taken from the chronicles: 'the French captains . . . with Pucelle in the dead time of the night, and in a great rain and thunder, with all their victual and artillery entered into the city' (Hall, page 148).

100   *gathered head* drawn their armed forces together

103   *power* army
       (stage direction) *groans*. This is probably meant to be
       prophetic of what Joan's presence will mean to the
       English.

107   *Pucelle or pussel* virgin or trollop
       Dolphin (a common Elizabethan pronunciation of
       'Dauphin', which is often spelt 'Dolphin' in F. The
       dolphin was highest among fish in the great Chain of
       Being.)
       dogfish (a small shark; often used as a term of abuse;
       here counterpoising the dolphin at the lower end of the
       Chain of Being)

110   *me* for me (the ethical dative)

111   (stage direction) *Alarum* (the sounds of the approaching
       French army)

I.5   The events of this scene and of I.6 are based on the
       chronicles' account of Joan's entry into Orleans, an
       English attack on the following day, Alençon's relief of
       the city and his capture of the tower at the end of the
       bridge, the repulse of the French by Talbot, and the
       English withdrawal from the siege in 1429 (Hall, pages
       148–9). There is no historical evidence for Talbot's
       encounter with Joan.

2   *stay* stop

4   *bout* (1) fight; (2) sexual encounter

5   *Devil or devil's dam* (proverbial)
       dam mother
       conjure control by means of an oath (oppose super-
       natural good against supernatural evil)

6   *Blood will I draw on thee – thou art a witch*. There was a
       common belief that drawing blood from a witch en-
       sured protection from her powers.
       on from

7   *him* (the Devil)

9   *suffer* permit
       hell so to prevail. Compare Matthew 16.18: 'upon this

rock will I build my church; and the gates of hell shall not prevail against it'.

12 *But I will* if I do not

14 *victual* supply with provisions

(stage direction) Joan here breaks past Talbot and leads her soldiers to the rear of the stage, which is viewed as Orleans.

16 *hungry-starvèd* perishing with hunger

17 *testament* last will

21 *Hannibal.* This Carthaginian general, according to Livy and Plutarch, once rescued his encircled army by driving two thousand oxen with firebrands tied to their horns into the Roman ranks, thus terrifying the soldiers.

22 *lists* pleases

23 *noisome* noxious

28 *Or tear the lions out of England's coat.* The English coat of arms bore three lions passant, quartered with the fleur-de-lis; see the second note to I.1.80.

29 *soil* country. The suggested emendation 'style' (meaning 'title') is attractive as a continuation of the heraldic sense of the previous line.

give sheep in lions' stead in place of heraldic lions, display sheep (as a symbol of cowardice)

30 *Sheep run not half so treacherous from the wolf.* In Holinshed it is the French that flee 'like sheep before the wolf' (page 164).

treacherous treacherously

32 *oft-subduèd* frequently defeated

33 *It will not be* it is hopeless

34 *consented unto* conspired together to effect

35 *his revenge* revenge for him

39 (stage direction) *Retreat* (a trumpet and drum signal to recall a pursuing force)

I.6.1   *Advance* raise aloft

4   *Astraea* (the daughter of Jupiter, and goddess of Justice, who lived among men during the Golden Age, but was forced by human wickedness to reascend to heaven during the Iron Age)

6   *Adonis' garden* (mythical gardens noted for their fertility; compare *The Faerie Queene*, III.6.29–50)

10   *hap* event

11–13   *Why ring . . . streets.* This is based on Hall: 'After this siege thus broken up . . . what triumphs were made in the city of Orleans, what wood was spent in fires, what wine was drunk in houses, what songs were sung in the streets' (page 149).

15   *replete with* full of

16   *played the men* shown ourselves to be full of manly courage

21   *pyramis* pyramid

22   *Rhodope's of Memphis.* Rhodope was a courtesan who became queen of Memphis and reputedly built the third pyramid.

25   *rich-jewelled coffer of Darius.* When Alexander overcame the Persian king Darius, he took from him a rich jewel chest and kept in it the works of Homer, which he considered his most precious possession. The story that Alexander had this chest always carried before him was well known in Shakespeare's time. Some editors prefer 'rich jewel-coffer' on the strength of a quotation from George Puttenham's *Arte of English Poesie* (1589) which tells the story.

26   *high* important

28   *on* in the name of
         Saint Denis (the patron saint of France)

II.1   There is no basis in the chronicles for Talbot's recapture of Orleans, though some details were suggested by the accounts of the recapture of Le Mans in 1428. See the notes to lines 11–12 and 38 (stage direction).

      (stage direction) *Band* troop of soldiers

3   *apparent* plain, obvious

4   *court of guard* guard-room

5   *servitors* common soldiers

6   *upon their quiet beds* peacefully in their beds

7   *Constrained* forced

      watch (1) keep guard; (2) go without sleep

      (stage direction) F adds 'Their Drummes beating a Dead March', but this is obviously inappropriate, as the forces are intent upon a surprise attack. See the note to the stage direction at II.2.6.

8   *Burgundy*. Philip the Good, Duke of Burgundy (1396–1467), became an ally of the English after the Treaty of Troyes (1420), the murder of his father in 1419 having caused his enmity to the Dauphin. He was named by Henry V on his deathbed as co-regent of France with the Duke of Bedford. In 1434–5 he shifted his allegiance to Charles VII (see III.3).

9–10 *By whose approach ... to us.* Burgundy's alliance with Henry V had also brought to the English side the forces of these territories in the Netherlands, which were friendly to him.

9   *By whose approach* because of whose coming (to join our cause)

11–12 *This happy night ... banqueted.* Compare Hall's account of Le Mans: 'The Frenchmen ..., now casting no perils nor fearing any creature, began to wax wanton and fell to riot' (page 143).

11   *happy* fortunate

      secure confidently unsuspecting

14   *quittance* repay

15   *art* magic

16–18 *Coward ... of hell!* Compare Holinshed: 'the Dauphin, whose dignity abroad [was] foully spotted in this point, ... for maintenance of his quarrels in war would not reverence to profane his sacred estate as dealing in devilish practices with misbelievers and witches' (page 171).

16   *Coward* (the Dauphin)
       wrongs his fame injures his reputation

17   *fortitude* strength, power

20   *so pure.* Compare Holinshed's 'a great semblance of
       chastity' (page 163).

22   *prove not masculine* (1) does not continue so manly;
       (2) shows her femininity (by becoming pregnant)

23   *underneath the standard of the French* (1) serving under
       the French colours; (2) lying down for the French
       penis

24   *carry armour* (1) wear armour; (2) lie underneath
       soldiers

25   *practise* (1) plot; (2) have sexual intercourse
       converse (1) talk; (2) be sexually intimate

29   *Not all together* not all going up one ladder but using
       several

30   *several* separate

31   *That* so that
       fail. Some editors read 'fall' to balance *rise* (line 32).

32   *rise against their force* scale the walls despite French
       opposition

34   *make his grave* (die)

36   *shall* it shall

38   (stage direction) The details here are from the recap-
       ture of Le Mans; compare Hall: 'about six of the
       clock in the morning they issued out of the castle
       crying "Saint George! Talbot!" The Frenchmen
       which were scarce up, and thought of nothing less than
       of this sudden approachment, some rose out of their
       beds in their shirts, and leapt over the walls, others
       ran naked out of the gates for saving of their lives,
       leaving behind them all their apparel, horses, armour,
       and riches' (page 143).
       À Talbot! See the first note to I.1.128.
       ready dressed

45   *venturous* daring
       desperate suicidal

47   *favour* look with favour on

48   *marvel* wonder
       sped fared
50   *cunning* magical skill
51   *flatter* encourage with false hopes
       withal with it
54   *impatient* angry
       friend (1) companion; (2) lover
55   *alike* the same
56   *still prevail* always be victorious
58–9   *Improvident soldiers! Had your watch been good, | This sudden mischief never could have fallen* (proverbial)
59   *mischief* catastrophe
       fallen happened
61   *tonight* last night
62   *charge* duty
63   *kept* guarded
64   *government* control
68   *her* (Joan's)
       precinct area of control
70   *About* concerned with
72   *Question* let us discuss
75   *rests* remains
       shift stratagem
77   *lay new platforms* make new plans
79–81 *The cry ... his name.* Compare Holinshed: 'his only name was and yet is dreadful to the French nation' (page 158); and see the first note to the stage direction at line 38.
80   *loaden me* laden myself

II.2   This scene takes place in Orleans.
2   *pitchy* black
3   (stage direction) *Retreat* (a trumpet signal for the withdrawal of forces)
5   *advance* raise on a bier
6   *centre.* F's 'Centure' (that is, 'belt') has been retained by some editors as meaning the central belt of the town.

(stage direction) *their drums beating a dead march*. In F
this phrase appears after the stage direction at II.1.7,
where it is obviously inappropriate for a surprise
attack. The theatre book-keeper may have mistakenly written it there instead of at the beginning
of II.2 because of the similarity between the character
entries at these two points. But it seems more appropriate to accompany the actual entry of Salisbury's
funeral procession.

8   *was* which was

10–17   *that ... France*. Salisbury was actually buried in
England; Hall says that his body 'was conveyed into
England, with all funeral and pomp, and buried at
Bisham by his progenitors' (page 145).

10   *that* so that
      hereafter future

16   *mournful* causing sorrow

19   *muse* wonder
      the Dauphin's grace his grace the Dauphin

20   *virtuous*. Talbot is being ironical.
      of Arc. F's spelling here is 'Acre', and at V.4.49 she
is called Joan 'of *Aire*'. Holinshed has 'of Are'; there
is no mention of any such title in Hall and Grafton. It
is possible that 'of Aire' was intended here.

22–5   *when the fight ... field*. See the first note to the stage
direction at II.1.38.

27   *For* because of

28   *trull* harlot

33   *power* armed forces

34–60   *All hail ... accordingly*. This event has no basis in the
chronicles.

37   *would* wishes to

41   *lies* lives

43   *report* (1) acclamation; (2) noise (of cannon?)

45   *comic* (1) mirthful; (2) with a happy ending (as in a
comedy)

46   *encountered with* (1) met; (2) wooed

47   *gentle* well-bred
      suit request

48   *a world* a large number

49   *oratory* eloquence

50   *kindness* courteous behaviour
        overruled prevailed

52   *in submission* obeying her request
        attend on visit

54   *manners will* etiquette requires

55–6   *unbidden guests | Are often welcomest when they are gone*
        (proverbial)

58   *prove* test

59   *perceive my mind* understand my intention

60   *mean* mean to act

II.3   This scene has no basis in the chronicles.

1   *gave in charge* ordered

6   *Tomyris* (a Scythian queen who defeated Cyrus and
        his army of 200,000 Persians. In revenge for his slaying
        of her son and to symbolize his blood-thirstiness, she
        threw his head into a wine-skin full of human blood.)

7–10   *Great is . . . reports.* Shakespeare seems to be alluding
        to the encounter between Solomon and the Queen of
        Sheba: 'And she said unto the King "It was a true
        word that I heard in mine own land of thy sayings and
        of thy wisdom. Howbeit, I believed it not, till I came,
        and saw it with mine eyes; and behold, the one half
        was not told me; for thy wisdom and prosperity
        exceedeth the fame which I heard of thee"' (1 Kings
        10.6–7; compare also 2 Chronicles 9.5–6).

7   *rumour* talk, report
        dreadful causing dread

10   *censure* judgement, opinion

11   *desired* requested

14   *scourge.* See the note to I.4.42.

15   *abroad* everywhere

16   *with his name the mothers still their babes.* See the note
        to I.4.43.
        still quieten

17   *fabulous* mythical

18, 19   *Hercules ... Hector* (classical examples of military strength)

19   *for* because of

       aspect (accented on the second syllable) facial appearance

20   *proportion* size

21   *silly* feeble, frail

22   *writhled* wrinkled. Talbot was sixty-five years old when he was killed at Castillon in 1453. All the extant portraits of him show a strongly marked face and an aquiline nose.

26   *sort* choose

30   *Marry* (a mild oath, originally meaning 'by the Virgin Mary')

       for that she's in a wrong belief because she is under a misapprehension

31   *certify* inform

       Talbot (the real Talbot; see lines 47–55)

34   *trained* decoyed, seduced

35   *shadow* image, portrait (contrasted often in Shakespeare with the physical substance; compare *The Two Gentlemen of Verona*, IV.4.115–17; III.1.174–84). See the variants below in lines 45, 49, and 61.

       thrall slave

37   *substance* actual person

39   *tyranny* cruelty

40   *Wasted* laid waste

41   *captivate* into captivity

43   *moan* lamentation

44   *fond* foolish

46   *severity* cruelty

51   *the smallest part* (an allusion to Talbot's small size)

52   *least proportion of humanity* least significant part of my total human substance (that is, the smallest part of my army)

53   *frame* (1) human structure; (2) body (of the army)

54   *pitch* (a term from falconry) height

56   *riddling merchant* purveyor of riddles
     nonce occasion
59   *presently* straight away
     (stage direction) *winds* blows
64   *subverts* destroys
66   *abuse* deception
67   *fame* report, rumour
     bruited noised abroad
68   *by* from
71   *entertain* receive
72   *misconster* misconstrue
73   *mistake* misunderstand
77   *patience* permission
78   *cates* delicacies
79   *stomachs* (1) appetites; (2) courage
     always serve them well are never lacking

II.4   This scene takes place in the Temple Garden. It has
            no basis in the chronicles. Shakespeare depicts the
            origin of the Wars of the Roses as being a legal dis-
            pute between aristocratic students of law.
            (stage direction) *Richard Plantagenet*. Plantagenet was
            the nickname of Geoffrey of Anjou, the father of Henry
            II, the originator of the dynasty that governed England
            from 1154 until the advent of the Tudors in 1485. It
            was apparently used by Richard, the third Duke of
            York, to bolster his claim to the throne against the
            Lancastrian line. Richard (1411–60) was the only son
            of Richard Earl of Cambridge, and thus the grandson
            of Edmund Langley, the fifth son of Edward III. He
            became the third Duke of York in 1415 and was Henry
            VI's lieutenant in France from 1440 to 1445. His
            attempts to claim the throne are detailed in *Part Two*.
            See Table 2.
               Historically Richard's personal conflict with Somer-
            set was spread over a number of years; but it was only
            on his return from Ireland in 1450 that it had serious
            consequences for the nation.

Suffolk. William de la Pole (1396–1450), fourth Earl and first Duke of Suffolk, served in the French wars under Henry V and later fought under the Duke of Bedford. At the death of Salisbury in 1428 he assumed command of the English forces in France. Inclined by his marriage to the widowed Countess of Salisbury to support the Beauforts, he emerged as the chief opponent of the Duke of Gloucester and desired that Henry VI marry Margaret of Anjou rather than the daughter of the Count of Armagnac (see V.3. and V.5).

3   *the Temple Hall* the hall of one of the Inns of Court
      were would have been

4   *convenient* fitting

6   *wrangling* (1) quarrelling; (2) formally disputing

7   *a truant* neglectful of study

8   *frame* adapt

11   *pitch* (a term from falconry) peak point of flight

12   *deeper mouth* louder bark

14   *bear him* carry himself

17   *nice sharp quillets* fine, subtle distinctions

18   *daw* jackdaw (proverbial for its stupidity)

19   *mannerly forbearance* courteous refusal to get involved

20   *truth appears so naked* (proverbial)

21   *purblind* partially blind
      find it out perceive it

22   *well apparelled* (in contrast to Richard's *naked truth*)

24   *a blind man* (in contrast to *purblind* in line 21)

26   *dumb significants* wordless signs

28   *stands upon* insists on

29   *pleaded* (in the legal sense) put the case for

30   *a white rose.* The white rose was the badge of the Mortimers, worn by Roger Earl of March, the father of Edmund Mortimer.

32   *party* (one side of the legal case)

33   *a red rose.* The red rose had been the badge of the House of Lancaster, and indeed of the Tudors, since the thirteenth century.

34   *colours* (1) hues; (2) corroborative evidence
      colour semblance, pretext

38	*held the right* argued the correct position
41	*cropped* plucked
42	*yield* (a legal term) concede
43	*objected* (a legal term) brought forward
44	*subscribe* concur (literally, by signing at the bottom of a legal document)
48	*verdict* (a legal term) decision
51	*fall on my side* find yourself demonstrating agreement with me
52	*opinion* judgement, conviction
53	*Opinion* reputation
54	*still* always
60	*meditating* contemplating
	that that which
62	*counterfeit* imitate
65	*that* because
68	*canker* (a green caterpillar that feeds on rosebuds)
69	*Hath not thy rose a thorn* (proverbial)
70, 71	*his* its
76	*fashion* (that of wearing the red rose)
	peevish foolish
	boy (an insult, as, for example, in *Coriolanus*, V.6.101–10)
77	*scorns* taunts
79	*turn . . . into thy throat* throw back (the slanders) into the throat from whence they came
81	*grace* (1) do honour to; (2) ennoble
	yeoman. The allusion is to the fact that Richard's father, the Earl of Cambridge, had been executed for treason by Henry V, which meant that his titles had become forfeit to the crown.
83	*grandfather* (actually his great-great-grandfather on his mother's side; but Edward III's fifth son Edmund Duke of York, was Richard's grandfather on his father's side; see Table 1)
85	*crestless* (1) not having the right to a heraldic crest; (2) without a top to his genealogical tree; (3) cowardly
86	*bears him on the place's privilege* takes advantage of the

fact that the Temple (being originally a religious house) is a place of sanctuary. Compare I.3.46; but, unlike the Tower, the Temple actually enjoyed no such privilege.

91   *late king* (Henry V)

92   *attainted* condemned by association

93   *Corrupted* legally deprived of title
      exempt excluded
      ancient gentry hereditary rank of gentleman. See the second note to line 81.

95   *restored* given back your lands and titles

96   *attachèd, not attainted.* Richard insists that his father was in fact arrested and immediately executed for treason by order of Henry V, and not indicted by Parliament on a full bill of attainder. He is suggesting that his father did not receive justice. See *Henry V*, II.2.

98   *prove on better men* establish through trial by combat with men of higher rank

99   *Were growing time once ripened to my will* if developing events provide me with the opportunity I desire

100   *partaker* ally, supporter

102   *apprehension* opinion, idea

104, 130   *still* always

108   *cognizance* badge

111   *flourish* (1) blossom; (2) succeed
      degree noble rank

114   *Have with thee* I'll accompany thee

115   *braved* defied
      perforce of necessity

116   *object* urge, bring forward

118   *Called for the truce of* summoned to make peace between

121   *in signal* as token

123   *party* side

125   *Grown to this faction* having swollen to this conflicting allegiance

128   *bound* indebted

II.5   The scene takes place in the Tower of London. There
        is no evidence for Richard paying such a visit, but
        the material of the scene is based on a passage in the
        chronicles: 'Edmund Mortimer, the last Earl of March
        of that name (which long time had been restrained
        from his liberty, and finally waxed lame), deceased
        without issue, whose inheritance descended to Lord
        Richard Plantagenet, son and heir to Richard Earl
        of Cambridge, [who was] beheaded ... at the town of
        Southampton' (Hall, page 128). Both the chronicles
        and Shakespeare are historically incorrect. The histor-
        ical Edmund Mortimer, fifth Earl of March, who was
        declared heir presumptive to Richard II in 1398, was
        not imprisoned when Henry IV succeeded to the
        throne, but served in France and was at his death in
        1425 Lieutenant of Ireland. Shakespeare confuses this
        figure with his uncle Sir Edmund Mortimer, who was
        imprisoned by Owen Glendower, whose daughter he
        married; and possibly also with Sir John Mortimer,
        who, after several years in prison in the Tower and at
        Pevensey Castle, was executed in 1424 for urging his
        cousin Edmund Mortimer's claim to the throne.

3   *halèd* dragged

5   *these grey locks, the pursuivants of Death* (proverbial)
        pursuivants heralds

6   *Nestor* (the oldest of the Greek leaders at the siege of
        Troy and a proverbial type of old age)

7   *Argue* give evidence of

8   *like lamps whose wasting oil is spent.* The combination
        of ideas here seems to come from 1 Samuel 3.2–3:
        'And as at that time Eli in his place his eyes began to
        wax dim, that he could not see. And ere the lamp of
        God went out, Samuel laid him down to sleep in the
        temple of the Lord'.

9   *Wax* grow
        exigent end, extremity

11   *pithless* (literally, without marrow) feeble

13   *stay is numb* support is paralysed. See the quotation in
        the headnote to this scene.

16   *As witting* as if they knew

17   *my nephew*. Richard's mother was Anne, sister of Edmund Mortimer, fifth Earl of March. See Table 2.

22   *his wrong* the injury done to him

23   *Henry Monmouth* (Henry V)

25   *sequestration* (1) imprisonment; (2) loss of property

26   *obscured* living in obscurity

28   *arbitrator of* (a legal term) provider of relief for

30   *enlargement* delivery to freedom

31   *his* (Richard's)
       expired at an end (like my life)

35   *ignobly* (1) badly; (2) contrary to your noble rank
       used treated

36   *late* recently
       despisèd treated contemptuously

37   *I may* so that I may

38   *latter* final

40   *kindly* (1) affectionately; (2) to one of my kinsmen

41   *stock* tree trunk (a genealogical reference; see Table 1)

44   *disease* (1) un-ease; (2) distress

47   *lavish tongue* uncontrolled language

49   *obloquy* disgrace

53   *alliance'* kinship's
       declare explain

56   *flowering* flourishing

59   *Discover* reveal

64   *nephew*. Richard II was Henry's cousin (see Table 1); the two terms were commonly interchanged.
       Edward (the Black Prince, eldest son of Edward III)

67   *whose* (referring to Henry IV)
       Percys (the Earl of Northumberland and his son, Harry Hotspur)

69   *Endeavoured* tried to procure

70   *moved* that moved

71   *for that* that (literally 'because')

73   *next* (in line to the throne)

74–91   *by my mother ... beheaded.* The source for this pedigree is the Duke of York's oration in the parliament of 1460 (Hall, pages 245–8), supplemented with Holin-

shed's account of the same (pages 409–12) and with
some extra material found in Stowe's *Chronicles of
England* (1580) concerning the agreements drawn up
between Henry and the Duke of York.

74–5   *by my mother I derivèd am | From Lionel Duke of
Clarence*. His grandmother, Philippa, was the daughter
of the Duke of Clarence. Shakespeare is again confusing this Mortimer with his uncle of the same name.

78   *but fourth of that heroic line*. Henry IV's father, John
of Gaunt, was Edward III's fourth son.

79   *haughty* exalted

84   *derived* descended

88   *Levied an army*. There is no historical evidence for this.
weening thinking

89   *diadem* crown

94   *issue* children

95   *warrant* assure

96   *thee gather* (1) to infer for yourself; (2) to gain yourself

98   *admonishments* warnings

101   *politic* prudent

103   *like a mountain, not to be removed* (an echo of Psalm
125.1: 'even as the Mount Sion, which may not be
removed')

104   *removing* departing

105   *cloyed* bored

106   *settled* firmly established

108   *redeem* buy back
passage passing

111   *except* unless

112   *give order* make arrangements

117   *overpassed* spent

121   *better than his life* is more appropriate to his rank than
was the treatment he received during his life

122   *dusky* extinguished

123   *meaner sort* people of lower rank (Bolingbroke and his
supporters)

124   *for* as for

128   *blood* hereditary rights

129   *make my ill th'advantage of my good* make my wrongs the instrument of working something to my advantage. The F reading, 'will' for *ill*, makes the phrase mean 'make some opportunity for advancement out of my sheer determination'; but Richard seems to be making the point that either he will have his name restored or he will use the wrong done to him as an excuse for advancing his ambitions.

III.1   The scene takes place in London in the Parliament House; but historically these events took place at Leicester, where the parliament of 1426 met.

    (stage direction) *offers* attempts, starts

    put up a bill bring forward a list of accusations

1   *lines* written statements

2   *pamphlets* documents

4   *lay unto my charge* charge me with

5   *invention* premeditation

    suddenly extemporaneously

7   *object* urge against me

8   *this place* (parliament)

10   *preferred* brought forward, set out

13   *rehearse the method of my pen* recount orally what I have written. 'Method' was a term in formal logic to describe the arrangement of matter for delivery.

14–18   *such is thy . . . peace.* Hall's character sketch of Winchester lies behind these lines: 'more noble of blood than notable in learning, haughty in stomach and high in countenance, rich above measure of all men, and to few liberal, disdainful to his kin and dreadful to his lovers, preferring money before friendship' (page 210).

15   *lewd* wicked

    pestiferous deadly

    pranks malicious deeds

16   *As* that

17   *usurer.* According to the chronicles, Winchester had

amassed a large fortune by embezzlement and his
rents from the Southwark brothels.

18   *Froward* arrogant

20   *degree* rank, position

21, 33   *for* as for

22–3   *thou laidest a trap ... Tower.* One of the items in
Gloucester's charge against Winchester in the 1426–7
parliament alleges: 'My said lord of Winchester,
untruly and against the King's peace, to the intent to
trouble my said lord of Gloucester going to the King,
purposing his death in case that he had gone that way,
set men of arms and archers at the end of London
Bridge next Southwark ... and set men in chambers,
cellars, and windows, with bows and arrows and other
weapons, to the intent to bring to final destruction my
said lord of Gloucester's person' (Hall, page 131).

24   *sifted* examined closely

26   *envious* evil

       swelling (with pride)

31   *haps it* does it happen that

32   *wonted calling* customary profession

34, 114 *except* unless

35   *that* that which

37   *sway* govern, have power

38   *about* in the company of

42   *bastard of my grandfather.* Winchester was John of
Gaunt's illegitimate son by his mistress, Catherine
Swynford, before she became his third wife in 1396.
See Table 1.

44   *imperious* acting like a ruler

45   *saucy* insolent

47   *keeps* resides (for his defence)

48   *patronage* defend

50   *Touching thy spiritual function* only in your ecclesiastical title

52–3   SOMERSET ... WARWICK. In F line 52 is spoken by
Warwick and line 53 by Somerset. Most editors
agree that that distribution of the speeches is faulty:

the sense of the lines indicates that after the Winchester–
Gloucester exchange, Somerset and Warwick take
sides with Warwick supporting Gloucester in line 51,
Somerset taking Warwick to task for his remark in
line 52, Warwick taunting Somerset in line 53, and
then parallel couplets of comment from both of them
in lines 54–7. C. J. Sisson (*New Readings in
Shakespeare* (1956), II, 69–70) justifies F's assign-
ment, but needs the emendation of 'so' for *see* in line
53.

52 *forbear* restrain yourself
53 *overborne* overruled
54 *my lord* (Gloucester)
55 *office* duty
    such (religious persons)
56 *his lordship* (Winchester)
57 *fitteth not* is not appropriate for
58 *holy state is touched so near* ecclesiastical position is
    affected so seriously
63 *bold verdict* insolent opinion
    enter talk engage in discussion
64 *have a fling at* make a verbal attack on
66 *weal* well-being
68 *love and amity*. This typically pious reflection by
    Henry is a quotation from the Book of Common
    Prayer.
70 *jar* quarrel
71 *tender years* youth. Henry VI was born at Windsor in
    1421 and ruled England through a council during his
    minority, with Gloucester as his Protector and Warwick
    as his Master. He took part in public functions as a
    child and was crowned at Westminster in 1429 and in
    Paris in 1431; he opened parliament in person in 1432.
    Historically Henry was only five years old at the time
    of this Gloucester–Winchester confrontation, and it
    was the Duke of Bedford who 'openly rebuked the
    lords in general, because that they in the time of war
    through their privy malice and inward grudge had

almost moved the people to war and commotion'
(Hall, page 130).

74   *uproar* public disturbance

76–85   *O my good lords ... our shops.* Hall (pages 136–7),
Grafton (I.567–70), and Holinshed (pages 146–54) all
deal with the Gloucester–Winchester quarrel and the
disruption caused by their followers; but the details
here seem to have been derived from Fabyan's account
of the events of 29 October 1425: 'the Mayor ... was
by the Lord Protector sent for in speedy manner.... he
gave to him a strait commandment that he should see
that the city were surely watched in that night following, and so it was. Then upon the morrow following, about nine of the clock, certain servants of the
forenamed Bishop would have entered by the Bridge
Gate.... In so much that the commons of the city, hearing thereof, shut in their shops and sped them thither in
great number. And likely it was to have ensued great
effusion of blood shortly thereupon, ne had been the
discretion of the Mayor and his brethren, that exhorted
the people by all politic means to keep the King's
peace.... This was cleped of the common people the
parliament of bats. The cause was for proclamations
were made that men should leave their swords and
other weapons in their inns, the people took great bats
and staves in their necks and so followed their lords
and masters unto the parliament. And when that
weapon was inhibited them, then they took stones and
plummets of lead and trussed them secretly in their
sleeves and bosoms' (pages 595–6).

78   *Bishop* Bishop's

79   *late* recently

81   *contrary* (accented on the second syllable) opposing
    parts gangs

83   *giddy* wild with rage

84   *windows* shutters

88   *mitigate* pacify

92   *peevish broil* foolish conflict

93   *unaccustomed* (1) unusual; (2) contrary to good order

97   *ere that* before

       suffer permit

99   *disgracèd* (1) insulted; (2) denied proper respect to his 'grace'

       inkhorn mate unworthy pedant

103   *pitch a field* (literally, supply a battlefield with defensive stakes)

106   *forbear* desist

111   *study* plan carefully

       prefer recommend, promote

113   WARWICK. Historically Warwick was in France at this time.

114   *repulse* refusal

117   *enacted* brought about

122   *privilege of* advantage over

124   *moody* arrogant, haughty

127–41   *Here, Winchester ... dissemble not.* Compare Hall: 'it was decreed ... that every each of my lords of Gloucester and Winchester should take either other by the hand ... in sign and token of good love and accord, the which was done' (page 137).

132   *kindly gird* fitting rebuke

137   *hollow* false, treacherous

139   *token* (handshake)

144   *contract* (accented on the second syllable)

145   *masters* (a condescending term for social inferiors)

149   *physic* medicine

151–80   *Accept this scroll ... York!* Compare Hall: 'the great fire of this dissension ... was thus ... utterly quenched out. ... For joy whereof, the King caused a solemn feast to be kept on Whitsun Sunday, on the which day he created Richard Plantagenet, son and heir to the Earl of Cambridge ... Duke of York' (page 138). Historically Richard succeeded his uncle Edward Plantagenet as third Duke of York in 1415 and in 1425 inherited the possessions of his uncle Edmund de Mortimer, fifth Earl of March.

153   *exhibit* (a legal term) produce for consideration

155   *An if* if

        circumstance detail

157   *occasions* reasons which

158   *Eltham Place.* See the note to I.1.170.

159   *force* compelling weight

161   *restorèd to his blood* reinstated in his titles and heredi- tary rights (as heir to the Earl of Cambridge)

165   *true* loyal

171   *Stoop* kneel

172   *reguerdon* requital

        duty act of loyalty

173   *girt* gird

178   *grudge one thought* have a single hostile thought

182   *to be crowned in France.* See the note to line 71.

185   *disanimates* disheartens

188   (stage direction) *Sennet* (a trumpet call to signal the arrival or departure of a procession)

191   *late* recent

192   *forged* pretended

194   *by degree* bit by bit

196   *breed* increase itself

197   *prophecy.* This is based on Hall's account of Henry V's premonition: 'But when he heard reported the place of his nativity, whether he fantasied some old blind prophecy, or had some foreknowledge, or else judged of his son's fortune, he said to the Lord Fitzhugh, his trusty chamberlain, these words: "My lord, I Henry born at Monmouth shall small time reign and much get, and Henry born at Windsor shall long reign and all lose"' (page 108).

200   *Henry born at Monmouth* (Henry V)

201   *Henry born at Windsor* (Henry VI)

202–3   *Exeter doth wish | His days may finish ere that hapless time.* In the chronicles Exeter's death occurs im- mediately after the reconciliation of Gloucester and Winchester.

203   *hapless* unfortunate, miserable

III.2 This recapture of Rouen is unhistorical. The city was
not lost until 1449; and Joan of Arc was burnt in 1431.
The events are similar to those recorded during the
capture of Cornill Castle by the English in 1441, which
Hall describes thus: 'the Frenchmen had taken the
town of Evreux, by treason of a fisher. Sir Francis
Arragonois, hearing of that chance, apparelled six
strong men like rustical people with sacks and baskets,
as carriers of corn and victual, and sent them to the
Castle of Cornill, in the which divers Englishmen were
kept as prisoners' (page 197). However, certain points
seem to have been taken from Fabyan's account of
the same incident (page 615), the details of which are
given in the notes on the relevant lines.

(stage direction) *four*. This is the number in Fabyan;
six in the other chronicles.

1 *These are the city gates*. The staging is presumably the
same as in I.5.

2 *policy* crafty stratagem

3 *place* arrange

4 *Talk like the vulgar sort of market-men*. In Fabyan the
disguised English soldiers talk like Frenchmen; this
detail is not in the other chronicles.

vulgar ordinary, common (without any pejorative
connotation)

5 *gather money*. Only Fabyan has 'to sell'.
corn. Fabyan has 'fruits' here.

7 *that* if

10 *mean* means

13 *Qui là?* who [is] there? F's '*Che*' for *Qui* is a version of
the regular medieval French form 'Chi'.

14 *Paysans, la pauvre gent de France* peasants, the poor
tribe of France. The modern French 'gens' (masculine
plural) was originally feminine, being the plural of
'la gent' meaning 'the race, tribe'.

15 *sell their corn*. See the first note to line 5 and the
quotation from Hall in the headnote to this scene.

16 *market bell* (to signal the opening of the market)

18   *Saint Denis.* See the note to I.6.28.

20   *practisants* conspirators

22   *Here.* This is often emended to 'Where', but the
      sense of the Bastard's lines is clear. He has indicated
      that Joan's party has entered the town at a specific
      point, *Here* (line 20), and he wants to know how she
      will signal to them that it is safe to follow her.

23   *By thrusting out a torch from yonder tower.* This seems
      to be based upon an incident at Le Mans in 1428:
      'When the day assigned ... was come, the French
      captains privily approached the town, making a little
      fire on an hill in the sight of the town, to signify their
      coming and approaching. The citizens, which by the
      great church were looking for their approach, showed
      a burning cresset out of the steeple, which suddenly
      was put out and quenched' (Hall, page 142).

24   *that* what

25   *No way to that, for weakness* no way is as weakly
      defended as that by
      (stage direction) *the top* (some elevated area above the
      stage doors representing the gates of the city)

28   *Talbotites* followers of Talbot

31   *shine it* may it shine

32   *A prophet to* presaging

33   *delays have dangerous ends* (proverbial)

34   *presently* immediately

35   *do execution on the watch* kill the guards
      (stage direction) *in an excursion.* Here soldiers pass
      fighting across the stage to simulate a battle.

39   *unawares* which has taken us by surprise

40   *That hardly* so that with difficulty
      pride arrogant forces

42   *fast* starve

44   *darnel* weeds, tares

46   *thine own* (that is, your own bread)

48   *starve* die

49   *let no words, but deeds, revenge this treason* (proverbial)

50   *greybeard.* Actually the Duke of Bedford did not die

until 1435, some four years after he had overseen the execution of Joan of Arc, at the age of forty-five.

51   *run a-tilt* make a lance charge

52   *hag* witch. Compare *Macbeth*, IV.1.47.
       of all despite full of malice

53   *Encompassed with* surrounded by

56   *bout* (1) armed combat; (2) sexual encounter

58   *hot* (1) angry; (2) lustful

59   *do but thunder, rain will follow* (proverbial)

60   *Speaker* (1) spokesman; (2) leader (of the 'parliament')

64   *Hecate* (goddess of the moon and the underworld, and thus guardian of witches). The word is trisyllabic.

68   *Base muleteers* mule-drivers of low birth

69   *footboys* (servants on foot accompanying a master on horseback)
       keep stay within

73   *bye* be with you

76   *fame* reputation

78   *Pricked on* goaded

81   *his father here was conqueror*. Henry V had captured Rouen in 1419 after a lengthy siege.

82   *late* recently

83   *Great Coeur-de-lion's heart was burièd*. Richard I 'willed his heart to be conveyed unto Rouen and there buried, in testimony of the love which he had ever borne unto that city for the steadfast faith and tried loyalty at all times found in the citizens there' (Holinshed, II, page 270). Richard earned the nickname when he was pitted against a lion by Leopold, Archduke of Austria, and thrust his hand down the animal's throat and tore out its heart.

86   *regard* take care of

89   *crazy* decrepit

92   *weal* welfare

95   *Pendragon*. According to Geoffrey of Monmouth's *Historia Regum Britanniae*, Uther Pendragon caused himself to be carried sick on a litter to join his people, who were thereby inspired to defeat the invading

Saxons. Holinshed's *History of Scotland* tells the same story of Pendragon's brother, Aurelius Ambrosius.

102   *out of hand* at once

103–8   This episode is fictitious. See the note to I.1.131.

106   *have the overthrow* be defeated

113   *scoffs* taunts

114   *fain* satisfied

    (stage direction) *carried in* carried off stage

121   *gentle* noble

122   *old familiar* customary demon (which serves a witch; the reference may be to Satan himself)

123   *braves* boasts

    Charles his gleeks Charles's taunts

124   *amort* dispirited

126   *take some order* make arrangements for the governing of the city

127   *expert* experienced

133   *exequies fulfilled* funeral rites performed. Bedford was buried at Rouen in 1435 (Hall, page 178).

134   *couchèd* carried in fighting position

135   *gentler* more noble

    sway exercise authority

III.3   This scene takes place near Rouen.

1   *Dismay not* do not be dismayed

    accident unhappy event

3   *Care is no cure* (proverbial)

    Care sorrow

    corrosive aggravating

5   *frantic* proud

7   *train* (1) followers; (2) peacock's tail (glory)

8   *be . . . ruled* follow instructions

10   *cunning* magic skill

    diffidence lack of confidence

11   *foil* set-back

12   *Search out thy wit for secret policies* employ your

intelligence to devise stratagems unexpected by the enemy

14–15 *We'll set ... saint.* Compare Hall, page 159: 'The citizens of Orleans had builded in the honour of her an image or an idol ... as a saint sent from God into the realm of France'.

16 *Employ thee* exert your powers

17–91 *Then thus ... the foe.* The defection of Burgundy, which took place in 1434–5, was not the result of Joan's action; the chronicles detail far more complex political motives for Burgundy's decision. Compare Hall: 'they thought to find a mean way to save themselves and their city from the captivity of their enemies, and devised to submit their city, themselves, and all theirs under the obeisance of Philip Duke of Burgundy, because he was brought out of the stock and blood royal of the ancient house of France; thinking by this means (as they did indeed) to break or minish the great amity between the Englishmen and him.

'After this point concluded, they made open and sent to the Duke all their devices and intents which certified them that he would gladly recieve their offer, so that the Regent of France would thereto agree and consent.'

But owing to some disagreement between the allies, 'the Duke of Burgundy began to conceive a certain privy grudge against the Englishmen for this cause, thinking them to envy and bear malice against his glory and profit, for the which in continuance of time he became their enemy, and cleaved to the French King' (page 147). Hall also notes that Burgundy inclined toward the Dauphin because 'the Duke of Bedford was joined in affinity with the noble and famous house of Luxembourg, by the which he saw that the power of the Englishmen should be greatly advanced' (page 168).

18 *fair persuasions* seductive arguments
sugared flattering

21   *sweeting* (an amorous term)

21–4   *if we could . . . provinces.* This seems to echo Charles's
        words to Burgundy in Hall: 'but by your help . . . we
        shall expel, clean pull up by the roots, and put out all
        the English nation out of our realms' (page 177).

24   *extirpèd* rooted out

25   *expulsed* driven out

26   *title* possession

29–36   *Hark . . . Burgundy!* From the stage direction *Drum
        sounds afar off* it would appear that Pucelle points off
        stage at the departing troops and that Burgundy enters
        after the parley is sounded. But F has no entry for
        Burgundy at line 36; and some editors have Talbot and
        his army enter and march across the stage followed by
        Burgundy, who drops out of the procession when
        Charles utters line 36.

30   *unto Paris-ward* in the direction of Paris

33   *his* (his soldiers)

34   *in favour* benevolently for us

36–9   *A parley . . . hence.* Compare Hall: 'the French King
        . . . not only sent for him, but . . . met him in proper
        person' (page 176).

40   *enchant* charm (by supernatural means)

41   *undoubted* fearless

44–57   *Look on . . . spots.* This passage seems to be based on
        Hall: 'the common people were slain, murdered, and
        trod under the foot, . . . towns were destroyed and
        wasted, town dwellers and citizens were robbed and
        exiled, beautiful buildings were cruelly brent, nothing
        was spared by the cruelty of Mars which by fire, blood,
        or famine might be catched or destroyed, beside a
        hundred more calamities that daily vexed and troubled
        the miserable French nation' (page 165).

44   *Look on* (in the biblical sense: 'look with pity on')

46   *wasting ruin of* destructive devastation by

47   *lowly* little (or possibly 'lying low in death')

48   *tender-dying* dying young

50   *unnatural* (because they are against Burgundy's own
        country)

52   *edgèd* sharp
       another way (against the English)

57   *stainèd spots* blots which stain (the reputation of France)

59   *nature* natural feeling

60   *exclaims on* loudly accuses

61   *progeny* ancestry

65   *fashioned thee* turned thee into

66   *Who then but English Henry will be lord.* Hall notes that it was contrary to Burgundy's expectation that 'the King of England, by the right course of inheritance, took upon him the whole rule and governance within the realm of France' (page 176).

67   *fugitive* deserter of one's own country. According to Grafton (I.604), patriotic considerations were Burgundy's chief reasons for deserting the English cause.

68   *Call we to mind* let us remember

72   *They set him free.* Charles Duke of Orleans was captured by the English in 1415 and was not actually freed in the circumstances described here until 1440, some five years after Burgundy joined the French forces. Hall explains the feud between the two families: 'John Duke of Burgundy, father to Philip, shamefully and cruelly caused Louis Duke of Orleans, father to this Duke Charles, . . . to be murdered in the city of Paris; for the which murder all the allies and friends to the Duke of Orleans had envy against the house and family of Burgundy, . . . for the surety . . . of the Duke of Burgundy [the English] kept still the Duke of Orleans in England' (page 194). Holinshed notes further that after Burgundy's defection the English devised how to deliver the Duke of Orleans to do 'displeasure to the Duke of Burgundy'.

75   *will* who will
       slaughtermen murderers

76   *wandering* (1) erring; (2) having wandered from your true allies

78–84   *I am vanquished . . . trust thee.* The suddenness of Burgundy's conversion may have been suggested by

> Hall: 'And so . . . without long argument or prolonging of time, he took a determinate peace' (page 176).

78   *haughty* lofty

86   *makes us fresh* endows us with new strength

88   *bravely* (1) valorously; (2) splendidly

90   *powers* forces

91   *prejudice* harm

III.4   The scene takes place in Paris.

4   *duty* homage, feudal allegiance

8   *esteem* noble rank

9, 11   *his* its (referring to *this arm* in line 5)

11   *Ascribes* attributes

17   *When I was young.* Henry VI was actually nine months old when his father died.

19   *stouter champion* more valiant warrior

20   *we* (the royal plural)
     resolvèd convinced

23   *reguerdoned* rewarded

25   *deserts* deservings

26   *We here create you Earl of Shrewsbury.* This elevation actually took place in 1442 (Hall, page 202), while Henry VI's coronation in Paris occurred in 1431.

28–45   *Now, sir . . . would.* See IV.1.89–97. This quarrel has no basis in the chronicles. The two characters are unhistorical, but both names are mentioned in the chronicles: John (or Peter) Basset was Henry V's chamberlain and biographer (Hall, page 113), and a Sir John Vernon was present at Chatillon when Talbot was killed (Hall, page 228).

28   *hot* angry

29   *Disgracing of* insulting
     colours emblems (of the white rose)

32   *patronage* defend

33   *envious* malicious

35   *Sirrah* (a contemptuous form of address)
     as for what

38   *the law of arms* (a reference to the law which forbade fighting within the precincts of a royal dwelling)

39   *present death* immediate execution (the punishment for violating *the law of arms*)

40   *broach* cause to flow

42   *liberty* permission
       wrong insult

45   *after* after the King's permission to duel has been granted

IV.1   The scene takes place in Paris. The chronicles note that in 1431 'In the month of November, he [Henry VI] removed from Rouen ... to the intent to make his entry into the city of Paris, and there to be sacred King of France, and to receive the sceptre and crown of the realm and country .... he was met at the Chapel, in the mean way, by Sir Simon Morver, Provost of Paris, with a great company .... And on the seventeenth of the said month ... he was anointed and crowned King of France by the Cardinal of Winchester' (Hall, pages 160–61). Historically Talbot, who had been captured at the Battle of Patay, was still in French hands; Exeter was dead; and Gloucester was in England.

4   *elect* acknowledge

5   *Esteem none* regard none as

6   *pretend* intend

7   *practices* plots

8   (stage direction) *train* attendants

9–47   *My gracious sovereign ... death.* Burgundy's letter to the King was delivered in 1435. Compare Hall: 'From this battle departed without any stroke stricken Sir John Fastolfe, the same year for his valiantness elected into the Order of the Garter. For which cause the Duke of Bedford, in a great anger, took from him the image of Saint George and his Garter; but afterward, by mean of friends and apparent causes of good excuse by

him alleged, he was restored to the Order again,
against the mind of the Lord Talbot' (page 150).

15   *Garter* (insignia of the Order of the Garter, worn at
this time just below the left knee)
craven coward

19   *dastard* coward
Patay. See the account of the Battle of Patay at I.1.105–
47 and Talbot's reaction to Falstaff's cowardice there
at I.4.35–7.

20   *but in all* all told

21   *that* when

23   *trusty squire* (a contemptuous phrase here)

25   *divers* various

30   *fact* evil deed

31   *common man* man below the rank of gentleman

33   *ordained* established

35   *haughty courage* lofty spirit

36   *were grown to credit* had achieved a high reputation

37   *for distress* on account of hardship

38   *most extremes* greatest extremities (of danger)

39   *furnished in this sort* endowed thus

43   *degraded* reduced in rank
hedge-born swain rustic of low birth

44   *gentle* noble

45   *Stain* blemish
doom sentence

46   *packing* off

48–63   *And now ... guile*. Compare Hall: 'the Duke of
Burgundy, which thought himself by this concord in
manner dishonoured, ... sent his letters to the King of
England, rather to purge and excuse himself of his
untruth ... not for any malice or displeasure which he
bare to King Henry or to the English nation. This
letter was not a little looked on ... of the King of
England and his sage council, not only for the weighti-
ness of the matter but also for the sudden change of the
man, and for the strange superscription of the letter,
which was: "To the high and mighty Prince, Henry,

by the grace of God King of England, his well-beloved cousin", neither naming him King of France nor his sovereign lord, according as, ever before that time, he was accustomed to do' (page 177).

49   *uncle*. The King's uncle, the Duke of Bedford, married Anne, the sister of the Duke of Burgundy.

50   *style* manner of address

53   *churlish* rude

      superscription address (on the outside of the letter)

54   *Pretend* import

56   *wrack* ruin

58   *feeds* preys

63   *such false dissembling guile*. Compare Hall: 'glozing and flattering words ... crafty deed and untrue demeanour of the Duke' (page 177).

64   *revolt* change sides

69   *abuse* deception

71   *prevented* anticipated

73   *strength* soldiers

      straight at once

74–5 *Let him perceive ... friends*. This seems to echo Holinshed, where the Duke 'might shortly find' the difference between 'an old tried friend' and 'a new reconciled enemy' (page 184).

74   *brook* tolerate

75   *offence* crime

      flout mock

76   *still* always

77   *confusion* destruction

78–122 *Grant me ... honourable Lord*. See the note to III.4.28–45.

78   *combat* trial by duel

80   *servant* follower (not a menial)

90   *envious* malicious

91   *rose* (red rose of Lancaster)

92   *sanguine* bloody, red

      leaves petals

94   *repugn* reject, oppose

95   *a certain question.* The reference is almost certainly to the question of York's right to the succession and his father's death for treason.

98   *confutation* (a legal term) refutation
      rude ignorant

100   *benefit of law of arms* legal privilege to fight a duel to defend my honour

102   *forgèd quaint conceit* false ingenious invention

103   *set a gloss upon* give a fine outward appearance to

105   *at* to

106   *flower* (white rose of York)

107   *Bewrayed* revealed
      faintness cowardice

108   *left* given up

113   *factious emulations* partisan conflicts

114   *cousins* kinsmen

118   *toucheth* affects

120   *pledge.* York here probably throws down his glove as his gage.

124   *prate* prattling

126   *immodest* audacious, arrogant

129   *objections* mutual accusations of criminal behaviour

130   *occasion* opportunity

131   *mutiny* riot, civil brawl

140   *within* among

141   *grudging stomachs* resentful passions

144   *certified* informed

145   *toy* trifle
      regard importance

149   *forgo* lose

151   *doubtful* worrying

154   *incline to* favour

161   *still* ever

162–5 *Cousin of York . . . foot.* See the quotation from Hall in the headnote to IV.3.

162   *institute* appoint

165   *foot* infantry

166   *progenitors.* Both Somerset and York were descended from Edward III; see Tables 1–2.

167   *digest* dissipate

173   *rout* rabble

174   *promise* assure

180   *An if* if

        wist knew for certain. Some editors emend F's 'I wish' to 'iwis', which gives the meaning 'if that was certainly true'; but this does not seem to be the sense called for by the context.

184   *deciphered* discovered

187   *simple* common

189   *shouldering* physical pushing

190   *bandying* verbal conflict

        favourites followers

191   *But that* but sees that. Some editors emend to 'But sees', which is not necessary, as 'sees' is understood from its occurrence in line 187.

        event outcome

192   *much* serious

193   *envy* malice

        unkind unnatural (because between kinsmen)

V.2   Historically Bordeaux had already been retaken by Talbot, but English tradition held it to be the site of his death. The events are based on the chronicles' account of the Battle of Castillon, where Talbot actually died in 1453, some twenty-two years after the coronation depicted in IV.1.

        (stage direction) *trump* trumpeter

        drum drummer

5   *would* desires

8   *bloody power* forces capable of bloodshed

10–11   *You tempt . . . fire.* See the quotation in the note to III.3.44–57. These lines seem to be derived from Henry V's words at the siege of Rouen: 'The goddess of war, called Bellona, . . . hath these three handmaids ever of necessity attending on her: blood, fire, and famine' (Hall, page 85). Compare also *Henry V*, III.3.1–43.

11   *quartering* dismembering, butchering

12   *even* level

13   *air-braving* defying the air, lofty

14   *forsake* refuse
      their. Presumably this refers to *famine*, *steel*, and *fire*,
      who are willing to withhold their fury if the town
      accepts Talbot's offer. The construction is awkward
      and some editors have emended to 'our' or 'his'.

15   *owl* (a bird of ill omen often prophesying death;
      compare *Macbeth*, II.2.3–4)

16   *their* our nation's
      scourge. See the note to I.4.42.

17   *period* end
      tyranny cruelty

19   *protest* declare

21   *appointed* equipped

23   *thee* of thee
      pitched drawn up in battle order

24   *wall thee* hem you in

25   *redress* relief

26   *front* face
      apparent spoil evident slaughter. *Spoil*, a hunting term,
      carries on the trapping metaphor used in line 22.

27   *pale* (the traditional hue of Death)

28   *ta'en the sacrament* (that is, sworn an oath)

29   *rive* (literally 'split') fire. The emendation 'rove'
      (meaning 'aim at a fixed mark') is attractive.

33   *latest* final

34   *due* grace, endue. F's 'dew' gives a meaning 'sprinkle,
      cause to descend on', which seems strained here.

35   *the glass that now begins to run* (proverbial)
      glass (hourglass)

36   *Finish the process of his sandy hour* complete the hour-
      long running of the sand (through the hourglass)

37   *well coloured* ruddy-complexioned (healthy)

39   *warning bell* (1) bell tolling for the dead; (2) bell
      heralding coming disaster. The image here might be
      the same as that employed in *Macbeth*, II.2.3, which

suggests the bellman sent to bid good night to condemned prisoners the night before their execution.

40	*heavy* sombre, doleful
42	*fables* lies
43	*peruse* reconnoitre
	wings flanking forces
44	*discipline* military tactics
45	*parked* enclosed (as a deerpark)
	pale fenced-in area
47	*Mazed with* confused, bewildered by
	kennel pack
48	*in blood* in vigorous condition
49	*rascal-like* (1) like lean worthless deer; (2) like unworthy men
	pinch slight nip (of hounds)
50	*moody-mad* wild with rage
51	*heads of steel* (1) antlers like swords; (2) helmeted heads
52	*aloof at bay* barking far off
54	*dear* (1) taken at great expense of life; (2) precious
56	*colours* banners

.3   This is based upon the situation recorded in the chronicles for 1436–7: 'the English ... began the war new again, and appointed for Regent in France Richard Duke of York .... Although the Duke of York, both for birth and courage, was worthy of this honour and preferment, yet he was so disdained of Edmund Duke of Somerset, being cousin to the King, that he was promoted to so high an office ... that by all ways and means possible he both hindered and detracted him, glad of his loss and sorry of his well-doing, causing him to linger in England, without dispatch, till Paris and the flower of France were gotten by the French King. The Duke of York, perceiving his evil will, openly dissimulated that which he inwardly thought privily, each working things to the other's displeasure' (Hall, page 179). Historically York's troops were on the plains of Gascony at this time.

3	*give it out* report
4	*power* army
6	*espials* spies, scouts
10	*supply* reinforcements
13	*louted* mocked, made a fool of (or, perhaps, a late usage of the meaning 'delayed', referring to Richard's sense of being unsupported, emphasized in lines 46 and 49)
14	*chevalier* knight
16	*miscarry* come to harm

(stage direction) *Sir William Lucy*. The chronicles make no mention of his being present in France at this time. It has been suggested that Shakespeare, perhaps using local oral tradition, introduced this worthy, who lived at Charlecote, near Stratford, and was three times Sheriff of Warwickshire in the time of Henry VI.

18	*needful* necessary
20	*girdled* encircled

waist (1) belt; (2) waste

25	*stop my cornets* hold back my cavalrymen (called 'cornets' from the curved pennants attached to their lances)
29	*remiss* negligent
30	*distressed* troubled with difficulties
41	*Vexation* anguish
42	*sundered* separated
43	*can* can do
44	*the cause* the person who is the reason why (Somerset)
46	*'Long all* all because
47–8	*the vulture of sedition	Feeds in the bosom*. The allusion is to the myth of Prometheus, whose punishment, decreed by Jupiter, was to have his liver devoured daily by an eagle or a vulture. It is also possible that the reference is to Tityus, whose punishment in hell was to have his entrails perpetually eaten by vultures.
49	*Sleeping neglection* careless disregard
50	*scarce-cold conqueror*. Historically Henry V had been

dead for thirty-one years; but Shakespeare throughout
the play contrasts the glories of his reign (as if they were
very recent) with the immediate disorders of his son's
reign.

51   *ever-living man of memory* man of ever-living memory
53   (stage direction) *Exit*. F has no exit here and no entry
     for Lucy at the beginning of IV.4, so it is possible that
     the action is continuous, with Lucy remaining on the
     stage while Somerset, the Captain, and the soldiers
     march on to the stage and discover his presence at IV.4.
     10. However, Somerset's words at IV.4.12 seem to
     suggest that Lucy enters afresh to plead with Somerset
     as he has with York at IV.3.17–30.

.4.2   *expedition* (against Bordeaux)
3   *rashly* carelessly
3–5   *All our ... buckled with* the whole of our forces might
       safely be engaged by the garrison of only the town
       itself
6   *sullied all his gloss* tarnished his fine appearance
7   *unheedful* careless
8   *set him on* encouraged him
11   *o'ermatched* faced by superior forces
13   *bought and sold* (proverbial, with an allusion to Judas)
       betrayed
14   *adversity.* This may be a late usage of the word meaning
       'opposition'.
16   *legions.* F's 'Regions' certainly appears to be erron-
       eous. The same possible error at V.3.11 suggests that
       initial 'R' and 'l' were similar in the manuscript from
       which the text was printed.
19   *in advantage lingering.* The sense intended here is not
       clear. Possible meanings are (1) finding every means
       possible to delay the action; (2) prolonging the action
       by remaining in a strong position; (3) trying to pre-
       serve as much strength as the situation allows.
20   *trust* guardian, trustee

21 *worthless emulation* senseless rivalry
22 *private discord* personal disagreement
23 *levied succours* raised reinforcements
25 *a world of* tremendous
27 *compass* encircle
28 *default* failure
30 *upon your grace exclaims* accuses you
31 *his levied host* the army raised for him
33 *might have sent and had the horse* had the necessary cavalry and might have sent them
35 *take foul scorn* think it a foul disgrace
36 *fraud* faithlessness
39 *betrayed to fortune* given up to chance
42 *ta'en* captured

IV.5 This scene takes place in the English camp outside Bordeaux. It follows closely the chronicles' account: 'the Earl . . . desiring the life of his entirely and well-beloved son . . . willed, advertised, and counselled him to depart out of the field and to save himself. But when the son had answered that it was neither honest nor natural for him to leave his father in the extreme jeopardy of his life, and that he would taste of that draught which his father and parent should assay and begin, the noble Earl and comfortable captain said to him "Oh, son, son, I thy father, which only hath been the terror and scourge of the French people so many years, which hath subverted so many towns, . . . neither can here die for the honour of my country without great laud and perpetual fame, nor fly or depart without perpetual shame and continual infamy. But because this is thy first journey and enterprise, neither thy flying shall redound to thy shame nor thy death to thy glory; for as hardy a man wisely flieth as a temerarious person foolishly abideth. Therefore, the flying of me shall be the dishonour not only of me and my progeny, but also a discomfiture of all my company;

thy departure shall save thy life and make thee able
another time, if I be slain, to revenge my death and
to do honour to thy prince and profit to his realm.''
But nature so wrought in the son that neither desire of
life nor thought of security could withdraw or pluck
him from his natural father; who, considering the
constancy of his child and the great danger that they
stood in, comforted his soldiers, cheered his captains,
and valiantly set on his enemies' (Hall, page 229).

4	*unable* impotent
5	*drooping* invalid
6	*ill-boding* presaging evil
8	*unavoided* unavoidable
11	*sudden* immediate
15	*To make ... of me* to make me act like
17	*basely* cowardly
	stood remained firm
22	*Your loss is great* the loss of you would be a great blow
	regard concern for your safety
23	*no loss is known in me* my loss would not be felt
27	*that* who (referring to the 'I' implicit in *mine*)
28	*vantage* military advantage
29	*bow* yield
31	*the first hour* at the first trial
	shrink give way in battle
32	*mortality* death
42	*charge* order
	stain moral blemish
43	*being* when you are
44	*apparent* inevitable, certain
46	*age* whole life
53	*eclipse* (with a pun on *son*/'sun')

V.6	The events of this scene are invented; the chronicles record only that Talbot's son, Lord Lisle, 'died manfully'.
2	*The Regent* (Richard Duke of York; see IV.1.162–3)

3   *France his* France's

9   *determined time* limited span of life
         date limit

10   *crest* helmet

13   *Quickened* revived
         spleen ardour

15   *pride* arrogant forces
         Gallia France

17–18 *had the maidenhood | Of thy first fight* (thus was the
first person to draw blood from you in your initiation
in war)

20   *in disgrace* insultingly

22   *misbegotten* illegitimately conceived

23   *Mean* inferior

24   *brave* fine

25   *purposing* while I was intending

29   *sealed* certified, confirmed

31   *stands me in little stead* is of small help to me

32   *wot* know

33   *To hazard all our lives in one small boat.* 'Venture not
all in one bottom' was proverbial.

35   *mickle* great, much

38   *our household's name.* Actually John was a younger son
by Talbot's second wife.
         household family

39   *fame* reputation

40   *stay* remaining

42   *smart* suffer

44   *On that advantage* in order to gain those benefits

48   *like me to* make me be like

49   *shame's scorn* the object of shameful scoffing

52   *boot* use

54–5 *follow thou thy desperate sire of Crete, | Thou Icarus.*
The allusion is to the mythical inventor Daedalus, who
made for himself and his son, Icarus, wings by which
they might escape from King Minos of Crete. The
feathers were fixed on the wings by wax, which melted
when Icarus flew too near the sun, so that he fell into

the sea and was drowned. Icarus was for the Eliza-
bethans the type of the aspiring mind come to grief.
The image may have been suggested by the wording of
Hall's account: 'the ... subtle labyrinth in the which
he and his people were enclosed' (page 229), for
Daedalus had also created the labyrinth for the Minotaur.

57   *in pride* with honour, glory

IV.7   Talbot's death is recorded in the chronicles (see Hall,
page 229); but the details here are invented.

3   *Triumphant* leading dead men in a triumphal procession
    smeared with captivity stained with the blood of
captives

5   *shrink* give way in battle

8   *rage* warlike fury
    impatience anger

9   *guardant* protector

10   *Tendering my ruin* being concerned for me in my fall
    of by

11   *Dizzy-eyed fury* anger which dazzled him

13   *clustering battle* swarming ranks of soldiers

14   *drench* drown

15   *over-mounting* too high-aspiring (like Icarus)

16   *Icarus.* See the note to IV. 6.54–5.
    pride glory

18   *antic* grinning grotesque figure, death's-head. Compare *Richard II*, III.2.160–70.
    here on earth

19   *Anon* soon
    tyranny cruelty

20   *Coupled in bonds of perpetuity* bound closely together
for eternity

21   *lither* yielding

22   *thy despite* spite of you
    'scape mortality avoid death

23   *become* make beautiful

23	*hard-favoured* ugly, hideous
25	*Brave* defy
27	*as who* as one who
32	(stage direction) *He dies.* Historically Talbot died some twenty-two years after Joan was burned.
35	*whelp* young dog (with a quibble on 'talbot' meaning 'hound')
	wood mad
36	*flesh* employ for the first time in battle
	puny previously unused in battle
38	*maiden* uninitiated in battle
41	*pillage* plunder, spoil
	giglot wanton, harlot
43	*unworthy* unworthy of
45	*inhearsèd* laid as if in a coffin
46	*nurser of his harms* man who fostered the power by which he was able to commit the injuries (done to the French)
47–50	*Hew them . . . dead.* This seems to echo Hall's report of the death of the Duke of Bedford and his burial in Rouen Cathedral: 'which . . . sepulture when King Louis XI, son to this King Charles, . . . did well advise and behold, certain noblemen in his company . . . counselled him to . . . pluck down the tomb and to cast the dead carcass into the fields; . . . King Louis answered again saying "... him whom, in his life, neither my father nor your progenitors with all their power . . . were once able to make fly one foot backward, . . . let his body now lie in rest, which when he was alive would have disquieted the proudest of us all"' (page 178).
53	*submissive message* petition of surrender
54	*mere* exclusively
55	*wot* know
58	*Hell our prison is* we have sent all our enemies to hell
60	*Alcides* (another name for Hercules)
61–71	*Valiant Lord . . . France?* All of these titles appear on Talbot's tomb in the Cathedral of Rouen; but the

first known publication of them in England is Roger Cotton's *Armour of Proof* (1596). This fact has been used to support the theory that the play was revised some time after this date; see the Introduction, pages 11–12.

61   *Earl of Shrewsbury*. The creation was in 1442.

63   *Washford* Wexford (a title Talbot inherited from his great-grandmother Elizabeth, wife of Richard, second Lord Talbot)

    Waterford. Talbot received this earldom when he was Steward of Ireland in 1446.

    Valence. One of Talbot's ancestors was Joan of Valence.

64   *Goodrig*. Talbot's father was Richard Talbot of Goodrich Castle in the march of Wales; Talbot succeeded to this title in 1421.

65   *Lord Strange of Blackmere*. Talbot was the sole heir of the last Lord Strange of Blackmere, which is near Whitchurch in Shropshire.

    Lord Verdun of Alton. Talbot held this title in the right of his second wife, Margaret.

66   *Wingfield* (in the county of Wexford)

    Lord Furnival of Sheffield. Talbot held this title in the right of his first-wife, Maud, daughter of Thomas Neville, Lord Furnival.

68   *Knight*. Talbot was knighted in 1413, and was made a member of the Order of the Garter in 1424.

69   *the Golden Fleece* (an order of knighthood established by Philip of Burgundy in 1429)

70   *Great Marshal* supreme commander

72   *style* manner of address

73   *Turk* (Sultan of Turkey)

75–6   *Him that thou ... our feet*. Compare Hall on the subject of Talbot's remains: 'after that he with much fame more glory, and most victory had for his prince and country ... valiantly made war ... [his] corpse was left on the ground' (pages 229–30).

77   *only* supreme. Compare Hall: 'which only hath been the terror and scourge of the French people' (page 229).

78   *Nemesis* (goddess of avenging justice)

84   *amaze* stupefy, appal

86   *beseems their worth* is proper to their rank

89   *have them.* F reads 'haue him', which some editors emend to 'have 'em' on the grounds that the compositor misread ''em' in the manuscript as 'him'; but such a confusion between the two words is unlikely in the handwriting of the period.

93   *phoenix* (the mythical bird which is unique and dies every five hundred years on a funeral pyre of its own making, its successor rising from the ashes). It has been suggested that this may be an allusion to the English expedition to Normandy in 1591–2; see the Introduction, page 9.

94   *So* as long as

        with them. F reads 'with him', which some editors emend to 'with 'em'; see the note to line 89.

V.1   The scene takes place in London. Shakespeare uses mixed historical materials: the peace-making efforts during the negotiations of Arras in 1435 (Hall, pages 174–5); the proposals for Henry's marriage to the Duke of Armagnac's daughter in 1442 (Hall, pages 202–3); the installation of Winchester as Cardinal in 1427; and an accusation made by Gloucester against Winchester in 1441.

1   *the Pope* (Eugenius IV)

2   *The Emperor* (Sigismund, Holy Roman Emperor and King of Hungary and Bohemia, who, with the Pope, intervened unsuccessfully in an attempt to secure a truce between France and England)

7   *affect* incline towards, like

        motion proposal

9   *effusion* spilling

10   *stablish quietness* establish peace

12–14   *It was . . . one faith.* This was an argument used by the Cardinal of Sainte-Croix at the negotiations of Arras in 1435.

13   *immanity* atrocious cruelty

14   *one* the same

15–45   *Beside, my lord ... England's Queen.* Compare Hall:
        'the Earl of Armagnac ... sent solemn ambassadors to
        the King of England, offering him his daughter in
        marriage, not only promising him silver hills and
        golden mountains with her, but also would be bound
        to deliver into the King of England's hands all such
        castles and towns as he or his ancestors detained from
        him within the whole Duchy of Aquitaine or Guienne
        ... offering further to aid the same King with money
        for the recovery of other cities within the said Duchy'
        (pages 202–3).

17   *near knit* closely related

21   *my years are young.* Historically Henry was twenty-one
        at this time.

23   *wanton dalliance* lovemaking

27   *Tends* which tends
        weal welfare

28–62   *What, is my lord ... mutiny.* Compare Hall: 'The
        Duke of Bedford ... landed at Calais, with whom also
        passed the seas Henry Bishop of Winchester, which in
        the said town was invested with the habit, hat, and
        dignity of a cardinal with all ceremonies to it apper-
        taining. Which degree King Henry V, knowing the
        haughty courage and the ambitious mind of the man,
        prohibited him on his allegiance once either to sue
        for or to take, meaning that cardinals' hats should not
        presume to be equal with princes. But now, the King
        being young and the Regent his friend, he obtained
        that dignity, to his great profit and to the impoverishing
        of the spirituality. For by a Bull Legative, which he
        purchased at Rome, he gathered so much treasure that
        no man in manner had money but he, and so was he
        surnamed the rich Cardinal of Winchester' (page 139).
        Historically this took place in 1427 and Exeter died in
        1424.

29   *degree* rank

30   *that* that ... which

30   *verified* proved true
31   *sometime* once
34   *several* various
38   *draw* draw up
39   *mean* intend
40   *presently* immediately
41   *for* regarding
42   *at large* in detail
43   *As* that
46   *In argument* as evidence
      contract (accented on the second syllable)
49   *inshipped* when they are put on board ship
51–4 *You shall first . . . ornaments.* There is no evidence in the
      chronicles that Winchester bribed his way into the
      College of Cardinals. These lines may be due to a
      misunderstanding of Winchester's purchase of 'a Bull
      Legative' (for which see the quotation in the note to
      lines 28–62).
54   *grave ornaments* dignified robes (of a cardinal)
56   *trow* think
62   *mutiny* rebellion

V.2   The location of this scene is the plains of Anjou. The
      loss of Paris, which according to I.1.61 fell to the
      French in 1422, actually happened in 1436.
2   *stout* strong, valiant
5   *powers* armed forces
      dalliance trifling, idleness
7   *Else ruin combat with their palaces!* otherwise let their
      palaces be destroyed. Andrew S. Cairncross emends
      combat with to 'come within' on the grounds of the
      similarity to the phrasing of Psalm 122.7: 'Peace be
      within thy walls, and plenteousness within thy palaces'.
9   *accomplices* associates
12   *conjoined* united
13   *presently* immediately
16   *I trust the ghost of Talbot is not there.* In F Burgundy

speaks this line as well as line 17. But it seems clear that
line 17 is uttered in response to line 16 and thus cannot
really belong to the same speaker. Two possible re-
arrangements suggest themselves: (1) line 16 is said by
Charles as a second thought about the suddenness of
the English attack, and line 17 is said by Burgundy in
reassurance; or (2) Burgundy expresses a fear of the
ghost of the man he has betrayed, and line 17 is the
first line of Pucelle's response to his fear, before she
goes on to give moral support to the Dauphin. I have
preferred the first of these because (a) both Burgundy
and Pucelle seem intent on bolstering the Dauphin's
confidence; (b) Pucelle's *Charles* in line 19 is more
typical of her manner of blunt speech than the *my lord*
in line 17.

18   *passions* emotions
20   *repine* be discontented
21   *fortunate* favoured by fortune

V.3   This scene takes place before Angiers, where historic-
       ally Joan of Arc was captured by the English and
       Burgundians.

1   *The Regent* (the Duke of York. According to Hall
      (pages 156–7), York was not present in the action
      before Angiers. Historically Bedford was Regent at
      this date, York going to France in 1436.)

2   *charming* working by magic incantation
      periapts amulets

3   *ye choice spirits.* Compare Holinshed: 'her campestral
      conversation with wicked spirits' (page 171).
      admonish me keep me informed, forewarn me

4   *accidents* happenings
5   *substitutes* subordinate spirits
6   *monarch of the north* (Lucifer; compare Isaiah 14.13:
      'I will climb up into heaven, and exalt my throne
      above beside the stars of God. I will sit also upon the
      mount of the congregation toward the north')

8	*argues proof* gives evidence
9	*diligence* careful service
10	*culled* selected
11	*legions.* F's 'Regions' gives a kind of sense, though it is puzzling to know why the underworld should be described as *powerful*. The same confusion at IV.4.16, where F's 'Regions' makes no sense at all, supports the emendation here.
12	*get the field* win the battle
14	*Where* whereas
	feed you with my blood. Witches were thought to feed their attendant spirits in this way.
15	*member* limb
16	*In earnest* as a token payment in advance
17	*condescend* agree
18	*redress* relief from trouble
19	*Pay recompense* serve as payment
21	*furtherance* assistance
23	*give . . . the foil* defeat
25	*vail* lower
	lofty-plumèd crest high-plumed helmet (signifying pride)
27	*ancient* former
28	*buckle with* combat
29	(stage direction) F has no entry for Pucelle here, but she obviously enters in the *Excursions* with Burgundy at the head of the French forces. Some editors believe *Burgundy* is a mistake for 'Pucelle'.
31	*spelling* incantatory
33	*the devil's grace* his grace the Devil (ironical)
34	*bend her brows* frown, glower
35	*with* like
	Circe (the enchantress from Homer's *Odyssey*, Book X, who turned men into beasts)
37	*proper* handsome
38	*dainty* fastidious
39	*mischief* misfortune
40	*surprised* attacked
42	*Fell* fierce

banning cursing

44 *miscreant* misbegotten

stake (where she will be burnt)

(stage direction) Some editors begin a new scene here, but the events are continuous, Suffolk's capture of Margaret being part of the same action as that in which Pucelle is taken. Both Suffolk's seizure of Margaret and their subsequent illicit love affair (which is fully explored in *Part Two* of the play) are unhistorical; but their exchanges here may have been suggested by some phrases in the chronicles (quoted in the relevant notes below).

in his hand by the hand

48–9 *I kiss these fingers for eternal peace, | And lay them gently on thy tender side.* The sense intended here is obscure. I take the lines to mean: 'I will kiss your hand in token of everlasting peace between us and then release your hand so that it may hang free by the side of your soft and smooth body'. Some editors reverse the lines, so that the meaning becomes 'and I will lay my hands on your sides (embrace you) and then kiss your fingers as a sign of everlasting peace'.

48 *for* in token of

52 *The King of Naples*. Historically, Reignier was only nominally King of Naples, the province having come into the control of Alphonsus of Aragon.

55 *allotted* destined

56 *save* protect

58 *servile usage* treatment as a prisoner

60–109 *I have ... quid for quo*. The distribution of asides (which are not in F) has been determined by the fact that some of the speeches appear not to have been heard by the other character (for example, lines 60–71 and 75–6), whereas others appear to have been overheard (for example, lines 86 and 89).

63 *Twinkling another counterfeited beam* reflecting back a second image of the sun's rays

67 *de la Pole* (Suffolk's family name)

67   *disable* undervalue (and so make impotent)

68   *Is she not here?* Many editors emend on the grounds of defective metre to 'Is she not here thy prisoner?', following the reading found in the second Folio (the first seventeenth-century reprint of the first Folio). However, the point being made by Suffolk is not that he has made Margaret prisoner – the role of captor he has already disowned in lines 46–50 – but that she is present and therefore available to be wooed if he can only bring himself to speak to her.

69   *a woman's sight* the sight of a woman

70   *such* such that

71   *Confounds* it confounds
       rough dull

75   *deny* refuse

79   *She is a woman, therefore to be won* (proverbial)

81   *Fond* foolish
       wife. Historically Suffolk married the widow of the Earl of Salisbury.

84   *There* by that fact (that he is married)
       cooling card (proverbial; that card in a game which dashes the opponent's hopes when it is played; hence 'check' or 'deterrent')

86   *dispensation* (special permission granted by the Pope to dissolve a marriage)

88   *I'll win this Lady Margaret.* Although there is no evidence at this point in the chronicles for Suffolk's personal infatuation with Margaret, Hall does note that the Earl was 'too much affectionate to this unprofitable marriage' (page 204); and that 'the Queen ... entirely loved the Duke' and called him 'the Queen's darling' (pages 218–19).

89   *wooden thing* (1) insensible thing (referring to the King); (2) stupid scheme

91   *fancy* amorous inclination

92   *peace established between these realms.* Compare Hall: 'the Earl of Suffolk ... without assent of his associates, imagined in his fantasy that the next way to come to a

perfect peace was to move some marriage between the French King's kinswoman and King Henry' (page 203).

93   *scruple* objection

94–5   *though her father ... poor.* Compare Hall: 'the Earl of Suffolk ... desired to have the Lady Margaret, cousin to the French King, and daughter to Reignier, Duke of Anjou, calling himself King of Sicily, Naples, and Jerusalem, having only the name and style of the name. without any penny profit or foot of possession' (pages 203–4).

98   *disdain they ne'er so much* no matter how much they despise the idea

101   *enthralled* enslaved

106   *cause* (a legal term) case

107   *women have been captivate ere now* (proverbial)
      captivate (1) taken prisoner; (2) strongly attracted

109   *cry you mercy* beg your pardon
      quid for quo tit for tat

111   *to be* if you were to be

112   *vile* worthless

113   *servility* slavery

114   *princes.* The word was applicable to women of royal blood as well as men.

115   *happy* fortunate

120   *condescend* agree

125   *choice* (1) choosing; (2) thing chosen

127   *An if* if

132   *what remedy?* can nothing be done about it?

133   *unapt* not inclined

134   *exclaim on* complain of

138   *Whom* (Margaret)

139   *easy-held* easily endured

141   *Speaks ... as he thinks* (proverbial)

142   *face* deceive (put on a false face)

143   *warrant* assurance

145   *expect* await

148   *happy for* fortunate in having

151   *her little worth* her who is scarcely worthy

153–6 *Upon condition . . . please.* Compare Hall: 'The Earl of
Suffolk . . . condescended and agreed to their motion
that the Duchy of Anjou and the County of Maine
should be released and delivered to the King her father,
demanding for her marriage neither penny nor farthing'
(page 204).

153   *quietly* in peace

154   *country.* This is F's reading, but it may be an error, for
Hall (page 119) has 'countries'. However, Reignier
may simply be thinking of the two provinces as a single
kingdom he wishes to possess.

157   *deliver* free

158   *counties* (domains of a count)

160   *again* in return

161   *deputy* (Suffolk)

162   *plighted* pledged

164   *traffic* business

166   *be mine own attorney* act on my own behalf

170   *it becomes* is fitting (for such a jewel)

179   *placed* arranged

     modestly directed. F's 'modestie directed' could mean
'controlled by modesty'; but the phrase seems to be
intended to balance *sweetly placed.*

183   *taint* tainted, tinged

186   *peevish* silly, trifling

189   *Minotaurs.* Minos, King of Crete, employed Daedalus
to create a labyrinth in which he kept the Minotaur, a
monster half man and half bull, which was the result
of the union between his wife Pasiphäe and a bull; see
also the note to IV.6. 54–5.

190   *Solicit* move, excite

     her wondrous praise praise of her wondrous qualities

191   *surmount* excel

192   *And.* F has 'Mad'. The emendation ''Mid' is attractive, but the word is not used in this way elsewhere in
Shakespeare's works.

     extinguish eclipse

193   *Repeat their semblance* recall repeatedly the image of her virtues by rehearsing descriptions of them

V.4   The location of this scene is the Duke of York's camp at Anjou. Historically Joan was captured at Compiègne in 1430 and tried and sent to the stake at Rouen in 1431. The peace negotiations (lines 94–175) are based upon the terms offered and rejected at Arras in 1435, and the truce negotiated by Suffolk at Tours in 1444. (stage direction) This is substantially the direction as it stands in F. Some editors move the entry of Pucelle and her father to follow line 1; but it seems obvious that the English peers enter with their soldiers guarding Pucelle, who is brought forward at York's command in line 1.

2   *kills* breaks

3   *country* district

4   *it is my chance* I have happened
     find . . . out discover

5   *timeless* untimely

7   *miser* wretch

8   *gentler* more noble

9   *friend* relative

10   *an* if it

13   *was the first fruit of my bachelorship* (that is, was illegitimately conceived)

15   *argues* gives evidence of

16   *concludes* (1) makes an end; (2) settles the truth

17   *obstacle* (malapropism for 'obstinate')

18   *a collop of my flesh* (proverbial)
     collop slice

20   *Deny* disown

21   *suborned* persuaded to commit perjury

23   *noble* (English gold coin, first minted by Edward III, worth about a third of £1)

29   *ratsbane* poison

30   *thou didst keep my lambs a-field*. This detail is found

only in Holinshed: 'she kept her father's lambs in the fields' (page 171).

30   *keep* tend

32   *drab* whore

37   *me.* It is possible that the emendation 'one', adopted by many editors, is correct; but Joan seems to be stressing her own uniqueness, so the F reading may stand.

38   *issued* descended

       progeny of kings royal ancestors

41   *exceeding* exceptional

43–5 *polluted . . . vices.* This is an echo of Ezekiel 23.17,30.

46   *want* lack

47   *straight* immediately

48   *compass* accomplish

49   *misconceived.* Pucelle is probably saying here that the notion she describes in lines 47–8 is a misrepresentation of the real truth of the matter, which she defines in the following lines. Some editors print no punctuation after the word, making it apply adjectivally to Pucelle as 'misunderstood Joan of Arc', with possibly a quibble on the second meaning, 'misbegotten'.

51   *in very thought* even in her thoughts

52   *rigorously effused* cruelly spilled

55–8 *because . . . shortenèd.* Warwick wishes Joan to feel the minimum pain and so bids the soldiers to employ the practice of making the fire smoke so that the victim died of asphyxiation rather than burned to death.

56   *enow* sufficient

59–85 *Will nothing . . . in vain.* This is based on Holinshed's account: 'she, . . . not able to hold her in any towardness of grace, falling straightaway into her former abominations (and yet seeking to eke out life as long as she might), stake not, though the shift were shameful, to confess herself a strumpet, and, unmarried as she was, to be with child' (page 171).

59   *turn* change

60   *discover* reveal

61   *warranteth* guarantees

       privilege (the right of a condemned pregnant woman to postpone her execution until her innocent child has been born)

67   *preciseness* morality, propriety

68   *juggling* (1) conjuring; (2) engaging in sexual play

69   *refuge* final defence

74   *Alençon, that notorious Machiavel?* This is an obvious anachronism, perhaps based on the fact that Niccolò Machiavelli's *The Prince* (1513) was dedicated to a later member of the Alençon family, Henry, who, as Duke of Anjou, was a suitor for the hand of Elizabeth I in 1570, and later became Henry III of France. In 1572 he had taken part in the Saint Bartholomew Day Massacre of the French Huguenots in Paris, an event which was unpopular in England and was believed to have been carried out in accordance with Machiavelli's political principles. There was little first-hand knowledge of Machiavelli's works in England at this time; and on the Elizabethan stage a 'Machiavel' was simply a stereotyped villain who either practised evil for its own sake or was crafty and ambitious.

78   *prevailed* persuaded me to have sexual intercourse

82   *liberal* wanton, loose

84   *brat* (with no derogatory meaning) child

87   *reflex* shed

89   *darkness and the gloomy shade of death.* This echoes Matthew 4.16: 'The people which sat in darkness saw great light; and to them which sat in the region and shadow of death light is sprung up'.

90   *mischief* disaster

93   *Thou foul accursèd minister of hell.* Compare Hall: 'an enchantress, an organ of the devil, sent from Satan, to blind the people and bring them in unbelief' (page 157).

       minister agent, servant

96–9   *the states ... French.* Compare Hall: 'The cry and noise of this perilous and insatiable war was ... detested through Christendom' (page 174); and in the twenty-second year of Henry VI 'all the princes of Christendom so much laboured and travailed by their orators and ambassadors that the frosty hearts of both the parties were somewhat mollified and their indurate stomachs greatly assuaged' (page 205).

97   *remorse of* pity for

100   *train* courtly followers

102   *travail turned to this effect* laborious efforts come to this end

105   *overthrown* destroyed

107   *effeminate* weak and unmanly

108   *most part* the bulk

114   *covenants* articles of agreement

115   *As* that

120–22   *boiling choler . . . enemies.* This confused image appears to be an allusion to the basilisk, a mythical creature which was reputed to kill its enemies with its gaze.

120   *choler* anger

122   *By* at the
       baleful deadly, mortal

124–75   *in regard . . . solemn peace.* The peace terms are derived from those offered and rejected at Arras in 1435 (Hall, pages 174–5), but are here used for the eighteen-month truce negotiated historically at Tours in 1444 by Suffolk (Hall, page 203).

124   *in regard* in so far as

125   *Of* out of
       mere pure
       lenity mildness

127   *suffer* allow

128   *true liegemen* loyal subjects

134   *coronet* small crown (not befitting a king)

135   *substance and authority* actual power

139   *Gallian* French

141–3   *Shall I . . . whole?* shall I, in order to gain possession of the part of France I do not already occupy, surrender my right of sovereignty so as to be reduced to the rank of viceroy of the whole of France?

141   *lucre* gain, acquisition

142   *Detract* take away

144–6   *I'll rather ... all* (an adaptation of the proverb 'All covet, all lose')

146   *cast* excluded
possibility of all the chance of possessing anything

149   *grows to compromise* approaches a peaceful solution

150   *Standest thou aloof upon comparison* are you withholding agreement through rhetorical quibbling over the details

152   *Of benefit proceeding from* as feudal beneficiary of

153   *challenge of desert* claim to the title as if by right

155   *in obstinacy* in being obstinate

156   *in the course of this contract* during the time this agreement is being negotiated
contract (accented on the second syllable)

159   *policy* course of astute political action

162   *proceeding* continuing

164   *your pleasure serves* it suits your own purpose

165   *condition* treaty provisions

167   *Only reserved* with the single reservation that

168   *towns of garrison* fortified towns

175   *entertain* accept

V.5   Historically this scene takes place in Westminster in 1443–4. It follows the chronicles' account very closely: 'the Earl of Suffolk ... came to the King to Westminster, and there openly before the King and his council declared how he had taken an honourable truce ... omitting nothing which might extol and set forth the personage of the lady, nor forgetting anything of the nobility of her kin nor of her father's high style; as who would say that she was of such an excellent beauty and of so high a parentage that almost no king or emperor was worthy to be her mate. Although this marriage pleased well the King and divers of his council, and especially such as were adherents and fautors to the Earl of Suffolk, yet Humphrey Duke of Gloucester, Protector of the realm, repugned and resisted, as much as in him lay, this new alliance and contrived matrimony, alleging that it was neither consonant to the law of God nor man, nor honourable to a prince, to infringe and break a promise or contract by him made and concluded, for the utility and profit of his realm and people, declaring that the King, by his ambassadors, sufficiently instructed and authorized, had concluded and contracted a marriage between his Highness and the daughter of the Earl of Armagnac upon conditions both to him and his realm as much profitable as honourable. Which offers and conditions the said Earl . . . is ready to yield and perform, saying that it was more convenient for a prince to marry a wife with riches and friends than to take a mate with nothing and disherit himself and his realm of old rights and ancient signories. The Duke was not heard, but the Earl's doings were condescended unto and allowed' (Hall, page 204).

2	*astonished me* filled me with wonder
4	*settled* deeply rooted
5	*rigour* strength
6	*Provokes* impels
	hulk ship
7	*breath* verbal descriptions
8	*arrive* reach the shore
10	*superficial tale* account of her most obvious qualities
11	*her worthy praise* the praise of her true worth
15	*conceit* imagination
17	*full* fully
25	*flatter* gloss over, extenuate
27	*another lady* (the daughter of the Earl of Armagnac)
28	*dispense with* set aside
	contract (accented on the second syllable)
29	*deface* soil, disfigure
31	*triumph* chivalric tournament
32	*forsaketh . . . the lists* leaves the combat or tilting arena

35   *may be broke* (the contract with her) may be broken

37   *better* higher-ranking

38   *excel* is outstanding

42   *As* that
       confirm strengthen .

47   *Where* whereas

50   *perfect love* love alone

53   *So* thus do

56   *attorneyship* legal haggling

57   *affects* desires

60   *It most*. F reads 'Most', and some editors let that stand; but it gives very strained sense.

62   *what is wedlock forcèd but a hell* (proverbial)

63   *age* lifetime

65   *pattern of celestial peace* image of heavenly harmony

68   *feature* figure
       birth royal birth

69   *Approves* proves

72   *answer our hope in issue of a king* will satisfy our expectations of royal children

75   *resolve* aspirations

79   *through force* by the strength

80   *for that* because

81   *attaint* sullied, infected

87   *post* hasten

88   *covenants* terms
       procure contrive

91   *anointed* (with coronation oil)

92   *charge* money for expenses

93   *a tenth* (a tax levy of ten per cent of value of personal property)

95   *rest* remain

96   *offence* sense of hostility

97   *censure* judge

97–8   *what you were, | Not what you are* what you were like when you were a young man, not what you are like now in your sober old age. The allusion may be to an incident in 1422 recorded by Hall: 'Humphrey Duke of Gloucester, either blinded with ambition or doting for love, married the Lady Jaquet . . . which was lawful wife to John Duke of Brabant then living, which marriage was not only wondered at of the common people but also detested of the nobility and abhorred of the clergy' (page 116); see also the note to I.1.39.

99   *sudden* hasty

100   *from company* alone

101   *grief* amorous pain

102   *grief* sorrow

103–6   *thus he goes . . . Trojan did.* Suffolk intends to imitate Paris, who stole Helen from her husband, Menelaus; but he hopes to avoid results similar to those which were a consequence of Paris's action – the Trojan War and his own death.

105   *the like event* a similar outcome

107–8   *Margaret shall . . . realm.* This is a link with *Part Two* of the play, which details Suffolk's and Margaret's manipulation of Henry.

AN ACCOUNT OF THE TEXT

THE play was first printed in the first Folio edition of Shakespeare's works (1623), where it appears as the sixth item in the Histories section under the title *The first Part of Henry the Sixt*. This is the only early text which has any authority; those in the later Folios of 1632, 1664, and 1685 are all based ultimately on the first printing. The text of the play in the second Folio contains an unusually large number of variant readings, some of which offer distinct improvements in sense and metre; but they can only be considered as conjectures originating in the printing house.

The text in the first Folio ('F') was set in type mainly by the principal compositor of the whole volume, with help in the later pages from another workman. While many of the characteristics and errors of the text can be attributed to idiosyncrasies in the workmanship of these two men, a number of features indicate that some of the irregularities and inconsistencies found in the text were probably also to be found in the manuscript copy from which they worked:

1. The text is divided into acts and scenes, but the division is very erratic. The indications for the beginnings of Acts I, II, III, and IV are accurate, as are the scene divisions of Act III; but the scene divisions of Act IV and the act division for Act V are certainly inaccurate. This may mean that some scenes are missing or that whoever prepared the manuscript for the press did an inept job of apportioning the play.

2. There is a more than normal variation in the spelling of proper names: for example, Reignier is also called 'Reigneir', 'Reignard', and 'Reynold'; Pucelle is variously 'Pusel', 'Puzel', 'Ione', and 'Ioane'; Burgundy appears also as 'Burgonie'; and Armagnac also as 'Arminacke'.

3. A good deal of inconsistency is found in the speech pre-

fixes: for example, 'Charles' becomes 'Dolphin' in I.2; Plantagenet is 'York' in II.4 and 'Richard' in II.5; and Sir William Lucy, although addressed by name by York, is indicated merely as '2 Messenger' in IV.3.

4. The stage directions are, in the main, descriptive and literary, some of them being taken straight from the wording of the chronicles. Some directions are missing, such as those for the exits of the First and Third Messengers in I.1 and Falstaff in IV.1, and the entries of Vernon and Basset in III.4 and Sir William Lucy in IV.4. Some are vague: '*others*' does duty for the entry of Gargrave and Glansdale at I.4.22 and for Vernon and the Lawyer in II.4. Some directions are incomplete; for example, Reignier does not appear at III.2.17, even though he has two speeches at lines 23 and 33. Still other directions are clearly erroneous or misplaced; for example, '*Their Drummes beating a Dead March*' at II.1.7 is obviously inappropriate for a surprise night attack on Orleans and was probably intended for Salisbury's funeral procession in II.2.

5. There are a number of inconsistencies between different parts of the play: for example, Exeter expresses surprise at Winchester's being a Cardinal at V.1.28–9, although he has already appeared in a Cardinal's habit in III.1, III.4, and IV.1 when Exeter was present; and there seems to be some doubt about how young King Henry is in the early scenes of the play, in contrast to his obvious young manhood in the final scenes.

Some of these features of the text, such as the variation in characters' names and speech prefixes and the descriptive nature of the stage directions, have persuaded scholars that the manuscript copy from which the printers worked was not a theatre prompt-book (which would have been tidied up for performance) but a manuscript which was in some way closely related to Shakespeare's own written version. However, other characteristics, such as the irregular act and scene division, the misplaced stage directions, the transposition of words and phrases, the dislocations of metre by the introduction of extra words, and peculiar lines susceptible of explanation as palaeographical or copying errors, seem to indicate that the printers' copy was perhaps an edited transcript, with some theatrical annotation, of Shakespeare's own manuscript.

Many of the peculiarities of the text have been claimed (most notably among recent editors by John Dover Wilson in his New Cambridge edition) to be the result of the play's being a product of multiple authorship, with Shakespeare reworking a version originally produced by Robert Greene, Thomas Nashe, and George Peele. Other scholars believe that the textual difficulties are the result of the play's having been revised some years after its original composition (for a discussion of the date and authorship of the play see the Introduction, pages 9–12). In recent years the prevailing view has been that Shakespeare was probably solely responsible for the play as we now have it.

The collations below list the substantive emendations made in this edition, two of which are new (at III.2.14 and V.2.16–17); plausible readings suggested by other editors; changes made in the F stage directions; and the act and scene divisions of F and the present edition.

COLLATIONS

The following lists are selective. The first Folio is abbreviated as 'F1' and its three seventeenth-century reprints as 'F2', 'F3', and 'F4'. Quotations from F are unmodernized, except that 'long s' (ſ) is replaced by 's'.

I

Emendations
Below are listed the more important departures from the text of F1, with the readings of this edition printed on the left of the square bracket. Most of these emendations were first made by eighteenth-century editors. Those found in F2, F3, or F4 are indicated. Corrections of obvious misprints are not recorded, nor are the straightforward regularization of F's speech prefixes and variant spellings of proper names.

THE CHARACTERS IN THE PLAY] *not in* F

I.1. 33 The ... prayed,] The ... it? | Had ... pray'd,
     47 dead.] dead,
     60 Rouen,] (*not in* F)
    141 slain? Then] slaine then?
    176 steal] send

I.2. 30 bred] breed
     37 Let's ... slaves,] Let's ... Towne, | For ...
        Slaues,
     99 five] fine
    113 rites] rights
    131 halcyon] (F3); *Halcyons*

I.3. 29 Humphrey] *Vmpheir*
     74 OFFICER] (*not in* F)

I.4. 10 Wont] Went
     27 Duke] Earle
     33 pilled] pil'd
   87-8 Sir Thomas ... him.] (*In* F *these lines follow line 89
        of this edition*)
     95 like thee, Nero,] like thee,

I.6. 22 of] or

II.1. 29 all together] altogether

II.2.   6 centre] Centure
      20 Arc] Acre

II.3. 27 What ... goes.] What ... now? | Goe ... goes?
      43 Laughest ... moan.] Laughest ... Wretch? | Thy
        ... moane.

II.4.   1 Great ... silence?] Great ... Gentlemen, | What
        ... silence?
      60 meditating that] meditating, that
     117 wiped] (F2 wip't); whipt
     132 sir] (F2; *not in* F1)

II.5.   3 rack] Wrack
  18, 33 GAOLER] *Keeper.*
      84 Cambridge then,] Cambridge, then
     129 ill] will

III.1. 51-2 WARWICK Roam thither then. SOMERSET My]
        Warw. Roame thither then. | My

53 WARWICK] *Som.*

165 alone] (F2); all alone

201 should lose] (F2); loose

III.2. 13 *Qui là?*] *Che la.*

14 *pauvre gent*] *pouure gens*

28 Talbotites] *Talbonites*

50–51 What . . . lance, | And . . . chair?] What . . . beard? | Breake . . . Death, | Within . . . Chayre.

107–8 Ay, | All . . . life.] (*as one line in* F)

III.3. 78 I . . . hers] I . . . vanquished: | These . . . hers

90 Now . . . powers,] Now . . . Lords, | And . . . Powers,

III.4. 38 Villain . . . such] Villaine . . . knowest | The . . . such,

IV.1. 19 Patay] *Poictiers*

133 It . . . friends.] It . . . Highnesse, | Good . . . Friends.

180 wist] wish

IV.2. 3 calls] (F2); call

15 GENERAL] *Cap.*

34 due] dew

50 moody-mad and] moodie mad: And

IV.3. 5 Talbot; as . . . along,] (F2); *Talbot* as . . . along.

17 LUCY] 2. *Mes.*

20 waist] waste

30, 34, 47 LUCY] *Mes.*

49 loss] losse:

IV.4. 16 legions] Regions

IV.7. 89 have them] haue him

94 with them] (F2); with him

V.1. 49 where inshipped,] (F4); wherein ship'd

V.2.16–17 I trust . . . there. BURGUNDY Now] *Bur.* I trust . . . there: | Now

V.3. 11 legions] Regions

57 her] (F3); his

179 modestly] (F2); modestie

192 And] Mad

V.4. 49 No, misconceived!] No misconceyued,

V.4.   49 Arc] *Aire*
       102 travail] trauell
       165 How ... stand?] How ... *Charles*? | Shall ...
            stand?
V.5.   60 It most] Most
       82 love] (F2); Ioue

2

Rejected emendations

The following list records a selection of emendations and conjectures which have not been adopted in this edition, but which
have been made with some plausibility in F2 or by other
editors. Many of the emendations suggested for this play have
been aimed at turning flat, mediocre verse into metrically
regular flat, mediocre verse; most of these have been ignored
in this list, along with various modernizations of F's grammatical forms. To the left of the square brackets are the readings
of the present text, and to the right of them F's readings where
they differ from this edition, and (in modernized spelling) the
suggested emendations. When more than one emendation is
listed, they are separated by semi-colons.

I.1.   49 moistened] moist (F2)
       50 nourish] marish
       56 –] Charlemagne; Hercules; Constantine
       62 man, ... corse?] man! ... corse
       76 third thinks] third man thinks (F2); third, he
            thinks
       83 her] their
       112 full scarce] scarce full
       124 slew] flew
       131 (and throughout) Falstaff] Fastolfe
I.2.   100 churchyard] church
I.3.   49 I] I'll (F2)
       82 cost] dear cost (F2)
I.4.   33 pilled] (F pil'd); vile
       60 grate] secret grate
       66 stands] stand (F2)

244

95 like thee, Nero,] (F1 like thee,); Nero like will (F2); Nero-like,

110 me] we

I.5. 6 art a] arrant

16 hungry] hunger

29 soil] (F Soyle); style

I.6. 2 English] English wolves (F2)

4 Astraea's] bright Astraea's (F2)

6 garden] gardens

25 rich-jewelled coffer] rich jewelled coffer; rich jewel-coffer

II.1. 31 fail] fall

II.2. 20 Arc] (F Acre); Aire

II.4. 57 you] law

76 fashion] passion; faction

102 this apprehension] misapprehension; this reprehension

132 gentle sir] (F1 gentle); gentlemen

II.5. 71 Richard] King Richard (F2)

75 third] the third (F2)

78 fourth] the fourth (F2)

129 my ill] (F my will); mine ill

III.1. 53 see] so

III.2. 13 *Qui là?*] (F *Che la.*); *Qui est là?*; *Qui va là?*

14 *la pauvre gent*] (F *la pouvre gens*); *pauvres gens*; *les pauvres gens*

22 Here] Where

117 Yet] Let

IV.1. 48 Lord] my Lord (F2)

180 I wist] (F I wish); iwis

191 that] sees

it] he

IV.2. 14 their] our; his

29 rive] rove

IV.4. 26 Burgundy] and Burgundy (F2)

31 host] horse

41 aid] (F ayde); side

IV.5. 39 shame] shamed

IV.7.   60 But where's] Where is

        70 Henry] our King Henry (F2)

        89 have them] (F haue him); have 'em

        94 with them] (F with him); with 'em

V.1.   59 or] nor

V.2.   7 combat with] come within

V.3.   44 (*Some editors start a new scene here*)

    48, 49 (*lines in reverse order*)

        68 here] here thy prisoner (F2); prisoner here

        83 I were] 'Twere

     154 country] county; countries

     192 And] (F Mad); 'Mid

V.4.   37 me] one

        49 No, misconceived! Joan] (F No misconceyued, Ione); No, misconceived Joan (F4); No, misconceivers: Joan

     101 some matter] the same

V.5.   39 lord] good Lord (F2)

        55 Marriage] But marriage (F2)

        60 It most] (F Most); That most; Which most

        64 bringeth] bringeth forth (F2)

3

Stage directions

The stage directions of this edition are either necessary additions or corrected or expanded versions of those found in F. The list below records the more important changes and additions, with the readings of this edition printed on the left of the square brackets, and F's readings on the right of them. Not listed are directions for speeches to be given aside or addressed to a particular character, all of which are editorial; simple expansions of proper names and ranks; and minor corrections such as '*Exeunt*' for '*Exit*'.

I.1.   0 *with heralds*] *not in* F

      45 *Exeunt heralds*] *not in* F

      56 *First*] *a*

  81, 161 *Exit*] *not in* F

172 *Exeunt all but Winchester*] *Exit.*

I.2.   60 *Exit Bastard*] *not in* F

       63 *and the Bastard*] *not in* F

I.3.   0 *in blue coats*] *not in* F

       4 *Servingmen knock*] *not in* F

  5, 7, 9 *within*] *not in* F

      88 *Gloucester and Winchester with their servingmen*] *not in* F

I.4.   22 *Sir William Glansdale, Sir Thomas Gargrave, and other soldiers*] *others.*

      56 *and exit*] *not in* F

      69 *Salisbury and Gargrave fall down*] *Salisbury falls downe.*

      89 *Exeunt attendants with Gargrave's body*] *not in* F

    111 *with Salisbury's body*] *not in* F

I.5.   0 *and exeunt*] *not in* F

      14 *she enters*] *enter*

II.1.   0 *French*] *not in* F

       on the walls] *not in* F

      5 *Exit Sergeant*] *not in* F

      7 *and soldiers*] *not in* F

       scaling-ladders] *scaling Ladders : Their Drummes beating a Dead March.*

      38 *The English . . . exeunt*] *Cry, S. George, A Talbot.*

      77 (F *has* 'Exeunt.' *after* 'them.')

       an English Soldier] *a Souldier*

II.2.   0 *a Captain, and soldiers*] *not in* F

      3 *sounded*] *not in* F

      6 *Enter a funeral procession with Salisbury's body, their drums beating a dead march*] *not in* F (*see* II.1.7 *above*)

      17 *Exit funeral procession*] *not in* F

      59 *He whispers*] *Whispers.* (*at the end of the line*)

II.3.   0 *of Auvergne and her Porter*] *not in* F

      26 *He starts to leave*] *not in* F

II.4.   0 *Vernon, a Lawyer, and other gentlemen*] *and others.*

II.5. 121 *Exeunt Gaolers, with Mortimer's body*] *Exit.*

III.1.   0 *and others*] *not in* F

III.1.   85 *Servingmen of Gloucester and Winchester] not in* F
         103 *They begin to skirmish again] Begin againe.*
         150 *Servingmen and Mayor] not in* F
III.2.   0 *dressed like countrymen] not in* F
          13 *within] not in* F
          16 *opening the gates] not in* F
          17 *into the city] not in* F
             Reignier, and soldiers] not in F
          28 *Exit] not in* F
          35 *They storm the gates] not in* F
             Enter Talbot in an excursion from within the town]
             Talbot in an Excursion.
          40 *Alençon,] not in* F
          59 *The English] They*
         103 *Exeunt all but Bedford and attendants] Exit.*
         109 *enter from the town and] not in* F
         114 *attendants] not in* F
             of the English soldiers] not in F
III.3.   0 *and soldiers] not in* F
          32 *Here sound a] not in* F
          36 *Enter Burgundy and troops] not in* F
III.4.   0 *Vernon, Basset, and other courtiers] not in* F
           9 *He kneels] not in* F
IV.1.   0 *of Paris, and others] not in* F
           3 *The Governor kneels] not in* F
           8 *Exeunt Governor and his train] not in* F
          15 *He plucks it off] not in* F
          47 *Exit Falstaff] not in* F
          50 *looking at the outside of the letter] not in* F
          55 *He reads] not in* F
          77 *Exit] not in* F
         152 *He puts on a red rose] not in* F
         173 *Flourish] (after 'Exeunt.' in line 181)*
IV.2.   2 *Trumpet] not in* F
        2, 41 *with his men] not in* F
          56 *Exeunt] not in* F
IV.3.   0 *(F has these two entrances reversed)*
          16 *Sir William Lucy] not in* F

46 *with his soldiers*] not in F
53 *Exit*] not in F
IV.4.　　0 *and a Captain of Talbot's*] not in F
11 *Enter Sir William Lucy*] not in F
IV.7.　　0 *by a Servant*] not in F
16 *soldiers*] not in F
50 *accompanied by a French herald*] not in F
V.1.　　27 *in cardinal's habit*] not in F
one a Papal Legate] not in F
50 *all but Winchester and the Legate*] not in F
55 *He steps aside*] not in F
V.3.　　29 *York then fights with Joan la Pucelle and overcomes her*] not in F
130 *a parley*] not in F
144 *Exit from the walls*] not in F
145 *below*] not in F
186 *Exeunt Reignier and Margaret*] not in F
V.4.　0, 91 *guarded*] not in F
93 *Enter Winchester with attendants*] *Enter Cardinall.*
115 *and attendants*] not in F
172 *Charles . . . Henry*] not in F
V.5.　102 *Exeunt Gloucester and Exeter*] *Exit Gloucester.*

4

Act and scene divisions
The act and scene divisions of the F text are erratic. The following list records the divisions of this edition on the left of the square bracket and those which appear in the Folio or an indication of omission on the right.

I.1] *Actus Primus. Scœna Prima.*
I.2–6] not in F
II.1] *Actus Secundus. Scena Prima.*
II.2–5] not in F
III.1] *Actus Tertius. Scena Prima.*
III.2] *Scœna Secunda.*
III.3] *Scœna Tertia.*
III.4] *Scœna Quarta.*

IV.1] *Actus Quartus. Scena Prima.*

IV.2–7] *not in* F

V.1] *Scena secunda.*

V.2] *Scœna Tertia.*

V.3–4] *not in* F

V.5] *Actus Quintus.*

GENEALOGICAL TABLES

TABLE I: *The House of Lancaster*

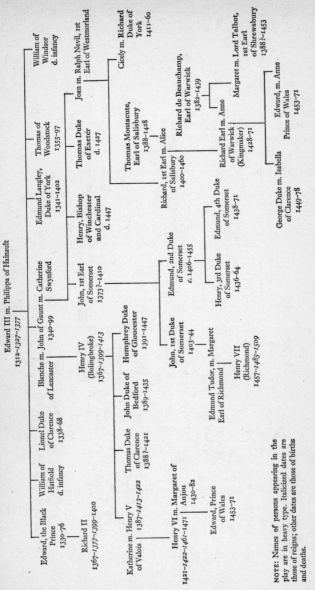

Edward III m. Philippa of Hainault
1312–1327–1377

Edward, the Black Prince 1330–76 · William of Hatfield d. infancy · Lionel Duke of Clarence 1338–68 · Blanche m. John of Gaunt m. Catherine Swynford of Lancaster 1340–99 · Edmund Langley, Duke of York 1341–1402 · Thomas of Woodstock 1355–97 · William of Windsor d. infancy

Richard II 1367–1377–1399–1400

Henry IV (Bolingbroke) 1367–1399–1413 · Thomas Duke of Clarence 1388?–1421 · John Duke of Bedford 1389–1435 · Humphrey Duke of Gloucester 1391–1447 · John, 1st Earl of Somerset 1373?–1410 · Henry, Bishop of Winchester and Cardinal d. 1447 · Thomas Duke of Exeter d. 1427 · Joan m. Ralph Nevil, 1st Earl of Westmorland

Katherine m. Henry V 1387–1413–1422 of Valois 1421–1422–1461–1471

Henry VI m. Margaret of Anjou 1430–82

Edward, Prince of Wales 1453–71

Edmund Tudor, m. Margaret Earl of Richmond

Henry VII (Richmond) 1457–1485–1509

John, 1st Duke of Somerset 1403–44

Edmund, 2nd Duke of Somerset c. 1406–1455

Edmund, 4th Duke of Somerset 1438–71

Henry, 3rd Duke of Somerset 1436–64

Thomas Montacute, Earl of Salisbury 1388–1428 m. Alice

Richard, 1st Earl of Salisbury 1400–1460

Richard de Beauchamp, Earl of Warwick 1382–1439

Richard Earl m. Anne of Warwick (Kingmaker) 1428–71

George Duke m. Isabella of Clarence 1449–78

Cicely m. Richard Duke of York 1411–60

Margaret m. Lord Talbot, 1st Earl of Shrewsbury 1388?–1453

Edward, m. Anne Prince of Wales 1453–71

NOTE: Names of persons appearing in the play are in heavy type. Italicized dates are those of reigns; other dates are those of births and deaths.

TABLE 2: *The House of York and the line of the Mortimers*

Edward III m. Philippa of Hainault
1312–1327–1377

Edward, the Black Prince
1330–76

Richard II
1367–1377–1399–1400

William of Hatfield
d. infancy

Lionel Duke of Clarence
1338–68

Philippa m. Edmund Mortimer, 3rd Earl of March
1355–c. 1380 | 1351–81

Elizabeth m. Henry Percy (Hotspur)
1364–1403 | 1364–1403

Roger Mortimer, 4th Earl of March
1374–98

Sir Edmund Mortimer
1376–1409

John, 7th m. Elizabeth Lord Clifford

Edmund Mortimer, 5th Earl of March
1391–1425

Anne m. Richard Earl of Cambridge
d. 1415

John, 12th Baron Clifford (Old Clifford)
1414–55

John, 13th Baron Clifford (Young Clifford)

NOTE: Shakespeare and the chronicles confused Sir Edmund Mortimer with his nephew

John of Gaunt
1340–99

Edmund Langley, 1st Duke of York
1341–1402

Edward of Norwich, 2nd Duke of York
1373?–1415

Constance

Isabella m. Richard de Beauchamp, Earl of Warwick
1382–1439

Richard Earl m. Anne Mortimer of Cambridge
d. 1415

Richard Plantagenet, m. Cicely Nevil 3rd Duke of York
1411–60

Edward IV m. Elizabeth Woodville (Lady Grey)
1442–1461–1483 | 1437–1492

Edmund Earl of Rutland
1443–60

George Duke m. Isabella of Clarence Nevil
1449–78

Richard III (Duke of Gloucester)
1452–1483–1485

Elizabeth m. Henry VII (Richmond)
1465–1503 | 1457–1485–1509

Edward V
1470–1483

Richard
1472–83

Thomas of Woodstock
1355–97

William of Windsor
d. infancy

TABLE 3: *Relationship between the French characters in the play*

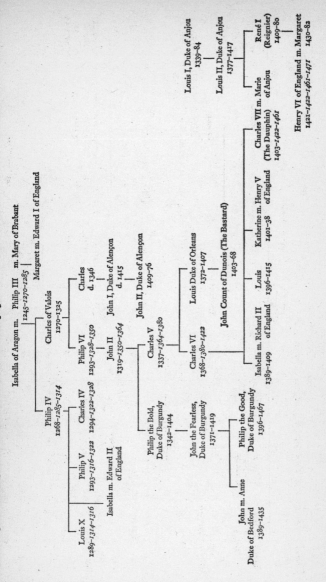

Isabella of Aragon m. Philip III m. Mary of Brabant
1245–1270–1285

Margaret m. Edward I of England

Charles of Valois
1270–1325

Philip IV
1268–1285–1314

Philip V
1293–1316–1322

Charles IV
1294–1322–1328

Philip VI
1293–1328–1350

Charles
d. 1346

John I, Duke of Alençon
d. 1415

Louis I, Duke of Anjou
1339–84

Louis X
1289–1314–1316

Isabella m. Edward II
of England

John II
1319–1350–1364

John II, Duke of Alençon
1409–76

Louis II, Duke of Anjou
1377–1417

Philip the Bold,
Duke of Burgundy
1344–1404

Charles V
1337–1364–1380

Louis Duke of Orleans
1372–1407

René I
(Reignier)
1409–80

John the Fearless,
Duke of Burgundy
1371–1419

Charles VI
1368–1380–1422

John Count of Dunois (The Bastard)
1403–68

Charles VII m. Marie
(The Dauphin)   of Anjou
1403–1422–1461

Philip the Good,
Duke of Burgundy
1396–1467

Isabella m. Richard II
1389–1409   of England

Louis
1396–1415

Katherine m. Henry V
1401–38   of England

Henry VI of England m. Margaret
1421–1422–1461–1471   1430–82

John m. Anne
Duke of Bedford
1389–1435